LAND OF THE GODS

(Joe Hawke #11)

Rob Jones

ISBN: 9781070574141

Other Books by Rob Jones

The Joe Hawke Series

The Vault of Poseidon (Joe Hawke #1)
Thunder God (Joe Hawke #2)
The Tomb of Eternity (Joe Hawke #3)
The Curse of Medusa (Joe Hawke #4)
Valhalla Gold (Joe Hawke #5)
The Aztec Prophecy (Joe Hawke #6)
The Secret of Atlantis (Joe Hawke #7)
The Lost City (Joe Hawke #8)
The Sword of Fire (Joe Hawke #9)
The King's Tomb (Joe Hawke #10)
Land of the Gods (Joe Hawke #11)
The Orpheus Legacy (Joe Hawke #12)
Hell's Inferno (Joe Hawke #13)
Day of the Dead (Joe Hawke #14)
Shadow of the Apocalypse (Joe Hawke #15)
Gold Train (Joe Hawke #16)
The Last Warlord (Joe Hawke #17)

The Avalon Adventure Series

The Hunt for Shambhala (Avalon Adventure #1)
Treasure of Babylon (Avalon Adventure #2)
The Doomsday Cipher (Avalon Adventure #3)

The Hunter Files

The Atlantis Covenant (Hunter Files #1)
The Revelation Relic (Hunter Files #2)
The Titanic Legacy (Hunter Files #3)

The Cairo Sloane Series

Plagues of the Seven Angels (Cairo Sloane #1)

The Harry Bane Thriller Series
The Armageddon Protocol (A Harry Bane Thriller #1)

The Jed Mason Series
The Raiders (Jed Mason #1)

The Bill Blake Series
An action-thriller series for fans of
Jack Reacher and Jason Bourne

The Operator (Bill Blake #1)
Against The Machine (Bill Blake #2)

The DCI Jacob Mystery Series
The Fifth Grave (A DCI Jacob Mystery)
Angel of Death (A DCI Jacob Mystery)

Visit Rob on the links below
for all the latest news and information:

Email: robjonesnovels@gmail.com
Twitter: @AuthorRobJones
Facebook: www.facebook.com/RobJonesNovels/
Facebook Reader Group: ADVENTURE HQ
Website: www.robjonesnovels.com

LAND OF THE GODS

CHAPTER ONE

Davis Faulkner peered over the top of his stylish browline glasses, a sinister smirk slowly taking up residence on his lean, hungry face. "I like it, Josh. I like it very much. We're sure we can make this stick, right?"

Joshua Muston gave a curt nod to the Vice President. They were sitting in the VP's formal residence at 1 Observatory Circle two miles northwest of the White House. Almost low enough to touch, a heavy bank of slate-gray cloud was skidding over the city, and rain lashed at the window. "We're sure, Mr. Vice President."

The smirk grew bolder as Faulkner's eyes crawled once again over the document Muston had just handed him. He was looking at his assistant's personal copy of the US Constitution, specifically Article II, Section 4.

The President, Vice President, and all civil Officers of the United States shall be removed from Office on Impeachment for, and Conviction of, Treason, Bribery, or other High Crimes and Misdemeanors.

Faulkner gave a sigh of satisfaction. The attempt to blow President Jack Brooke right out of the sky while taking off in Air Force One over England had failed, and so had the more recent attempt to take him out during the Five Eyes Conference in Miami Beach. At each turn, ECHO had thwarted his bid to remove the president and assume power but the manifest beauty of this plan was obvious.

After so many years of waiting, it was about to happen.

He jabbed at the worn cover of the leather-bound book

in his lap. "ECHO can't stop this, Josh. That's why I like it so much. Not only that, but we can get to them in the process."

"I don't understand."

"If we can't get to them in the meantime when we remove Brooke from office, the god-*damned* ECHO team will crawl out of the woodwork to save their man. Then we get them too. This pleases me very much." His voice started to trail away, a nervous tremor gently shaking his words. "I don't like to disappoint him."

Muston offered an anxious smile. He was uncomfortable when his boss talked about *him*, a distant figure of power Faulkner sometimes mentioned in passing but never elaborated on.

"Yes, sir."

Faulkner sniffed. "Treason then?"

"We can't prove treason, Mr. Vice President."

Faulkner was visibly deflated. "Damn it all. Why the hell not?"

"Way too much work to cook the books on that one, sir. The Constitution's definition of treason is remarkably narrow, specifically to stop people…" he paused, and swallowed uncomfortably.

The VP fixed a fiendish stare on his Chief of Staff. "To stop people using it as a political weapon, Josh?"

"Yes, sir."

"Article III, Section 3 is very clear on this," he said, licking his dry lips as he read from the tiny book. "*Treason against the United States shall consist only in levying war against them, or in adhering to their enemies, giving them aid or comfort*." He looked up at Josh again. "And we can't get the son of a bitch on that – giving our enemies aid or comfort?"

Muston shook his aching head. "Just too hard to cook something up in that area, as I said. I think we're looking at something in the high crimes and misdemeanors ballpark, sir. I already assembled a small team of constitutional legal experts and they think that we can manufacture something in that area that will get him out of the Oval Office and into a whole mess of trouble for a long time."

Faulkner was silent.

"Sir?"

The sinister smile now grew sly. "I'm not so sure about the treason thing."

"I don't understand."

"What about all those executive orders? He signs those things like checks, and we know he's given financial and weapons support to ECHO, right?"

"Sure."

"ECHO is not a United States operation, Josh."

"It has US citizens in it."

"Still not a US project. ECHO is an international operation run out of London." He cut off the end of one of his famous cigars and swiped a chunky gold lighter from his desk. The grind of flintstone and a burst of sparks, a metallic *clunk* as he flipped the lid down and tossed it back onto the desk.

Dragging the smoke through the long, expensive cigar, he leaned back in his leather captain's chair and swung his boots up on the desk. "I don't think it's the craziest thing in the world to paint ECHO as a terrorist organization, and then…"

Muston winced. "I don't know, sir."

"C'mon, Josh! This has been my thinking for a long time." He was lying. It had been the thinking of the man pulling his strings, the Oracle – but Joshua Muston did not need to know it.

"Seems too risky."

"Seems like you're losing your nerve."

Muston sighed and flicked aimlessly through the book in his hands for a few seconds to buy some time.

"Well?"

"It *could* work, but you'd need to make a clear case that ECHO was an international terror group who had actively attacked the United States. Then you'd need a paper trail linking all that shit right up to the Oval Office."

"Wrong, *you* would need to do it, not me. That's what I pay you for."

"Yes, sir." He shook his head and blew out a trembling breath.

"The attempt to blow him up while he was flying on Air Force One over England failed, and the attempt to drown him in Miami with the tsunami failed. They failed because the ECHO team is good… *damned* good, but what we're doing is playing on their home turf, Josh. This way is *my* way. The first those assholes will hear about anything is when Brooke is done and dusted and out of this office. If we can take ECHO out at the same time, what a glorious side dish that would be." Another deep drag on the cigar, and the smoke clouded in his mouth like a white fog in a tunnel.

Josh shifted in his seat and fiddled with his hands. "The problem we have is most Americans – and people all around the world – see ECHO as the team that saved the President's life from Kiefel. They're heroes."

"Wrong! From now on they're treasonous rats, Josh – and you're gonna prove it, and fast. I want Brooke's desk and I want it now. How is the kill order you put on them working out? I hope you arranged the full package just like I said."

"Yes, sir. It's going just fine, but I still say the full package seems a little *excessive*."

"When you cut the head off a snake, Josh, that head can still bite you. You have to crush it. When you take out a team like ECHO, you make damned sure you take out all their friends and families for the same reason. The full package does that, it will be as if none of them or anyone they ever knew existed."

Josh nodded.

"Good, and now I'm ordering you to make a case against Brooke for aiding and giving comfort to an international terrorist group. A case tighter than a hangman's knot on execution day – you got it?"

Joshua Muston gave another curt nod.

He got it, but he didn't like it.

CHAPTER TWO

Athens was enjoying a long, heavy rainfall. In the middle of a drought, it was a welcome relief and many people walked outside in the rain just to feel it on their bodies. All across the ancient city, children played in the puddles and danced in the downpour. Among this excitement, the ECHO team was standing under the shelter of a bitter orange tree opposite the Theatre of Dionysus.

High above them, the Acropolis was still sealed off and under repair after Kruger's helicopter assault on the rocky outcrop. Hawke was studying the scaffolding over the south side of the Parthenon when he heard a heavy car pull up on the cobblestone surface of Dionysiou Areopagitou behind them. Turning, he saw Sir Richard Eden and Magnus Lund stepping out of a chauffeur-driven Mercedes limousine.

He nudged Lea's elbow. "Heads up."

She watched the two men extend umbrellas and walk into the ancient ruined theatre. It was good to see her old friend back on his feet after the long recovery from the coma and especially nice to see he no longer needed a cane to walk. After her father's murder, Eden had stepped into his shoes and looked after her when she was growing up. Through a rocky childhood and turbulent teenage years, he'd always been there on the end of a phone. She kissed him on the cheek and smiled. "Good to see you, Rich."

"It's good to be back," he said.

"You're feeling all right now?" Lexi said.

"Yes, thank you, Cairo."

For a moment they thought he'd made a mistake, but then they saw the look on his face and they all burst into laughter.

"Funny." Reaper gave a nod of appreciation at the gag.

Ryan frowned. "Hey – I make the jokes around here!"

"Do you?" Scarlet said. "I hadn't noticed."

Ryan raised his middle finger. "You're much more aggressive when you're starved of sex, Cairo – do you know that?"

"If I'm starved then you're in the middle of a famine."

Another peal of laughter, but Scarlet was missing Jack Camacho and Ryan had hit a nerve with his comment. The former CIA man had traveled back to the US after Alex Reeve had contacted them. The president's daughter had heard rumors about some sort of plot in Washington DC and Eden had decided it would be prudent to send her some back-up.

With laughter still in the air, Eden moved things along and introduced the somber man beside him. "Magnus Lund here you already know."

They exchanged a polite nod with the enigmatic Dane. "So let's move straight to business," Lund began. "We found your story about the Alexander Codex very interesting indeed and I can only wish you'd had longer with the text before Dirk Kruger stole it. Using what little information you were able to extrapolate from the text before losing it, we know there is a Citadel, some kind of ancient power base used a capital city long before human history as we know it was capable of building such a place."

"Which is mind-blowing stuff," Eden said. "I think we can all agree on that, and we also know that access to the Citadel's gateway can only be had with the use of eight golden idols. We have those idols, but the location of the Citadel remains a mystery."

Lund took over. "That's what the Codex is for. When time was running out for him on board the Anshar, Wolff sacrificed the idols for the Codex, and this is very telling. He made the snap decision that it was better to know where the Citadel was and to hide its location from us than to have the idols."

Lexi crossed her arms and looked down at her hand. The steel prosthetic nails were still something alien and unwelcome in her life and she tucked them under her arm to keep them out of view. Everyone knew the torture she had undergone in China, but they still made her self-conscious. "Makes sense. There's no point having a key to a door if you don't know where the door is."

"Right," Eden said, taking back over. "We have the keys, but only he knows where the door is. I suspect he plans to locate and secure the gateway and then divert resources to hunt us down and take back the idols."

Lea laughed. "Yeah, like that's going to happen."

Others joined in, but Lund didn't share the moment. "Mr. Bale, I understand you had a short time to study the Codex before Kruger snatched it in Amphipolis?"

Ryan's hesitant voice spoke up in the empty theatre. "Yes, but not for long. I only had a few minutes with it."

"Tsk, tsk," Scarlet said. "Why are you on this team again?"

"And how quickly can *you* translate ancient Greek in faded ink on crumbling papyrus?"

She raised an eyebrow. "As you were."

He couldn't resist smirking at her as he shook his head. "As I was saying, the time I had with the Codex was limited, but it wasn't all a waste of time."

Reaper rubbed his hands together. "This is where things get interesting."

"The start of the Codex was a description of the idols and why Alexander wanted them so badly. It details his struggle to find them, and why he took his armies over so much of the ancient world. He was hunting the idols but also several rings. The ring I found on Alexander the Great's finger is one of eight, and the odds are good that those eight rings are integral to locating the Citadel."

"And we already have the idols to open the gateway," Lexi said.

"Bloody hell," Scarlet said. "We get those rings and we've nailed the whole thing."

Hawke scratched his head. "Just one problem though. We need the Codex to locate the seven other rings, and Wolff has the Codex."

"And that could be anywhere," Lexi said.

Eden spoke up. "It *could* be anywhere, but it's also *somewhere*, and we know where that specific somewhere is."

Hawke looked across at Lea. Catching her eye, he returned her smile with a conspiratorial wink.

"Well, where is it?" Scarlet said.

"Meteora, in the monastery."

Ryan was confused. "You mean the Monastery of the Holy Trinity, as in that amazing old building perched on the massive stack of rock in the Aegean Sea?"

"I do, or at least the *former* Monastery of the Holy Trinity. For some months Wolff has been in the process of acquiring it from the Orthodox Catholic Church. He closed the deal a few weeks ago and set up his new headquarters there. All our intel points to the Codex being kept in the monastery's vaults."

Reaper raised his eyebrows. "Sounds exciting."

"I should bloody well say so!" Ryan said. "That's where they filmed the final sequence of *For Your Eyes Only*!"

Scarlet rolled her eyes. "How many times, Ryan. You're not James Bond."

Ryan's shoulders visibly sloped. "I know, *dammit.*"

Lund seemed to relax. "Getting the location of Wolff's new HQ wasn't easy. It cost the life of a good man in the Greek National Intelligence Service, but it gave us a serious break. As far as we know, Wolff and the rest of his cult are under the impression Meteora has not been compromised. This gives us a real opportunity for a surprise raid, and the sooner we do it the better. We can only surmise, but my best guess is when he deciphers the Codex and has the information he needs about the other rings, he'll move out and probably for good."

Hawke found Lund's optimism troubling. Given how hard the mission had been to this point, he saw no reason why the Oracle wouldn't fight harder than ever to protect the Codex, and after translating it they could expect a savage assault aimed at retrieving the idols.

Hawke started to ask Lund a question, but his phone rang. The Dane took the call and wandered around the outside of the theatre with his umbrella.

"Where are the idols right now?" he asked Eden.

"All eight of them are in the secret gold vaults of the Bank of England," Eden told him. "And that's where they're staying until we have the other rings and know where the Citadel is. Then they'll be transported under heavy military guard to the location of the gateway. After that, it's anyone's guess what's on the cards."

Hawke looked around the theatre at his friends. After the devastating death of Danny Devlin in Miami Beach, they were more dedicated than ever to taking the Oracle out of action and discovering the Citadel.

"When do we start?" Lea asked.

Lund walked back over to them and slid the phone back into his suit pocket. "That was Nikos Katrivanos, the Greek Minister of the Interior," he said. "And he says you have permission to fly to Meteora and make an assault on the monastery."

"Thank fuck for that," Hawke said. "We never do anything unless we get permission first."

Eden gave him a wry smile. "All right, thank you."

Lund missed the sarcasm. "And he added that it would be ever so nice if you could try and minimize the damage to the building itself, please. It was built in 1475 and he doesn't want a repeat of the Parthenon if that's okay with you."

They all turned and looked up at the scaffolding on the ancient temple perched above high them.

"What?" Lea said. "Us?"

"Yes," he said with emphasis. "You."

"Okay, let's make this happen," Hawke said. "It's high time we took Wolff out of the equation for good."

"There's something else," Eden said. "Something you all need to know about Danny's death."

The silence that followed his words echoed the deep sadness they all felt about their old friend's brutal murder.

"What do we need to know?" Lea said.

Eden seemed hesitant. "He was killed with a marked bullet, one that had his name on it. We've run tests on the round and I can say it was a .408 bottlenecked cartridge, solid bullet with a non-lead core. Copper-nickel alloy round. The ballistics report concludes that it was fired on a CheyTac M200 Intervention."

"Holy shit," Lea said. "That's pretty much the most powerful sniper rifle in the world."

"You're saying this is some kind of vendetta?" Hawke asked.

Eden's answer was now without hesitation. "In my view, his death was a professional hit carried out by an extremely skilled sniper, probably ex-military. As for who ordered it, the best guess has to be the Oracle, but all bets are now off. Worse, there was a threat implying that the rest of us are also in danger."

"We're all targets?" Lea said, shocked.

"Looks that way."

"So there's a psycho sniper out there with the world's most lethal rifle and a hit list full of our names?" Ryan said. "You always think it's going to happen to someone else."

Lea rolled her eyes. "This is serious, Ry."

"Lea's right," Hawke said. "Until we find the killer, literally none of us is safe. The shooter could be anywhere."

"We're in the open now," Scarlet said, glancing around the area.

"We can't spend our lives hiding in a basement," Lexi said. "We have to find the bastard and take him out, but not before finding out who hired him."

By the time they all heard the crack of the shot, Magnus Lund had already been struck and knocked to the ground. As blood spilled out of the dead man's head, the team scattered to anywhere they saw cover, shocked to the core at the timing of the murder.

Hawke studied the way Lund had fallen and twisted his head around to the top of the theatre. "Over there," he called out. "No sign of the shooter but that's where the round was fired. I'm going up."

"Are you insane?" Lea said.

"He won't fire twice," he said. "Now it's about escape and evasion until the next time."

Hawke scrambled up the stone terraces of the theatre, stumbling here and there as he made his way up to the top. He heard the sound of a Vespa two-stroke receding into the distance, and by the time he crested the rise at the top of the theatre and reached the base of the Acropolis, it was in time to see nothing but a trail of dust twisting up from an empty road leading back down into the city.

He cursed and kicked a pile of gravel out into the road. With a sense of mounting fury, he padded back down to the rest of his team and gave them the bad news while Lea called an ambulance. They knew it was too late, but there was nothing else they could do.

"I can't believe it!" Lexi said. "I can't believe they killed Magnus."

Once again shattered by the violence of another sniper's round, the team rapidly pulled themselves together as the sound of sirens approached from the south.

"How fast can we get to this monastery?" Hawke asked.

"As fast as a chopper can fly," Eden replied.

Scarlet flicked her cigarette butt to the ground and crushed it under her heel. "And where do we rendezvous?"

"I've got a little boat in the Med," Eden said.

"Then let's get on with it – not just for Danny, but for Magnus because at this rate there might not be any of us left to fight anyone pretty soon."

CHAPTER THREE

Disregarding the charged political atmosphere surrounding her, Alex Reeve pushed her wheelchair slowly along a corridor outside the Cabinet Room. It seemed like forever since her father had become President of the United States but she would never get used to living in this place. It was nothing like in the movies, but a mostly quiet, boring place of work populated by straight-faced bureaucrats and steely Secret Service agents.

She was heading for the Oval Office to see her father when Agent Brandon McGee called out to her from behind. She turned and smiled, but there was no reciprocation. He looked concerned and anxious as he walked over to her.

"Hey, Brandon."

"Alex, hi. We need to talk."

She twisted her head as her eyes narrowed. "What about?"

"In private."

"We can go to my apartment in the Residence."

He thought about it, then shook his head. "I think we need to go for a drive."

She gave a nervous laugh. "What's going on, Brandon?"

He leaned over, flicked the brake off her wheelchair, and moved around behind her to grab hold of the push handles. "We'll talk when we're on the road."

He wheeled her along the corridor, each second getting closer to the Office of the Vice President. "Are we going to see Faulkner?"

A pause.

"No, no we're not. Besides, he's not here. He's at his private residence. I checked with his Secret Service detail less than an hour ago."

He steered her to the right and headed toward the main entrance to the West Wing.

"Why would you do that?"

"On the road, Alex. We'll talk on the road."

"You're making me nervous."

He showed his pass to the door security and they stepped outside. Parked up on the circular drive was a black Secret Service Escalade. A drizzle fell as McGee pushed down the brakes on the chair and opened the passenger door. Lifting Alex into the vehicle he paused to scan the building for something and then hopped into the driver's seat and fired it up.

He accelerated around the sweeping drive and headed to the northeast gate. Passing another layer of security he pulled out onto Pennsylvania Avenue and headed west to the river. The traffic was heavy and progress was slow, and inside the Escalade the atmosphere was somber as the windshield wipers moved across the rain-streaked glass.

"Why the cloak and dagger, Brandon?"

"Your room could be bugged."

"Huh?"

"You room, back in the Residence." He shot her a serious glance. "There's a good chance it's bugged."

"You can't be serious?"

"I am serious. I swept this car just before getting you so I know it's safe."

"But my *room?*"

"Sorry."

"Who would do such a thing?"

Brandon sighed.

"Not my *father?*"

"No, not your father. President Brooke is a good man."

She frowned. Her heart started to quicken in her chest. She wondered if she was having a minor panic response. They'd gotten worse since she was back in the chair. "Then who?"

The word fell from McGee's lips like an anvil hitting a concrete floor. "Faulkner."

For a few seconds, she didn't know what to say. When she'd had the time to process the information, she still couldn't bring herself to believe it. "You can't possibly mean Vice President Davis Faulkner?"

"I mean precisely him," he said in his rounded baritone voice.

"Holy shit. I'd heard vague rumors about a plot but nothing was confirmed."

"It is now."

"That's against the law, Brandon."

"Oh yeah," he said, steering the Escalade neatly around the roundabout at Washington Circle. "Big time."

Now the confusion and fear were giving way to anger. "What the goddam hell for?"

"This is difficult, but it looks like he's trying to move against your father."

She opened her mouth to speak but no words came.

"I know what that must sound like, but I just had to tell you, and now before things get out of control."

"I don't understand what you mean."

McGee cruised the Escalade past the Swedish Embassy and Bangkok Joe's, signaling to take the exit ramp down to Canal Road. Checking his mirror, he narrowed his eyes. Was that Chevy Suburban following them? He drove for another minute or two and then pulled off at the Abner Cloud House. Sweeping around in the gravel car park, he watched the Suburban cruise past them to the west. He pulled into a parking space with a view of the Potomac River, killed the engine, and sighed deeply.

"I mean Faulkner's planning to invoke the Twenty-Fifth Amendment and remove your father from office."

In the enclosed space of the SUV, his words sounded ridiculous. "What the fuck?"

"I know what it sounds like, but my intel is good."

"Who?"

"One of Muston's security detail. I've known him since we were in the army together."

Muston was Faulkner's Chief of Staff. "This just gets worse… so he's in on it too?"

McGee nodded. "Looks that way, yeah."

Alex ran her hands over her face and into her hair. She was struggling to make sense of it all and had a million questions pulsing in her brain and giving her a migraine headache. "But why?"

"That's the part we don't know. We all thought Faulkner was a dog with no teeth, but now we know different. Kusumoto thinks it's part of a wider conspiracy."

"Kusumoto?"

"She's my army buddy on Muston's detail. Suzie Kusumoto. She comes from Chicago just like me. That's why we got to be buddies in the army."

Alex tightened her hands into iron fists and smashed one down onto her dead legs. "A wider fucking conspiracy? Jesus fucking Christ, Brandon!"

The big man shook his head in sympathy at the shock she must be feeling. "I know, Alex. I know."

"What else do you know?"

"Not much. Suzie says she thinks Faulkner's either working with someone else or even working *for* someone else."

"The Vice President of the United States works for the American people and my goddam father, Brandon!"

"Not on this occasion."

"And who is this mysterious third party?"

"We don't know. Suzie's vague because Muston is a very careful man. Some of these guys talk when their security's in the room and some don't. Muston's the sort who doesn't, so she's only got this information through overhearing tiny fragments of conversation and observing his behavior."

Now she rubbed her temples. She realized she'd been staring at the rain sliding down the windshield for several minutes without blinking. "This is just nuts. Does my dad know?"

"Not yet."

She turned to him and wrinkled her face up. "Don't take this the wrong way, Brandon, but why the fuck not?"

"Apart from you and the President, I don't know who I can trust and I decided to talk to you about it first. Remember, your father isn't in any mortal danger. This isn't a threat to the life of the President. This is a political move against him." He turned to her and twisted his lips in uncertainty. "In other words, way above my pay grade."

"But invoking the Twenty-Fifth?" She looked puzzled. "He hasn't done anything to merit that. No way can that son of a bitch use the Constitution to get into the Oval Office. No frigging way."

McGee checked the mirror. A big black Cadillac CT6 pulled into the car park and crunched on the gravel as it pulled up beside them. Tinted windows. He checked his weapon in the holster but said nothing to Alex.

"I wouldn't be so sure about that," he said. "Suzie thinks this is the real deal and there's a good chance it's going to happen soon, as in the next day or two. That's why I came to you now."

She felt dizzy. She had to control her breathing to stop

hyperventilating. She did what she always did, forming her lips into a small oval and blowing the breath out in long controlled bursts with her eyes closed. When the dizziness had subsided, she opened her eyes again and noticed that her cheeks were flushed. She had to fight the panic.

"We have to tell my Dad right away," she said, fighting to control her breathing. "And I need to tell Joe Hawke, too!"

CHAPTER FOUR

"Today we fight."

Hawke scanned the faces of his team. They had fought many battles together, and many good friends had fallen on the way. The war against the Oracle and his Athanatoi cult had ground them down, stripping them of everything except their hope. Their team had been shattered, their home had been destroyed and any innocence they had left was crushed out of existence.

"And we fight hard," he turned from the team to the enormous rock formation looming over his shoulder. The Monastery that the Oracle and the Athanatoi high command had appropriated was nestled at the very top of this place. On the center of this island in the Aegean Sea, he had built his inner sanctum atop a towering column of rock nearly two thousand feet high.

"Do we fight any other way?" Scarlet dragged on the last of her cigarette and flicked the butt into the shore's shallow waters. "I mean, Ryan fights like a girl, but it's unwise to fuck with the rest of us, right?"

Ryan slowly extended his middle finger. "Spin baby, spin."

"You know what, boy?"

"What?"

"Since your balls dropped I'm starting to like you."

He blew her a kiss. "Maybe one day I can say the same of you."

"Ouch," Lexi said. "With an ego like yours, Cairo, that's gotta hurt."

Scarlet smirked. "At least since they dropped I finally

have something to kick."

"Fifteen all," Hawke said. "Now back to business."

Scarlet smacked a magazine into her machine pistol. "Forty-thirty actually… to me."

Hawke gave her a weary look and shook his head. "Right, gather round. We all know what's at stake here. At the top of this cliff is the ancient monastery which Wolff has converted into his latest headquarters. He's using it because of the inaccessibility, but that's not going to stop us. We go up silent and then we go in hard."

"Stop it, Joe," Lexi said. "No one wants to hear about our night in Zambia together."

Hawke opened his mouth to speak, and then closed it again, speechless.

Lea said, "You can look, Hun, but you can't touch." She waved the engagement ring in the air and the sun caught the diamonds, making them sparkle. "He's mine now." She walked over to the Chinese assassin and leaned into her ear, lowering her voice to a whisper. "Mine all mine, got it?"

As she and Lexi exchanged a glance, Scarlet broke the tension. "We do this for Danny and Magnus."

Hearing the names out loud stopped Hawke in his tracks. None of them had known Magnus, and while Danny Devlin had never been a full member of the team, he'd risked his life on countless occasions to save theirs and died making sure Hawke and Ryan could board the Oracle's airship over Biscayne Bay.

When Lund had told him that their friend had been killed by a marked bullet his blood ran cold. When he told him there was a threat to kill other members of his team engraved on the other side, it had almost frozen in his veins. Somewhere out there, trailing them… maybe monitoring them right now was one of the world's sharpest shooters. Knowing any of them could get shot dead at any minute by a silent, invisible killer was not an easy burden to bear at the best of times, but on a mission like this, it took a lot to hold things together. And that wasn't easy with a sniper on your tail. It was the one thing that could strike fear into any soldier.

And things were getting more dangerous by the day. With the murder of Magnus Lund, brutally cut down right in front of them in the heart of Athens, they all knew their new enemy was getting bolder. Each of them had started looking over their shoulders in search of the phantom killer and it was starting to spook them all out, but Hawke knew the only way forward was to go without fear.

Lexi slung her weapon over her shoulder and winked at Lea. "We ready to go?"

"Yeah, let's do it," the Irishwoman said with confidence, staring up at the monastery.

The ancient rock formation twisted up into the sky. A sheer rockface towered above them, but they were spared the problem of trying to scale it with ropes. The ancient monastery at the top had been inhabited for centuries, and in that time goat tracks had formed various winding approaches to the top.

The climb was not easy. The towering rockface was almost vertical in places and required all the climbing skills and strength they could muster. For what seemed like an eternity, life was nothing but climbing anchors, carabiners, and chalk bags while the ancient Aegean Sea churned far below them, crashing into the rocks at the base of the cliffs.

At the top, they tucked down beside a low wall of juniper growing among some craggy boulders and got their breath back while they prepared the guns and got ready to make their move.

Today there would be no playing games. With murdered teammates in their graves and the idols in their possession, the only thing that stood between them and the Citadel were the eight rings, and finding them meant taking back the Alexander Codex. They had the element of surprise on their side. No one knew they were here and it was dusk. The light was low and visibility was poor.

And they were angry.

It started when Hawke gave the sign to attack. He kicked things off and leaped over the boulders, submachine gun held tight to his body. Leading from the front, he executed a superfast crouch run and reached the monastery's western wall unseen and unheard.

The rest of his team were seconds behind him, armed and ready to fight as they moved through the half-light with the setting sun at their backs. When Ryan slammed up against the honey-colored stone wall, the team was all in place and ready to go inside the monastery.

The next move was clear. A winding goat track at the base of the building led around to a shady cloister. From there, access to the interior of the monastery would be simple. They crouch ran along the track in stony silence, the only sound being the crunch of gravel chips as they headed toward the cloister with their deadly cargo gripped in their hands.

Inside the shelter of the cloister now, Hawke signaled to the team that it was time to go inside. He led the way, vaulting over a low internal wall and then slipping through a stone archway. Gathered in a narrow corridor, it was time to divide the team. Hawke, Lea, and Lexi were going to the Oracle's quarters on the top floor and Scarlet, Ryan, and Reaper were going down to the vaults. The Codex could be in either place and it was essential they hit both at the same time.

Scarlet and Ryan stood aside as Reaper took his pump-action shotgun to the door that led down to the vaults. The rounds obliterated the old wood to sawdust and when the air cleared all that was left were three rusty hinges hanging off the door jamb.

Scarlet was the first to breach the gloomy darkness, gun raised into the aim as she moved down the cold, stone steps toward the monastery vaults far below. At her back, Ryan also held his weapon ready for action, and behind him, Reaper took up the rear, checking no one followed them down.

"This place is not nice, Cairo," Ryan said.

"Put it on Trip Advisor if you feel that strongly about it, boy."

Reaper suppressed a chuckle. He was too apprehensive to relax at a time like this, but it was good to know Scarlet's notorious sense of humor was impossible to kill.

They reached the bottom of the steps and cast their flashlights around the small, grimy place. It was cold and damp, and a foul musty smell filled the air. Ahead of them were several wooden doors.

Then they heard it.

"What the hell was that?" Ryan said.

"Sounded like a ghost," said Reaper.

Scarlet raised her gun and stepped toward one of the doors. "It was no ghost. There's someone behind this door."

Closer now, they all heard the sound of a man calling out but Scarlet couldn't recognize the language. "What's he saying?"

"It's Greek," Ryan said. "He's calling out for help, but it's not good Greek."

"We need to get in there," she said.

"Are you crazy?" Ryan said. "We can't rescue him!"

"Why not, because his grammar's wrong?"

He rolled his eyes. "No, because it could be a trap."

"They don't even know we're here, Sherlock," Scarlet said. "How could they be planning a trap?"

"Elle a raison," Reaper said, and smashed the door in with his boot.

In one of the corners, a monster of a man was chained to the wall. A torn shirt revealed a chest like an iron barrel, and the muscles on his arms would have made most professional wrestlers tremble in fear.

He looked up at them and spoke in Greek.

"He wants to know who we are," Ryan said.

"You speak English?" the man said.

"Sure do, I'm from the States."

Scarlet took a step closer to the man, her gun still firmly gripped in her hands. "And what the fuck are you doing in here?"

Without batting an eyelid, he said deadpan, "I just like the feel of the chains."

She sighed and rolled her eyes. "All right, Mr. Funny Cuts, it was a stupid question."

"I was rock climbing here a few days ago when these crazies burst out of nowhere with a bunch of guns and took me prisoner. They shot my buddy, Mark when he tried to escape."

"Jesus," Ryan said. "Why didn't they shoot you, too?"

The Texan gave a wry smile. "I never tried to escape, but what the hell they plan to do with me… I have no idea, man. Judging from the screams I hear at night, let's just say I'm glad you guys turned up."

The gnarled former Foreign Legionnaire crouched beside him, his silver stubble shining in Scarlet's flashlight beam. "You know how to shoot a gun, mon ami?"

"Are you kidding me? I'm a tank commander! Ex 7th Cavalry out of Fort Hood, Texas. Give me a gun and watch me go, man."

Reaper stood back up and looked at Scarlet. "Your call."

Scarlet stared down at the man. Yes, it could be a trap, but that was unlikely. It was true that no one knew they were coming and if it was a trap it was ridiculously elaborate. No, he was telling the truth, and there were always those arms to think about. Plus the hands, she thought as her eyes crawled down his arms. Bigger than boxing gloves and great muscle tone.

She snapped out of it and thought about Jack Camacho. "All right, get the chains off him."

Reaper gave a Gallic shrug. "Turn your head, mon ami."

He blasted the chains with the shotgun and ripped them to pieces, instantly freeing the man who now picked up an old battered cowboy hat and sunglasses and got to his feet. Standing at his full height he was even bigger than he had looked when chained to the wall.

"Thanks, guys. You saved my life. They were only feeding me once a day. I'd have been dead inside a week."

Ryan said, "They're not known for their hospitality."

"So who the hell are they?"

"It's a long story," Scarlet said. "More pertinent, darling – who the hell are you?"

"Ezekiel Jones," he said, holding out one of those hands. "Great to meet you, ma'am."

"It's Cairo to my friends," she said, taking the hand.

Golly, that's a firm grip.

Think of Jack Camacho, idiot.

"Friends call me Zeke."

"And this is Reaper and the Boy."

"Hey, guys."

"Actually my name's Ry—"

"Listen," Scarlet said, butting into Ryan. "Any idea where someone could hide a very valuable book around here?"

He shook his head. "Not exactly. They had a bag over

my head when they brought me down here, but maybe there's one thing that could help. It's pretty quiet down here and when you're waiting for food or the shit bucket to be emptied…"

"Oh, let's not go there, please," Ryan said.

"Sorry," Zeke said, grinning. "Anyway, locked in here you get to notice every little sound, and I can tell you guys that there's a lot of coming and going past this cell down to the end of the corridor outside. My best guess would be if there's anything valuable, then maybe try down there. If you need an extra pair of hands, count me on board. No one wants to blow their asses off more than I do. They killed my buddy."

Reaper pulled a pistol from his belt and threw it at him.

Zeke grabbed the gun with one hand, popped the catch, and slid the magazine out. "Empty."

"Just wanted to see if you knew how to use a gun," the Frenchman said, tossing him a magazine.

The Texan smacked the mag into the grip and gave them a big, broad smile full of strong white teeth. "Let's go kick some ass." On cue, the deep thump of an explosion boomed out high above them. "You guys didn't come alone, did you?"

"No," Scarlet said. "And it sounds like the other half of our team could use our help."

CHAPTER FIVE

Hawke dived to the floorboards and cradled his head with his arms. A shower of debris from a grenade explosion rained down over him as he now rolled to the cover of an archway a few yards to his right. He was swiftly followed by Lea who now slammed into his side while Lexi was further back along the corridor providing cover fire from her handgun.

"Gotta love these days," Lea said. "Something to tell the kids."

Hawke spun his head around to her, a startled look on his face. "Wait, you're not…"

"No," she said, rolling her eyes. "But it's great to know that when I am you'll have the same look on your face as you did when Klaus Kiefel attacked Washington."

Another round of gunfire stopped his reply, and looking ahead he saw the Athanatoi slam the Oracle's door shut. "We've got to get in there!" he called out.

Lexi sprinted over to them and they fired on the door together, blasting the lock to hell.

Hawke tried the handle but it wouldn't budge. "They've pushed something up against it!"

"What is it?"

He peered through one of the gaps in the wooden panel blasted out by the gunfire. "Looks like a bookshelf or something."

"Meanwhile Otmar Sodding Wolff is getting away with the Codex!"

Hawke shoulder-barged the cabinet out of the doorway as a hail of automatic gunfire ripped the piece of furniture to pieces. He crashed to the floor on top of it and landed in a carpet of splintered wood and smashed glass. Momentary surprise at his recklessness stunned the Athanatoi, giving him the half-second he needed to propel himself away from the danger with a classic parkour forward shoulder roll.

Bullets nipped at his heels as he came out of the roll at high speed and dived behind the cover of an upturned leather sofa running along the far wall. His bravery had paid off just as he had planned. Drawing the cultists' fire gave Lexi and Lea the time they needed to fall in behind him and break away to the right and left.

Lea was first into the fray, taking on a monk in black robes while Hawke and Lexi kept his associates pinned down with cover fire. The man was a skilled fighter, and she was instantly reminded of all those years she had wasted improving her Tekken skills. As he spun through the air, his black robes billowed out behind him like shadows, and then his boot was almost in her face.

She yanked her head back to dodge the blow and reached for her gun but it was too late.

The man used the momentum of spin and twisted at the waist as he came back to earth. Bringing his hand around like a scythe, he belted the gun from her grip and it flew across the room and out of an arched window.

Now he was still again, squaring up to her and confidently assuming the ready stance. He raised his right arm and beckoned for her to come closer. "Fight!"

She shook her head. "Christ, it's not *actually* Tekken, you know!"

He narrowed his eyes, confused, and then she struck. Firing a feint strike with her left hand while powering her right hand into his jaw.

He ducked, but too slow. The impact of bone on bone was hard, and she felt her knuckle crack and her finger dislocate as the acolyte staggered back a step and fought to regain his balance.

Behind her, Hawke was still using cover fire to keep some monks from entering the room while Lexi was now pounding another cultist with a brutal remorselessness. She quickly gained the upper hand and never relented, powering blows into his face and stomach until he fell and knocked himself out when his skull hit the tiled floor. Spinning, she saw Lea struggling with the other man in black robes, and she ran to help her.

"Thought you could do with some help," she said.

"Thanks," Lea said. "I think maybe I'm getting too old for this."

The two of them went to work on the acolyte, attacking from different angles as he fought hard to fend them both off. But it was an impossible task, and they soon got the better of him, with Lea hammering him hard until his eyes rolled back into his head and he toppled backward and crashed into the table behind him.

Hawke fought the others back and wedged the door shut with the upturned sofa. "That won't keep them out for long," he said, running deeper into the room in search of the Oracle's escape route. Up ahead was a double-door, which now swung open to reveal two more men in black robes holding submachine guns. They each opened fire, spraying the room with lead and sweeping their weapons from side to side to make sure none of the enemy survived.

Lea and Lexi were far enough back to dive behind two large stone support columns but Hawke was directly in the line of fire. Thinking on his feet, he tipped up the colossal briefing table in the middle of the floor and crouched down behind it as the bullets pelted and ripped and pinged all around him.

"Sometimes I ask myself exactly why I do this," he

muttered, ducking his head down just in time to avoid a speeding bullet.

"You love it really!" Lea slammed down beside him, and Lexi a moment later.

Gunfire chattered away somewhere below them deep inside the monastery.

"Sounds like someone got on Cairo's bad side." Lexi ducked her head down as she reloaded her gun, steeling herself for more action but momentarily distracted by the sight of the steel fingernails on her left hand. Every time she looked at them, she saw Pig's face and the pliers in his sweaty hands. She hated it, and she wondered how long it would be before she could finally banish the ghost of his chubby face from her mind.

When the shooting stopped, they took a second to get their bearings. Peering over the table, Hawke saw the men were gone, and he got his first proper look at the room. The Oracle's private suite was dominated by an enormous, formal room that might have looked more at home in the Vatican than a monastery on a Greek island.

A series of high, arched windows punctuated one of the walls and gave a breathtaking view of the sun setting over the Aegean Sea. The other wall was decorated with original artworks, some of which he recognized as masterpieces of Rembrandt and Caravaggio, and standing in front of them in stony silence was a series of statues from the ancient world – Poseidon, Amphitrite, Mars, Odin, Osiris, all the way down to the end.

But there was no sign of the man himself or any of his guards.

Lea raised her head from behind one of the upturned tables. "Where the hell did they go, Joe?"

"Bugger knows," he called back. "But they went that way!"

CHAPTER SIX

He scrambled to his feet and dusted himself off as he sprinted toward the double doors at the far end of the room. With Lea and Lexi at his back, he ran into the other room and was met with a meaty fist to the center of his face.

He felt his head jerk backward and fought hard to stay conscious. He blinked a couple of times and through the stars, he saw another fist rapidly approaching. This time he ducked and the fist smashed into the wooden paneling of the door behind him.

The man in robes grunted as he withdrew his grazed and shattered fist, but before he had time to survey the damage Hawke delivered a hefty headbutt into the middle of his head and splattered his nose across his face.

This got more than a grunt, and the howling man now cradled his head in his hands and scuttled away before the Englishman caused any more damage. But there was no break in the fighting, and now two more men in black robes flew through the air and landed right in front of them.

Lea felt the anger rise, as one of the men raced toward her. "They're holding us back while he gets away, dammit!"

The other attacked Lexi and now a third and fourth arrived from a side door and launched themselves at Hawke. The fighting intensified, each of the ECHO team members being pushed to the max just to survive against some of the fastest and most aggressive hand-to-hand combat they had ever experienced.

"We're in trouble, Joe!"

"Not with the cavalry here!"

Turning, she saw the welcome faces of Scarlet, Ryan, and Reaper burst around the corner, followed by a man-mountain of epic proportions. Bronzed, tattooed arms and a torn t-shirt barely containing a muscle-bound chest, and a pair of tight blue jeans fixed at the waist with a Lone Star belt buckle, it was topped off with a torn, sweat-stained ten-gallon cowboy hat.

"What the fuck?" Lea said.

"Wonder where he's from?" Lexi spun around and kicked her opponent in the stomach, sending him doubling over in pain.

"Meet Zeke," Scarlet said, rolling her eyes as she waded into the fray. "Zeke, meet the weaker half of the team."

"Hey everyone!"

"Good to meet… hey!" Lea said, kicking one of the monks in the balls. "Fuck off with that! We're the best half."

"And does the best half of the team have a plan?" Ryan said.

Hawke ducked a punch and turned to Ryan. "Just keep going forward until we stumble onto the truth, to be honest mate."

The fight wore on, and the ECHO team gradually overcame their opponents, desperate to get after the Oracle before he got away with the Codex. The man fighting Lea drew a blade from a holster on the prayer rope around his waist. A look of hatred curdled his young face and struck terror into her, but she never flinched.

He lunged forward, but she was ready for him. Side-stepping the attack, she brought the back of her hand down hard on his wrist and disarmed him, hooking her leg around his and throwing him down to the floor.

As they gathered around him, he scrambled for his knife and shocked everyone to the core by slashing at his wrists.

"Damn it!" Lea yelled. "Don't die!"

Lexi ripped some material from her shirt and tried to create two tourniquets around his cut wrists.

A sad, but satisfied smile appeared on his lips. "It's too late. You can't torture me for information now. I'm dying…"

She crouched down beside him and twisted the fabric of his cowl around in her fists. Blood bubbles popped at the corners of his mouth and his eyes were rolling back into the back of his head. "The Alexander Codex! Where is it?"

Now a much crueler smile spread on his split, bruised lips. "Why should I tell you?"

Reaper crouched down beside Lea. "Because if you don't, I can make the end of your life so painful you will wish for *la mort*, you understand me?"

"This is pretty heavy," Zeke said. "I only came here to hitchhike the Greek islands!"

Confusion spread on the man's agonized face as the blood streamed out of his wrists despite Lexi's improvised tourniquet. "You would torture a dying man?"

Reaper gave his famous Gallic shrug. "Unfortunately, *oui*."

"Just tell us where it is, arsehole," Hawke said, kicking the man's legs.

The Athanatoi warrior coughed blood up over his lips and wheezed for air. He tried to hoist himself up on his elbows but crashed back down to the floorboards. "I will never tell you where it is. I will never disobey my master."

"Oh, Christ," Hawke said. "One of them. It's so bloody frustrating."

Scarlet smacked her hands together and started

stretching her leg. "You want me to take your frustration out on his balls?"

"Where is the Oracle?"

"He's not here, you fools."

"Where is he?"

The man shook his head. "You're going to lose this war."

"Where, dammit?!"

"Not here. He left hours ago."

"Then you be a good little lad and tell us where he is and we might save your life."

The man gave Scarlet a strange, patronizing look. "I don't want my life saved. I now go to a better place where I can walk in eternal peace."

"You'll be walking with an eternal limp if you don't start talking."

"It's too late," Lea said, lowering the man's head to the floor. "He's gone." She got up and paced away from the dead man, leaning up against the wall near a stone archway. Damn it all, we're buggered again."

"Look out!"

Lea turned sharply to see the oncoming threat but it was too late. A black-robed acolyte was already upon her, quickly whipping a garotte around her throat and wrenching it as tight as he could.

Lea struggled to pull the leather strap from her throat, but it was too tight.

Hawke sprinted toward her but the man hurriedly twisted the garotte.

The man called out. "Get back or I will tear it right through her windpipe!"

He skidded to a halt, his heart thumping in his chest. "You hurt her and I'll kill you where you stand."

The man made no reply, but gradually walked backward, pulling his terrified hostage into the darkness of the archway.

And then the blood-streaked tip of a blade poked through his throat.

He released the garotte and Lea stumbled forward, doubling over as she heaved breath into her lungs.

The man fell to his knees and the blade tip vanished again. Hawke ran to Lea, reaching her just as another man in brown robes stepped out of the shadows.

"Get back!" Hawke yelled, reaching for his gun.

The man dropped the blade and raised his hands. "I am no threat. I surrender."

"What the hell just happened?" Lexi asked.

"He saved my life is what…" Lea wheezed between breaths.

The man stayed perfectly still, his empty hands still held high above his head. He looked down at the corpse of the man in black robes with contempt. "His name was Konstantin," the man said. "And I am glad he is dead."

"Who was he?"

"One of the Oracle's closest guards, along with his brother Kazimir." He nudged his chin at the dead man with the slashed wrists.

"And who are you?"

"My name is Nikolai, and I offer you my loyal service. If you want to kill me, then do so now." He drew a sword from beneath his robes and handed it to Hawke. Kneeling before the Englishman, he pulled his robes forward to expose his neck. "But I beg you, make my execution fast."

"No one's getting executed on my watch," Hawke said. "Least of all an unarmed man who just risked his life to save us. On your feet, Nikolai."

The man stood, a look of grave confusion on his face. "I don't understand. The Athanatoi would have executed you if this situation was reversed."

"Which is exactly why we're going to win this thing,"

Lea said.

Hawke extended his hand. “And you’re welcome to join us, Nikolai.”

They shook hands. “My friends call me Kolya.”

“Then, thank you for saving my fiancée’s life, Kolya, but we have to go. Your Oracle has something that belongs to us and we need to get hold of it in a hurry.”

Nikolai looked concerned. “No, he does not have what you seek.”

Hawke and Lea exchanged a deflated glance. “Then where is it?”

A wise but mischievous smile appeared on Nikolai’s face. He reached into his robes and pulled out the Alexander Codex. “It’s right here, in front of your eyes.”

“Didn’t see that little baby coming!” Zeke said.

“I’ll say.” Ryan stared at the ancient codex. “Hello again, old friend.”

Nikolai handed the book to Lea. Hawke could hardly believe what had happened and got busy calling Eden back at HQ. “We’ve got the Codex,” he said into his mic. “Repeat, we have the Codex.”

CHAPTER SEVEN

The Royal Navy Wildcat hovered precariously above the warship as the pilot fought a strong crosswind. Regaining level flight he lowered the chopper through the air and touched down on the aft deck of HMS Duncan. The Type 45 air-defense destroyer was in the Aegean Sea on exercises when the Ministry of Defence had taken the call from Sir Richard Eden.

Lieutenant Brian Robinson met them on deck and after a short round of professional introductions, Ezekiel and Nikolai were taken to their private quarters while the ECHO team were led into the ship and taken to the wardroom. When they stepped into the comfortable mess cabin, the familiar face of Eden was already waiting for them.

Hawke looked at Eden and laughed, repeating his words back to him. "I've got a little boat in the Med, indeed!"

Eden shrugged. "It's not much, but it does the job."

After a good-natured chuckle, Eden skipped the small talk and got straight to business. They all knew the value of keeping their humor, but the recent losses of Danny Devlin and Magnus Lund had made that harder than ever. "So, you have the Codex?"

Without speaking, Ryan slung the canvas bag off his shoulder and dumped it on one of the tables in the center of the wardroom.

"Little bastard's in there," Scarlet said. "Can you smoke in here?"

Eden shook his head and pointed to the large NO

SMOKING sign on the door. Then he opened the bag and pulled the heavy, leather-bound tome from the tattered, dusty bag. Weighing it in his hands, a rare smile crept on his face. "Very good work, team. I am impressed."

Scarlet sniffed. "Well, I don't know about anyone else but that's why *I* risked my life to get it back."

Eden gave her a sour look. "It was merely a compliment, Cairo."

Ryan laughed like a child and pointed his finger at her face. "Ha, you got told off by your boss."

Scarlet tipped her head and pouted. "Go fuck a hot teapot, boy."

"Damn!" Ryan said. "I *knew* you put a pinhole camera in my kitchen."

Reaper howled with laughter and high-fived Scarlet while Eden shook his head and gave a long, disappointed sigh.

"And we're the people who are going to save the world?" Lea said to herself.

Eden was sanguine. "Hey, it works, and getting back to the subject – have you had time to look at the Codex, Mr. Bale?"

Ryan nodded and slumped down in one of the chairs. Lifting his dirty boots onto the table he crossed his arms behind his head and scanned the room. "But anything to eat around here?"

The Maritime Logistics Chef took one look at the disheveled young man in the leather jacket and torn Megadeth t-shirt and raised his eyebrow. "Breakfast's not for another hour."

"Great."

Eden cleared his throat. "You were about to tell us what you have derived from the Codex, Mr. Bale."

"Oh yeah, right. Sorry – I was thinking about food. Is it a cooked breakfast or that oatmeal crap?"

"A full range of breakfasts will be served, sir," the chef said as he left the room.

"Back to work, Ryan," Hawke said. "Tell the boss what you have so far."

"First, according to Alexander's writings in the Codex, King Midas was real and was also hunting the idols. Alexander wrote that Midas managed to secure three of the idols. Ra in Egypt, Brahma in the Indus Valley in north India, and Pangu on the Tibetan-Chinese border. He then returned with them to Pavlopetri, but then the city sank into the ocean, taking with them the idols he had looted from Egypt and Asia."

"Now *that* is bad luck," Reaper said.

"It sure is," Ryan continued. "And it helps clear up a long debate about whether or not Midas was real or a legend, and when he lived. Of those who say he was real, some say he lived in the second millennium BC and others much later. Now we know he was real and the fact he was in Pavlopetri before it sank dates him much earlier than we believed."

Lexi yawned. "I wish I'd sat at the back now."

Ryan frowned. "But Alexander knew from Midas that there were eight idols in total, the other four being Tanit, Tinia, Viracocha, and Buri, but he never found them."

"No, we did," Lea said.

Eden was impressed. "Back in Athens, you mentioned something about there being eight rings?"

"The Rings of the Gods," Ryan said, his voice rising in confidence. "I had snatched some info about them before Kruger stole the Codex from me. A longer reading on the journey here today has thrown more light on the subject. The Codex describes how there are eight rings to match the eight idols. There is almost certainly a link here to the eight gates surrounding the ancient city of Babylon and the eight-pointed rosette star of Inanna we see all over cuneiform tablets from ancient Sumer, some of which refer to gods who lived among the people and flew in the skies. Anyway, the number eight was highly significant to the ancient Sumerian culture."

"The plot thickens!" Scarlet said.

Ryan smiled. "And the Sumerians invented beer, so Cairo should feel right at home here."

"But I thought the number seven was the big mystical number?" Hawke said.

"Seven also has a great mystical significance to many ancient cultures," Ryan said, "but today we're all about the number eight."

"Oh my *God*," Lea said, aghast. "You're a numbertard! I had no idea."

Scarlet and Lexi laughed. "Leotard, more like," said the Chinese assassin.

"Very funny, Lexi," Ryan said. "Had any luck in the boyfriend department lately?"

She looked daggers at him. "As a matter of fact, I dumped someone just last week."

"Was he offended?"

"He was when I told him that I faked every orgasm."

"Hey, don't feel too sorry for him," Ryan said. "He probably faked the whole relationship."

"You want a slap?"

"Just commenting on the course of true love," he said. "If love is chemistry then sex is physics, right?"

"Please," Scarlet said. "No sex or violence, I'm British."

Hawke spat out his coffee. "That's a good one, coming from you!"

"Whatever are you trying to say?" she said with a smirk on her lips.

Ryan and Reaper shared a high five, but Eden was less impressed with the jokes. "What's the significance of these rings?" he asked, bringing the subject back on track.

Ryan continued, unfazed by the ribbing. "Each ring belonged to one of the eight deities of the Land of the Gods, and when put together they reveal the location of their Citadel. According to the Codex, each ring is forged from pure, 24-carat gold, and on the face of each ring is one section of a map that reveals the Citadel's location. Alexander said that the faces of these rings tesselate..."

"Fit," Lea said.

"...fit together perfectly to form the map."

"So we get the rings and we're all set to find the Citadel," Lexi said.

"Right," Ryan said proudly. "And the idols are the keys which open the Gateway and give us access. Easy as pie."

Hawke raised a skeptical eyebrow. "Somehow I doubt that. For a start, where does the search for the rings begin?"

"With me, Joe," the young hacker said with a cocky wink. "With me."

CHAPTER EIGHT

Lea was leaning on the Duncan's taffrail and looking out to sea and taking in a magnificent ocean dawn. After a long night, they were charting a course south to the Mediterranean, and just off the starboard side she could see the faint outline of Skyros. Two Hellenic Air Force Mirage jets roared over the ship and headed to the island's air base. It seemed like everything was moving except them, and she sighed. They'd been on the ship several hours waiting while Ryan and Eden tried to work out the location of the divine rings and she felt like taking a walk to relieve the boredom.

Scarlet stepped out onto the aft deck and yawned. Giving one of the Wildcat's Sea Venom missiles a loving pat as she walked past the chopper, she joined Lea at the stern and pulled a packet of cigarettes from her pocket.

"If you do jump, can I have your ring?"

Lea gave her a look. "Funny."

"Let's have another look at it, then."

Lea reluctantly held her hand up on the rail, but couldn't resist staring at it herself when it sparkled in the sunshine.

Scarlet lit her cigarette and slipped the lighter back into her pocket. Exhaling the smoke into the sea air, she looked at the ring. "Woah, and I thought Hawke was a tight bastard."

"He thought about giving me Liz's."

"Oh."

"He didn't."

"Good or bad?"

"Good. That ring was hers, and another part of his life. It was good he wanted to start over, don't you think?"

"I never think, darling, especially when men are involved. Better to go with your gut."

Lea was quiet for a long time. "You think we'll find the Citadel?"

"We found everything else we ever looked for."

"I know, but if we do, then what next?"

Scarlet stretched her arms and yawned. "Early retirement for me, babe. You?"

She shrugged. "Dunno, maybe go back to Ireland with Joe. He never talks about his family in London so I don't think he'd mind making a new home. Maybe even start a family."

"Christ, a miniature Joe Hawke."

Lea turned. "What's wrong with that?"

"Nothing, darling, nothing at all."

Lea gave her a look. "Retirement, huh?"

"You'll find me on my little island in the Caribbean, fast asleep with a daiquiri in each hand and a straw hat over my face." She turned to her. "And if any of you bastards phones me up about any pissing treasure I'll go nuts. Now, shall we go inside and see if the boy has worked out where these rings are?"

*

Freshly showered, Hawke was second back onto the wardroom. First back had been Ryan, and now he saw the young man slumped forward, fast asleep on a table. In front of him was an empty plate covered in grease and ketchup streaks and the Codex opened somewhere in the middle and tipped upside down beside a pad of paper covered in Ryan's illegible scrawl.

Seeing his old friend out for the count reminded him

how hard they had all worked to get this far and if maybe the end of this mission would be a good time to call it quits. He and Lea were engaged, for one thing, and she had been dropping some pretty unmissable hints about maybe trying for a baby, but she was right about him – being a father scared him more than an outright assault on a machine gun nest.

He walked over and nudged him. "Wakey wakey, eggs and bakey, Ryan."

The young man's head jerked up to reveal two sleepy red slits where his eyes could usually be found. "What the fuck?"

"You fell asleep, mate."

The others walked into the wardroom. "Aww," Lexi said. "He looks like a teddy bear."

"Piss off, Zhang."

"Woah," her face crumpled up in mock horror. "An aggressive teddy bear."

Eden walked in and closed the door. "Right, to business everyone. Ryan and I made good progress so listen up."

Ryan took over. "As we all know, there are eight golden rings, and these eight rings will somehow reveal the location of the Hidden Citadel. We already have one – the one we found on Alexander's finger, but we have to locate the other seven and we all know who else wants to find them."

"The Oracle," Hawke said.

"Exactly," Eden said, resuming his presentation. "When he was a young man, Alexander was tutored by the famous ancient Greek philosopher Aristotle. It's during this time he learned not only about the ancient civilization at Sumer but also about the far older civilization that was there before, including the Citadel."

Sipping his coffee, Ryan started to come back to life.

"The Codex tells us so much. The Citadel was the capital city of an ancient civilization that far predates even Sumer. As far as I can make out from what is at times some pretty cryptic writing, this ancient civilization was the first to harness the power of immortality, and its leaders were sent to seed the world and spread their civilization around the world."

"Holy shit in the Pope's miter," Lea said. "This is getting real."

"It's going to get a lot more real too," Ryan said. "As with Sumer, the cradle of this civilization started on the banks of the Euphrates, and we think the purpose of the idols was to enable their priests and holy class to take an image of their gods to the new lands they were seeding. That's why the idols are always of the creator gods or goddesses of the various cultures around the world, and why they all share the same symbols and features, including the intricate ziggurat in the base which we believe is some kind of key."

"I like keys," Scarlet said. "They open doors to treasure."

"Always about the money," Ryan said, sighing. "Anyway, the statues that archaeologists have been finding in these places were reproductions of these idols, and that was how they spread their culture. Whether or not they were gods or just their kings or queens, the Codex isn't clear."

A groan of frustration went around the wardroom.

Ryan raised his palms. "This just means that Alexander the Great never knew, that's all. It's his Codex remember, and his research. I suspect we'll find the answer to this question and a whole lot more when we finally locate the Citadel."

Reaper smacked his hands together. "And it all starts with the rings, mes amis!"

"So where are they?" Lexi asked.

"That's the interesting bit," Ryan said. "As we now know, Alexander only found one of the rings, but he moved heaven and earth to locate the other seven."

"So why did we only find one on him?" Lea asked.

"Because he died before he could secure them for himself, and then he had their location buried with him in this Codex."

"I ask again," Lexi said with a sigh. "Where are they?"

"According to Alexander, the seven rings had traveled down through the ages and found their way into the possession of various great rulers – Tutankhamun, Ramesses II, and Akhenaten in Egypt, Cyrus the Great of Persia, Romulus and Remus in Rome and King Sudas in India. Alexander the Great's ring makes eight."

"But if I'm not very much mistaken," Lea said, "all of those people's tombs have been opened and cataloged."

Eden shook his head. "Not when Alexander was alive, no. He spent his life searching for them and never found them."

"But today, yes, they've been found and excavated," Ryan said.

Lexi looked confused. "So the rings could be anywhere?"

Ryan smiled. "These tombs have been discovered and opened and their contents cataloged, but there are problems. First, there's never been any way to tell if they'd been raided before their official discoveries, and second, many of the relics from these hoards were stolen after their discovery. What we *can* say is that the rings Alexander described never made it to the official inventories of these hoards."

Eden tried to control his excitement. "But thanks to the Codex, we've been able to ascertain that the rings are all very different in appearance."

"And Alexander was very specific in describing them," Ryan said. "So we took the descriptions of the various rings Alexander wrote in the Codex and got busy while you were all sleeping."

Eden tossed his pen on the wardroom desk and lifted his coffee cup to his lips. "After a somewhat tedious process involving online searches and several telephone calls to various auction houses and security service contacts, I can tell you that the first ring is accounted for, so no groping around in dark tunnels."

"I'm sorry for you, boy," Scarlet said. "I know how much you enjoy groping around in dark tunnels."

"Pack it in, Cairo," Lea said.

"And pack your bags, too," Eden said. "Because you're going to Malaysia."

"Eh?" said Hawke.

"Malaysia," Eden repeated. "One of that country's richest criminals is an avid collector of ancient world relics and we've already worked out that he has Tutankhamun's ring. He's especially obsessed not only with ancient Egypt but also with anything from Sumer or the Indus Valley, and he's rumored to have some sort of a god-complex. Thinks he's descended from a long line of Sumerian gods."

"That makes even your ego look normal, Cairo," Ryan said.

"Not even bothering to look at you, boy."

"Where in Malaysia?" Hawke asked.

"We're not one hundred percent sure because he has several properties in the country, but he, and more to the point his guards, divide most of their time between his luxury apartment in the Petronas Towers and a large rubber plantation in the Temenggor jungle." The corner of Eden's mouth twisted up as paused a beat, and then he said, "So guess what?"

"We're paying him a visit?" Reaper said.

"You are," Eden added. "There is no way for us to know in which of the properties he is keeping the ring. However, we think it's more likely he's securing it in the diamond safe in his apartment in the towers, so you're going there first. I'll stay here on the Duncan and work on the location of the second ring."

Eden saw the concern on their faces as they learned the Codex would be out of their hands. "We've made a copy of the Codex so Mr. Bale here can work on it while you're on the road, so to speak, but it's worth all of us remembering that this Codex was in the Oracle's hands for more than long enough for him to make his own copy and work out the location of the rings just as we are doing."

"In other words," Lexi said, "this is going to be a race to the finish to secure the rings and find the gateway?"

"And one hell of a battle," Hawke said.

"And if that weren't bad enough, there's more," Eden said. "In the last hour, I received a call from Alex Reeve in the United States. You're all aware that she'd heard rumors about some kind of plot?"

Lea nodded. "That's why we sent Kim and Camacho over."

"Right," he said firmly. "It appears we're no longer dealing with simple rumors. Alex had been briefed by US Secret Service Agent Brandon McGee concerning quality intel regarding the plot. It appears it's real and that the Vice President is behind it, but we're very short on details."

"Oh my God!" Lea said.

"Exactly my sentiments," Eden said. "Kim and Jack Camacho are on their way, but this has the potential to turn into something very nasty indeed. Of course, I'll be monitoring it and will keep you updated, but for now, I want you to focus on the rings."

Lea could hardly believe what she was hearing. "Thanks, Rich."

Hawke looked his team in the eye. "It's time to start that battle."

CHAPTER NINE

The US Marine Corps Super Stallion raced over the surface of the warm waters of the Malacca Strait on its way to the military airbase at Kuala Lumpur. Crossing the border over the private island resort of Pulau Tengah, Hawke was astonished all over again by the beauty of the Malay Peninsula.

Tropical white-sand beaches lined with coconut palms encircling emerald-green isles were jewels set in a dazzling turquoise sea, but things became less beautiful as they flew at low altitude over Port Klang. He saw jaded, crumbling buildings and pot-holes in the streets, but no one else was looking out the windows. Sitting in the back of the heavy-lift cargo chopper, the rest of the team had prepared for the landing and were sharing a few laughs. Even Zeke and Nikolai, both of whom had begged to come on the mission, were settling in and sharing jokes.

Scarlet was searching through her pockets for a lighter while Reaper was studying Lexi's new steel fingernails. He called them talons and she nearly slapped him, but then laughed. Lea and Ryan were leaning back in their seats with their eyes closed, trying to get some shut-eye before the trouble started. If this was like any other mission, sleep would be hard to come by for the next few days, and something told him it was going to be a hell of a lot worse than just any other mission.

On top of the worries here in South East Asia, he was also thinking about Alex and what his old friend was up against in Washington DC. Sending Kim and Camacho back was a good move by Eden. Both strongly trusted by the President and Alex either would fight to the death to protect him. He just prayed it wouldn't come to that, and cursed Faulkner for trying to get Brooke out of the Oval Office. What the hell was going on over there? He had no idea, but at least now it was all starting to make sense. The US black ops guys who attacked Elysium must have been sanctioned by someone near the top, and now that someone had a name: Davis Faulkner.

Damn, is he working with the Oracle? That was something Alex, Kim, and Camacho would have to work out under the command of the President. The ECHO team was here in Malaysia with a different fish to fry, and his name was Razak.

They flew over the Brickfields district and swung around to the north over the Ritz-Carlton before descending and landing on the shores of Simfoni Lake. Climbing out of the chopper, he stared up. All eighty-eight floors of the enormous Petronas Towers loomed up above them in the sweltering Malaysian sky. Completed in 1996, the towers were the tallest in the world until 2004, standing at a dizzy 1,483 feet in height and Razak's apartment was at the top of the east tower.

"That's a long way up," Reaper said.

Lea shielded her eyes from the sun and looked up into the sky. "Serviced by an elevator."

"Plus the bastard doesn't know we're coming," Hawke put in.

As they were expecting, Eden's contact Farish Awang was waiting for them at the base of the towers. A young man in his twenties with a crew cut, he and the two men beside him were dressed in civvies so as not to attract any unwanted attention.

"How's it going?" Hawke said.

"We don't know if Razak's in there or not," Farish

said. “He’s a very private man and the building is not normally under surveillance. He may be on his rubber plantation.”

Hawke heaved out a sigh. “No biggie. We want the ring more than Razak, and this is where he keeps his diamond safe.”

“These towers are beautiful,” Lea said. “Never seen them before.”

“Each tower is based on traditional Islamic geometry,” Ryan said. “Their floor-plates are formed of two squares on top of each other to produce an eight-pointed star. That’s why they’re in this amazing shape.

“There’s that number again,” Reaper said. “Huit…”

They followed Farish across the expansive lobby, a stunning space combining postmodern glass and steel architecture with traditional Malay songket weavings. The Special Actions Unit officer flashed his badge at the people on the front desk and spoke to them in quiet Malay for a few moments.

He turned. “The bad news is that they don’t know if Razak’s in the apartment or not either.”

“And the good news?” Lea asked, hopeful.

“The warrant we have allows us access without any problems.” He held up a plastic key-card in front of their faces. “So we can walk right in.”

Farish led them over to the executive elevators and they stepped inside. The high-speed, double-decker elevators could carry up to fifty-two people, but they were traveling in one of the four plush executive elevators. It rapidly whisked them up inside the building to the sky lobby. Here they changed to another elevator that took them the rest of the way to the upper zones. “One more change,” Farish said with a smile.

He slotted the key-card into the side of Razak’s private elevator and moments later they were stepping out into the deep, patterned carpet of the top floor.

"This is the life." Scarlet traced her finger over a golden lion sculpture.

Farish slapped her hand away from the lion. "Please, it could be alarmed."

They continued walking down the wide corridor until they reached a large set of double doors with polished golden handles. "This whole floor is Razak's," Farish said. "But through here is where his private residence is."

Using a keycode obtained from the front desk, Farish opened the penthouse suite door, and the team filed inside the luxury apartment. A plush room of thick white rugs and polished mahogany floorboards stretched in every direction. The entire floor was double-story height and diamond chandeliers hung down from the ceiling, each one worth hundreds of thousands of dollars.

Farish glanced at the schematics of the apartment on his phone. "The safe is through here. Follow me."

They followed him into Razak's private study, a smaller space filled with studded leather chairs and paneled wooden walls. On one of the walls hung an original Pissaro landscape which instantly captivated Ryan's attention. "Nice – I presume the goodies are behind here?"

Farish shook his head. "No, the safe is built into the floor – here."

He bent over and pulled a large circular rattan rug away from the center of the floor to reveal the brushed steel door of a safe. It was neatly incorporated into the study floor, perfectly flush with the floorboards and hidden from the world – unless you knew it was there.

"Anyone know the combo?" Lea said.

"I do," Hawke said, reaching into his bag. "It's C4."

She smiled. "I do love you, Josiah."

"Everyone take cover," he said, placing the explosives

around the safe door.

"Maybe we could get a safe cracker," Farish said, looking nervous. "Is this really the best way?"

"Nothing ventured, nothing gained." Hawke winked as he detonated the C4 and blew the doors from the safe. The sound generated by the explosion was deafening in the enclosed study and the force ripped the door from one of its hinges so now it was hanging from the other one, bent and scorched.

"Christ, I'm going to need to get some ear-canceling headphones," Ryan said.

Lea ran forward and peered inside the safe. "Good news if you like diamonds or what is obviously counterfeit American dollars, but bad news if you're looking for an ancient ring that once belonged to a god-king."

Scarlet sighed. "You're fucking kidding?"

She turned. "Nope, not unless he keeps it under his pillow because it's not in here."

"Then that means the plantation," Ryan said, deflated by their failure to locate the ring.

Farish radioed in the failure to his team leader and turned to Hawke. "As far as that goes you're on your own. We're only authorized to facilitate the search of this penthouse."

"I hope everyone packed their mosquito repellent," Hawke said. "Because things are going to get nasty out there."

CHAPTER TEN

The dense jungles of Western Malaysia are some of the most remote and rugged on the planet. At over 130 million years old, the steamy, lush slopes of these regions host one of the world's oldest rainforests. Some parts have been tamed for tourists and offer river cruises, and some parts offer tours of the highland tea plantations.

But not this part.

Razak's rubber plantation was buried in Belum-Temenggor, the deepest tropical rainforest on the peninsula. The jungle here was thick and luscious and a hundred shades of green. Teeming with insect life, it gave an atmosphere of danger and foreboding.

Hawke swung the machete for the thousandth time, hacking his way through the rattan vines. Their spiny tendrils flicked back on him and scratched at his face as he cut ever deeper into the tropical nightmare.

"Are you sure this is the right way?" Ryan said.

"Yes." He sounded like he was in a bad mood.

Skirting a mangrove swamp filled with leeches, they continued on their path east toward Razak's plantation.

"It's just that if we'd turned left instead of right back at the entrance to Dulles Airport last time we were there we'd all be hanging out in a New York bar right now instead of, well... *here*."

"Shut it, Ryan," Lea said. "I don't think Joe's in the mood."

Scarlet slapped the back of Ryan's head as she walked past him to the front where Hawke was savagely beating a giant pandan into submission with his machete. A lizard darted across one of the seven-meter leaves as he finally hacked a way around it.

"Having fun?"

"Oh, *yes*. This is my favorite thing to do of all time," he said.

"We should have just driven down the drive," Zeke said.

Reaper laughed. "Good one."

"As plans go," Scarlet said. "That's a real turd rolled in glitter, boy."

"Eh?"

"The drive to this property is three miles long, *boy*," said Scarlet. "With a gatehouse at both ends. Something tells me we might just get rumbled before reaching Razak if we tried your plan, don't you?"

"All right, take it, easy woman."

Scarlet was holding her machete at shoulder height ready for another swing when she turned and looked at Ryan, her lips pursed.

"Cairo," he squeaked. "I meant take it easy, *Cairo*."

Scarlet said nothing. She turned and continued hacking away at the jungle up beside Hawke.

Lexi laughed. "You're such a pussy cat, Bale."

Some token laughs, but everyone was getting tired. The air was hot and humid and the sun burned down through the tropical canopy, scorching their necks and backs. Ezekiel and Nikolai surprised everyone with their strength. Neither whined or complained and they never fell a step behind the rest of the team.

"What made you join the Athanatoi, Kolya?" Lea asked.

He paused before speaking, and when he did his thick Russian accent sounded odd in the steamy jungle. "My family were killed in Moscow when I was a child. They were killed by accident in a gangland drive-by shooting."

"My God," Lea said, her voice soft and respectful. "I'm so sorry."

He shrugged. "I was a small child and I barely remember them or my older sister, but I know that until that day life was perfect. They loved me and I loved them. They both worked hard in their restaurant business and provided me with a solid childhood. I never went hungry and we had lots of friends who came and went into the restaurant scrounging for free dinners. It was a good time, but when they died I was an orphan with no family and the state put me into the care system."

"Tough," Hawke said.

"Yes, very tough. The little boy from the restaurant who raised a laugh serving customers and who helped his papa clean the dishes or wash the windows found himself in a brutal dog-eat-dog place where you had no friends. I was beaten and thrashed and robbed until I joined a gang and swore allegiance to the same sort of scum that had killed my parents."

"Man," Zeke whistled. "Talk about a shitty time, Kolya."

"I got strong. I vowed when I was older, I would find any way I could to get my revenge on the gang who killed my parents. If you search hard enough, you always find and I found the Athanatoi while I was still a teenager. They sensed my vulnerability and drew me under their wing. I started to work my way through their hierarchy."

Nikolai stopped dead on the spot, his eyes hardening like steel. "And one day when I was strong enough I killed every last member of the gang who murdered my parents, and then the next day I killed every single one of the boys who had bullied and tortured me at the orphanage. I do not regret it."

A long silence followed his words, which seemed to hang from the trees surrounding them like dead animals in traps.

"I don't blame you," Scarlet said. "I know what it's like, Kolya. My parents were murdered when I was a child too."

"I am sorry."

She gave him a reluctant smile. In the wildest of circumstances, she had found someone who understood what had happened to her all those years ago.

"But why betray the Athanatoi?" Ryan asked.

"Betray?"

"Back in the monastery," he said. "When you killed the man trying to kill Lea."

"I did not betray the Athanatoi. They betrayed me. When the Oracle found out I had murdered those people without his sanctioning their deaths, he told me I had betrayed the Order and would never have the power of immortality revealed to me. That is why I was in brown robes."

"I wondered about that," Reaper said. "Most of the cultists wear black robes or black suits."

"The brown robes are for the lower orders. We are the servants, not full acolytes. I realized I had been hurt again, and decided to end my association with them. That is why I killed him and helped you. That is why I gave you the Codex. If the Athanatoi ever finds me, I will be executed where I stand."

"Holy crapola." Zeke took off his cowboy hat and wiped his brow. "Nasty."

"You're with us now," Hawke said. "We don't tolerate dishonesty or treachery, but if you're straight with us then you're in. You heard it from the boss himself back on the ship."

"Yes, but after this mission, I will return to Russia. I must leave this world behind. All I want is a farm in the countryside to the south of Moscow."

"Up to you, mate."

Merciless tropical heat crushed them like a vice and drained their energy like they were running a marathon. This was a steamy landscape itching with cockroaches and silkworms and mosquitoes. Ryan pointed out a praying mantis to a yawning Scarlet. Hawke kicked his way around a patch of blood-red bromeliads.

Another punishing hour passed before the rainforest started to thin out and allow an easier passage through to the western approaches of Razak's sprawling plantation.

"We did a lot of this in the Legion." Reaper untied his skull and cross-bones bandana and wrung out the sweat before tying it back on. "It's not so bad."

Hawke laughed for the first time that day. "If you say so, Vincent."

"Hey, it's…"

Before he could say it, the rest of the team answered in unison. "It's Reaper… I'm on a mission!"

Now Reaper laughed. "Am I that predictable?"

"Yes."

Reaper gave a token laugh as he lit a cigarette, struggling to ignite the match in the damp air. "Tell me, Ryan," he said, thinking of his twin boys. "If it's real, what does this Land of the Gods mean for us, for my kids?"

"Theories of antediluvian civilization aren't uncommon. The word antediluvian itself just means 'before the deluge' and by that, we mean flood – as in the Bible."

Scarlet hacked at some undergrowth, the sweat running off her back. "Here beginneth the lesson."

"Tell me more," Lexi said. "Those of us who can read are interested."

A howl of laughter.

"Those who went to Sunday School will already know

that the two major events in Genesis describe the creation and fall of humans and then the massive global flood. What makes this so fascinating is how these flood myths aren't restricted to the Christian Bible and are found in cultures all over the world."

"Like where?"

"Most ancient cultures do, to be honest. Aztecs, Mayans… even Australian Aboriginal Dreamtime stories. The most important one is found carved in the Sumerian King List."

"What is that?" Nikolai said.

"It's a stone tablet from the Bronze Age which lists all the various kings of ancient Sumer, and it includes references to antediluvian kings. Some dispute these were real rulers but instead just legends, but I think we all know better than to believe this now. Anyway, tucked away on this tablet is a very clear reference to a king named Ubara-Tutu of Shurupakk. He was the very last king of antediluvian Sumer and his reign of over eighteen thousand years was brought to a brutal end by the deluge, just like Noah's father Lamech. It says so right there on the stone tablet – *and then the flood swept over*."

"Sorry, he was king for eighteen thousand years?" Lea asked.

"Eighteen thousand, six hundred to be exact."

Hawke stopped hacking and turned. "So, he was another of these immortals."

Ryan shrugged. "Either that or he had a hell of a health plan."

"I remember reading about how people at the beginning of the Bible all lived for a very long time," Reaper said.

"There were seven in all, Ryan said. "Each of them lived over nine hundred years – in order, these were Adam, Seth Enosh, Kenan, Jared, Methuselah, and Noah.

The most important detail was that they were all born in the time before the great deluge."

"People just don't live that long anymore," Lexi said.

"Not even if they quit smoking," said Scarlet.

Lexi sighed. "I was *going* to say, that it's like it was a different world back then."

"That's the heart of the antediluvian theory," Ryan said. "That another civilization or world, if you prefer, existed before the history books. That a different culture inhabited this planet that we know nothing about."

"Freaks me out how all those cultures had flood myths," Lea said. "They were all so far apart they couldn't be sharing each other's stories."

Ryan turned to her with his serious face. "Oh yeah, the deluge story is real. There's no doubt. Fact is, we teach our kids that humans developed over a certain period, essentially evolving from the domain Eukaryota just over two billion years ago. So far so good. This evolved into the family of great apes around twenty-eight million years ago, and then to chimpanzees around twelve million years ago but it wasn't until maybe five million years ago that the subtribe *hominina* split away from chimps and slowly morphed into the genus *homo*. That happened around two and a half million years ago. Humans as we know them only turned up around three to eight hundred thousand years ago."

"*As we know it* is the bit that scares me," Zeke said.

"But are we getting to the end of this lecture?" Scarlet said. "Your droning is almost as tiring as this humidity."

"My *point*," he said with emphasis, "is that we pretty much date human history, and therefore the history of civilization back to just a few hundred thousand years ago, but what if there was another branch of humans – or something similar to us – evolved from the great apes ten or twelve million years ago? Our entire history would be wrong. If there were intelligent, civilized cultures on this planet millions of years ago, everything we thought we knew about ourselves would be wrong."

He turned to Reaper with a look of apology on his face. "That's what it all means for your kids. They could simply be the latest in a long line of cyclical civilizations, each one either dying off or wiping itself out before the next cycle begins."

Ryan's words were subdued in the dense thicket, almost drowned out by the howl of insects. The moment was ended when Hawke finally broke through the last wall of heavy vegetation, his boots crushing the damp earth of the jungle floor beneath. He paused where he stood before turning to the rest of his team. "Looks like we're here, kids."

When he stepped out of the way, they all saw the corpse at the same time. It had once been a man but was now almost skeletal. Tied to an enormous kempas tree with ropes, the blindfolded man had been killed where he sat.

"This is odd." Hawke crouched down in front of the skeleton until he was face to face with the skull.

Lea stepped over. "What?"

"If you look through the eye socket you can see a perfect hole burnt right through the trunk."

"Oh yeah!"

Ryan looked confused. "Eh? Let me have a look."

He leaned forward with his hands on his knees and peered through the eye socket. "Looks charred inside the tree."

"What did this?" Lexi asked.

"I know it sounds crazy," Hawke said. "But the first thing that struck my mind was a laser of some kind."

"Me too," Ryan said.

"I know of no such weapon that could do this, mes

amis."

Zeke shook his head. "Me neither. Kolya?"

"Nyet."

"But look here." Hawke pointed at the man's rib cage. "Those are normal crossbow bolts, so it looks like he was attacked with more than one kind of weapon."

Scarlet looked at the skeleton without pity. "Whatever killed him, his body was just left here for the insects to devour."

What was left of his skin was now dried leather stretched in patches across his sun-bleached bones. A hand-painted sign hung around his neck, and his lower jaw was hanging off at a grim angle. When Hawke touched it with the toe of his boot a cockroach scuttered out of one of the eye sockets.

Lea grabbed her mouth and turned away. "I think I'm going to be sick."

"What does the sign say, mate?"

Ryan stepped up to the base of the towering kempas tree and squinted. "Pencuri is Malay for a thief. The other words are damaged by the rain. Looks like *saya seorang pencuri* though." He turned to the others. "I am a thief."

Hawke pulled one of the normal crossbow bolts from a gap between the man's ribs. "Looks like our Mr. Razak has a zero-tolerance approach to employee misbehavior."

Lexi raised an eyebrow. "I can hardly wait to meet him."

Hawke silenced her with his hand and signaled everyone to crouch low on the ground. He scanned the tree line to the east. "I think we have company."

His words were punctuated by the sound of a crossbow bolt racing past them and shooting through one of the skull's eye sockets, shattering the skull and burying itself an inch deep in the trunk of the kempas tree.

"Take cover!" Hawke yelled.

CHAPTER ELEVEN

"No! Stay where you are!"

The command echoed around the jungle. Gradually, Hawke noticed at least two dozen heavily camouflaged men break through the tree line surrounding them. Each was holding a submachine gun.

"And drop your weapons!"

He signaled to the others to lower their guns and take a step back, raising their hands as they did so. The leader of the small army walked over to them, a pistol in his hand and a cruel smile on his lean, sweaty face. He stared at Hawke before turning to the skeleton lashed to the tree trunk. "I see you met Ibrahim. How's he doing? He's not very talkative these days."

"Most people with a crossbow bolt through their eyes aren't."

"Bring them back to the base!"

Hawke held Razak's eyes as his goons cuffed their hands behind their backs and ordered them to march through some long grass and into some trees to the east. The walk was short but hot and tiring. When they arrived, they saw a small clearing with some military tents dotted around.

"Welcome to my field HQ." Razak gestured for Hawke and the others to step inside one of the tents. "Please, come out of the heat and away from the mosquitoes." He turned to a man at his side and ordered that he remove their cuffs. "You're not going anywhere in this jungle, that's for sure."

Lea scowled at him. "You can't do this to us, *Razak*."

He slipped his hands in his pockets and strolled to where the mosquito mesh draped down to the ground. "Am I supposed to be impressed that you know my name? Many people do. Ibrahim over there certainly did. He tried to sleep with my daughter. Big mistake."

"You should be in prison, you psycho!" Zeke said.

He laughed. "Men like me do not go to prison – we're too busy searching for rings."

Hawke caught the fear in Lea's eyes. "What did you just say?"

"Oh, you thought I believed there was just one ring?" There was a smugness in his voice and a fiendish sparkle in his eye. He was delighting in toying with them. "Please, you're not so conceited to think that only the great ECHO team knows the value of these rings?"

"I don't understand," Lea said. "The Codex was…"

Hawke gripped her arm. "Don't tell him anything. He's fishing."

Razak's smile faded. "I don't go *fishing*, Englishman. Neither am I as stupid as you seem to think I am. Do you think you can break into my apartment or raid my plantation without me knowing about it? Without knowing who you are and what you want?"

Now, for the first time, he brought his hand out of his pocket and held it up in front of their faces. They all saw it at once, sparkling dully in the diffused light of the tropical thunderstorm.

"The ring!" Lexi said.

Lea couldn't take her eyes off it. "My God…"

"My *Gods*," Razak emphasized, and then laughed again. "When I was a young man I inherited this rubber plantation from my father. As you can see, it's a very substantial property and we are a very wealthy family and if you know your commodity prices then you will know that the price of rubber has gone up considerably in the last twenty years."

"This is fascinating," Ryan said. "I wish I had a notebook."

"Silence!" Razak snapped.

"Don't be too angry with him," Scarlet said. "He's always had a thing about rubber."

Razak smacked his hand down on the table and brought the laughs to an abrupt end. "If this is amusing you perhaps one of you would like to see how young Ibrahim died, *first hand?*"

A man with a crossbow stepped forward, pulled a string back on his weapon, and slotted a sharpened bolt down in the flight groove.

Razak waited for silence. "I thought not… As I was saying, the price of rubber is better now, but when my father died I was a very young man, and back then the price of our commodity was flatlining, as you say."

"What's the point of this lecture?" Hawke said.

Razak ignored him. "I decided to expand the business and go into palm oil."

"So you love orangutans as much as I do, then," Lea said.

"Spare me, please," Razak looked at her with contempt. "You couldn't go fifteen seconds without using a product made with my palm oil. It's a fascinating substance, but it requires the clearing of vast amounts of land to plant the oil palms. We started work the day after my father's funeral, clearing some jungle in the north of the property, and that's when we found it."

"The ring?" Reaper said.

Razak gave a deep belly laugh. "No, not the ring. We were digging a meter-deep irrigation ditch along the border of the field when we found a strange blue sphere."

Hawke and Lea exchanged a glance.

"Yes, you heard me correctly. It was deep in the earth,

so it was naturally covered in soil and mud. At first, I thought it was simply a strange rock. Then I thought it must be a meteorite, but when we cleared the mud away we saw it was a perfect sphere, and made of something similar to glass, and more than that, when I touched it, a faint bluish glow started to pulse deep inside it."

He turned and faced his beloved jungle, shaking his head in disbelief at his memory.

"And then the very earth under my feet shook. We all felt it. It was an immediate reaction to my touching the sphere, and when I touched it again there was another earthquake right under our feet. I dropped the thing out of fear and shock, and when it hit a rock on the ground without sustaining any damage, I knew it wasn't glass."

"Did it have any symbols on it?" Ryan asked.

Razak spun around. "No, it was smooth like glass. I already told you that. What do you know about symbols?"

"Nothing, I…"

A smile crept over the Malaysian's face. "I know about these symbols."

"How?"

"You think I'm stupid? You think I just stopped digging when we found the sphere?"

"What else did you find?" Hawke asked.

"You wouldn't believe it."

"Try me."

Razak looked at the SBS man with something approaching respect. "When the earthquake had subsided, I ordered my men to go down another three meters. They found nothing, so I ordered them to use the digger again and go down two more meters, and that's when they found it."

"They found what?"

"The crossbows."

Lea felt her blood run cold. She looked at her friends

and they were having the same reaction.

"That's right, five meters under the floor of the Temenggor rainforest we found a cache of high-technology crossbows with heat-seeking bolts, and they were covered in strange symbols." He locked eyes on Lea and his jaw tightened. "Care to explain that?"

She lowered her head. "I don't know what to say…"

"Then, let me try." Razak took a seat behind his desk and casually sipped his *teh tarik*, or pulled tea. He sighed with satisfaction and set the glass back down on the desk. "We didn't stop digging when we found the crossbows, naturally. We kept on going, not just deeper but wider, and that's when we started finding other things – shields, tridents, and other ancient weapons, but not like weapons from *our* ancient time. These all had strange technologies that made them sharper, faster… somehow *intelligent*. Far ahead of anything we have created even with today's latest digital technology… Are you certain you won't have some of the tea?"

"No thanks," Lea said. "I'm too gripped by your little story."

"Eventually we found a tomb covered in these strange symbols, and in that tomb, we found a sarcophagus, and in there we found a skeleton." He paused a beat, clearly anxious at the memory. "Besides the skeleton, we found a stack of journals, and on that skeleton, I found this ring."

"Wait," Lexi said. "Am I really here?"

"You're really here, Lex," Scarlet said.

Razak sighed and drummed his fingers on his desk. "We worked hard to translate the symbols on the tomb. I nearly bankrupted the family business finding and paying experts to translate and decipher them, but it was worth it."

"Whose tomb was it, Razak?" Hawke said.

"Pangu's."

Ryan's eyes widened. "The Chinese creator god?"

Razak nodded.

"But why was he here in Malaysia?"

"According to the journals, he was seeding a new civilization here."

"From China?"

"No, not from China. Pangu wasn't from China, he just seeded the Chinese population. That's why he was their creator god. After starting the Chinese civilization he ranged down through southeast Asia and seeded more civilizations there."

Lea felt like she was drowning in questions. "So if Pangu wasn't from China then where was he from?"

"From the Citadel, of course," Razak said.

Lea gasped. "You know about that, too?"

"I do. According to the manuscripts, Pangu lived there like all the other creator gods around the world. They lived in this Citadel, the capital of the world's first civilization in what they called the Land of the Gods. It was an antediluvian culture that existed long before our current history books even date the start of humanity."

"Sounds like you're bang up to speed, darling," Scarlet said.

Razak ignored her. "When we had finally finished translating the manuscripts, I was able to work out that the most valuable thing we discovered was this ring." He held it up again. "After a great deal of deciphering and translation, it became clear that this was just one of eight rings, each one belonging to a creator god or goddess, and that when all put together, they would somehow reveal the location of the Citadel."

"Sounds like you're good to go, Razak, and won't be needing us," Lea said, turning to leave. "Bye then!"

"Stay where you are!"

"Sorry…"

"But yes, I am *good to go* except for the fact the Citadel remains undiscovered. Can you imagine the kind of technology, weapons, and knowledge that would exist in such a place if a simple jungle field in a place like this contained the treasure and weapons we found?"

"I'm beginning to form an idea," Hawke said.

"When I find the Land of the Gods I will have control of all of these magnificent treasures and be the most powerful man on the planet. Perhaps even more powerful than the President of the United States with all the military at his command."

Hawke stepped forward. "You're not the only one searching for this Citadel, Razak."

"What do you mean?"

"There's a cult of immortals run by a man named Wolff."

"I have not heard of him."

"He calls himself the Oracle, and he claims to be thousands of years old. He thinks things like your little ring are his birthright and he'll kill anyone to get to them."

"He won't kill me," Razak said confidently. "If he gets in my way I will sweep him aside, however old he is. I didn't spend my entire life searching for these rings to give up now." He paused and scratched at his neck before turning to Hawke. "You realize I cannot of course let you live?"

"Spoilsport," Scarlet said.

He laughed sarcastically. "Maybe, maybe not. I see it more as pest clearance. Now, it's time for your executions," he said casually. "Competing against this *Oracle* for the rings is one thing, I don't need to be fighting another army at the same time. Lim! You and Rafizi are to take this thieving scum outside into the jungle and kill them. They seem to know so much about these weapons, it's only fitting that they should be executed by them, so use the ancient crossbows."

"Yes, sir."

Lim raised a sleek, white, and silver crossbow and ordered them outside the enormous tent.

Hawke studied the weapon, but he had never seen anything like it before.

"Move!"

They stepped outside. Away from the fans, the humidity soon enveloped them again and Lea felt the sweat forming all over her body.

"I said move, scum!" Lim pushed the crossbow's cocking stirrup in the small of her back and nudged her forward toward the center of the clearing.

"Hey! Get off me!"

"Shut up!" Lim snapped. "And say your prayers because your death is only seconds away."

CHAPTER TWELVE

Lea tensed as she heard Lim stepping through the grass behind her. Somewhere beyond him she now heard Razak give the kill order from over at the tents, his voice echoing in the steaming canopy ahead of her. She knew what she had to do – they all did. She dived into the long grass and rolled to the tree line as fast as she could.

Lim and Rafizi fired their weapons at her, unleashing strange neon-blue crossbow bolts in their direction as they raced to the trees.

Lea got there first, just managing to dive to the ground in time as one of the bolts raced over her head and flashed past her. She rolled in the undergrowth as the bolt twisted in the air like a heat-seeking missile and turned to find her once again.

Speeding toward her and aimed directly for her heart, she lifted the thick piece of bark to her chest at the last second and the bolt rammed into it. She gasped in fear as the lethal projectile's razor-sharp tip tore a hole through the bark and poked out the other side before stopping half an inch from her chest.

Her heart thumped as she dropped the bark to the ground and tucked herself down behind one of the oil palms. To her right, Lexi was trying to dodge another of the bolts by diving behind the trunk of a kempasa tree. Beyond, in the clearing, Lim and Rafizi were reloading their weapons and firing on them again.

"We've got to take them out!" Lexi said.

"No shit, Sherlock!" Ryan called over.

Zeke wiped the sweat from his brow. "But how?"

Another bolt tore past Lea's hiding place and burned a hole through a nearby trunk, and then another so close it scorched her cheek before burying itself in the undergrowth behind her head. She gasped and dived into the dirt as the rest of the ECHO team scattered in the jungle. Wiping blood from her cheek, she scanned the immediate area of the jungle for any sign of Lim and Rafizi or any other of Razak's men.

Zeke dived through the air to avoid one of the neon bolts and slammed down next to her.

"Holy shit!" he yelled. "I thought that Razak son of a bitch was all hat and no cattle but when he said execute us he meant it!"

"Where the hell is Joe?" Lea asked.

"I don't know," Zeke said. "But I think I see Razak – is that a river?"

She saw it now, running further north. "I think so."

"Well, that asshole Razak's right over there by the river. He's holding one of those crazy crossbows."

"But I still can't see Joe," she said. "I hope he's not wounded."

A bolt flashed over their heads and ripped a path through the jungle to their east. Leaving a scorched trail of blackened undergrowth in its wake, it exploded a few hundred meters away. In response, they heard what sounded like Nikolai and Scarlet screaming.

"This is getting out of control!" Lea said.

Zeke scrambled to his feet and clamped a heavy hand on Lea's shoulder. "I'm going to take that son of a bitch out!"

"No!" she called back.

It was too late. She watched the Texan tank commander vanish into the undergrowth, its broad green leaves and slender tendrils closing back up again as if it had swallowed him alive. "Dammit!"

Ezekiel Jones pounded through the jungle like a leopard. Spying Razak ahead of him, he leaped onto another fallen trunk to gain some elevation and sprinted along it until he was exactly behind and above him. The Malaysian hadn't noticed him. He was too engrossed in aiming his crossbow bolt at Hawke and some of the others taking cover on the south bank of the rushing river.

Zeke launched himself from the trunk and slammed down onto Razak's back, pulling him down to the ground and piling a heavy-duty punch into the back of his head.

Razak went out like a light, giving Zeke time to take the ring from his hand and snatch up his crossbow. As he turned, Lea was now standing at the edge of the small clearing.

"You got the ring!"

"Here," he said, tossing it over to her. "Means jack shit to me." Hefting the crossbow in his hands, he grinned. "This baby on the other hand is mine all mine."

"You see Joe yet?" Lea's heart was full of hope.

"Sure did – he's over on the riverbank up there with Ryan. Looks like the others are making their way toward them."

They heard a scream echoing in the canopy. Instinctively, Lea slipped the ring into her pocket and looked over to Zeke. "That sounded like Lex. We have to help her."

"Where did it come from?" Zeke asked.

"Over there, by the river. This is chaos!"

They ran north until reaching the river bank, just in time to see Lexi bobbing up and down in the rapids. She was calling out for help but struggling to keep her head out of the rushing water.

Lea gasped. "Oh my God!"

"There's a man on the bank firing at her. I think it's Rafizi."

"And there's Joe and the others!" Lea said, pointing further along the river.

"They're further along than when I saw them." Zeke lifted the crossbow and aimed at the Rafizi. "Here goes nothing!"

He fired the ancient weapon, gripping it hard as the air flashed with static and blue lightning. He winced and shielded his eyes as the bolt ripped out into the humid air and raced after its target. "Godspeed, you little bastard!"

Rafizi saw it, and his eyes opened wide with terror as he tried to sprint into the jungle. The crossbow bolt reacted instantly, bending in the air like a biased bowl and lining up behind the fleeing man. A second later it tore through his back and burst out of his chest, exploding his heart and sending him crashing to the ground amid a scream of terrified agony.

"This is like the goddam Predator movie!" Lea said.

Up ahead, Hawke and the others were diving into the river.

"What the hell are they doing?"

Then they heard the gunshots.

"There are more goons coming, Lea, and it sounds like they're armed with regular weapons," Zeke said. "They jumped in to get away and I think we should do the same – besides, Lexi's in there!"

Lea knew they had no choice and gave a reluctant nod. She wasn't going to lose Joe Hawke in the middle of the Malaysian jungle. "Let's do it, Ezekiel!"

A bolt flashed over their heads, and then the chatter of submachine gunfire. "It's Zeke to my friends!"

They jumped in and crashed into the water, instantly being dragged by the current into the center of the river. Thrown about like a pathetic straw doll, Lea worked hard to keep her head above the surface as she strained to breathe. Zeke was gone and no one else was in sight either. Only the screams of her friends reassured her that she was not completely alone as the mighty power of the river swept her toward the rushing rapids up ahead.

And then she saw it.

She was about to go over the top of a waterfall.

*

Hawke was no stranger to long runs with a heavy pack. It was such a central fact of life in the Royal Marines Commandos that it even had its own slang name - yomping. The dreaded yomp was a long-distance forced-march with full kit on your back The most famous yomp was when the Commandos landed at San Carlos in the Falkland Islands and proceeded to march nearly sixty miles in just three days, loaded down with packed bergens, weapons, and ammo.

With every pace he pounded out along the side of the riverbank he thought about his days in the marines and what he had gone through to win the coveted green beret. Legs pumped up and down and his breathing hardened as he looked around for his friends. Ryan to the left and Lexi somewhere behind. Scarlet and Nikolai were to the right, but further away. All of them had been flushed out of the jungle and toward the river, but there was still no sign of Lea or Zeke, and Reaper was AWOL too.

"Into the water!" he yelled. "It's our only chance!"

He launched into a racing dive position and flew through the air, neon bolts tracing inches above him as he cut through the surface of the river like a hot knife through butter. Spinning around in an explosion of bubbles, he swam to the surface just in time to see the last of his team crashing into the water, including Reaper. Already carried at speed away from the river bank by the current, Razak's goons were rapidly being left behind, and then he saw Lea and Zeke further behind.

Ryan called out from up ahead.

Hawke fought to keep his head above the rushing water. "Say again?"

"Waterfall!"

Then Hawke saw it. They were speedily approaching what looked like some heavy-duty falls, and there was absolutely nothing he could do about it.

*

By the time she reached the overhang, Lea realized she was the last of her friends to go over the edge. With froth and water in her eyes and ears and the deafening noise of the rushing water raging all around her, she gulped a deep breath of air and held on for her life.

Sliding over the edge was painless, but now came the hard part. She felt her stomach floating up inside as she tumbled through the saturated air. How high were the falls? How long would she fall? She had no answers and clamped her eyes shut to pray for her survival.

When she hit the bottom, she was sucked down into the plunge basin at the bottom of the waterfall. More froth and bubbles and confusion. She almost passed out. Was that someone's leg kicking in front of her face? The cascading water crashed around her as she struggled to work out which way was up and swim to the surface. When she finally got there, she saw the rest of her team crawling over wet rocks to reach the riverbank.

Exhausted and frightened, she followed suit and swam across the plunge pool where a relieved Hawke helped her out of the water and pulled her up into his arms. "Late again, Donovan."

"I sure earned my pay on this mission!"

“Time to get moving, non?” Reaper said.

*

They marched for another hour through the jungle before they were certain that Razak and his men were no longer pursuing them. Reaching another clearing and with the weakest of signals, Lea set her iPhone to speakerphone and set it on top of a fallen tree trunk, and put a call through to Richard Eden. As they grouped around it, she increased the volume so they could hear his voice above the raging cicadas.

“Go ahead, Rich,” she said. “You’re on speaker.”

“I have determined the location of another ring.”

The team reacted with joy. “Just as well,” Ryan said. “My copy of the Codex is what you might call water damaged.”

“I won’t ask,” Eden said.

“Where do we go?” Lea asked.

“Tokyo.”

Hawke caught Lea’s eye. “Tokyo?”

“The Ring of Cyrus the Great is in the possession of a family of treasure hunters.”

“How I hate treasure hunters,” Scarlet said. “They’re always so greedy.”

Ryan furrowed his brow. “Is she being sarcastic or not?”

“I have spoken with the treasure hunter’s daughter. She says it’s a sad story, but she may be able to help us with the ring, and there’s more,” Eden said.

“Let us have it,” Hawke said.

“I’ve had some intel from MI6 that the Oracle has sent a large number of Athanatoi to Hawaii.”

“Funny time for a surfing holiday,” Ryan said.

“It’s no surfing holiday, Mr. Bale. We’re looking into

it and so far, it seems the intel is good. At least two dozen heavily armed men took off from Athens a few minutes ago in a private plane registered to a holding company linked to Otmar Wolff. The flight plan has it stopping in Anchorage."

Ryan scrunched up his nose. "Eh? Now he's surfing in Alaska?"

Scarlet sighed. "It's a refueling stop, Dumble."

"Ah."

"From there it's due to land at Honolulu and onto a property owned by a man named McKenna. I think it's safe to assume this is a serious move by the Oracle to secure one of the rings. He has a copy of the Codex and is more than capable of translating it."

Lexi said. "We've known right from the start that this was going to be a race and the idea we'd just get all the rings one by one was like Ryan's haircut."

"What does that mean?"

"Ridiculous," she said deadpan.

Hawke laughed. "Not only do we now have two of the rings already, but we also have all the idols. It's a great start and we're winning, but we can't afford to give the Oracle even an inch or he'll destroy us. We're going to need to split the team. Lea, Reap and Kolya come with me to Hawaii and Cairo takes Ryan, Lexi, and Zeke to Tokyo."

"And what about getting out of here?" Lexi said.

Eden's voice crackled over the tiny speaker. "A chopper from the Royal Malaysian Air Force is already tracking the GPS signal on this phone. If the battery fails, stay where you are or they'll never find you."

"Great stuff." Hawke slapped his hands together. "All set?"

"All set, locked and loaded, darling."

CHAPTER THIRTEEN

Scarlet's half of the ECHO team landed at Narita Airport in a pink Tokyo dawn. The discovery of the second ring in Malaysia had been welcomed in Washington and London but no one was celebrating yet. With six more rings to locate there was still a lot of work to do, no one could be sure the Oracle hadn't already secured any of the others.

At least they still had the idols.

Taking a cab to the Shinjuku Gyoen Park just south of central Tokyo, they were soon strolling along a tree-lined path waiting to meet their contact. The sun streamed through the cherry leaves and blossom blew on the breeze. People talked quietly as they passed them by, and no one had the faintest idea why these strangers were in their land, or what was at stake for the world.

Scarlet took a brief call. "That was Jack," she said. "As in Camacho, not Brooke, and he says they're just about to take off for Washington. When they get there the plan is to go straight to the White House. When they meet with Alex and the President someone will get back to us. Now, where the hell is Rich's contact?"

"What about that guy?" Zeke pointed at a man sitting on a nearby bench.

"Did you not hear Eden's briefing?" Ryan said. "We're looking for a woman."

"Story of my life," the Texan drawled.

"There," Lexi said sharply. "She's over there, in the denim jacket. Three o'clock."

"Ouch," Zeke said. "No longer any need to look for a

woman."

"Do try and contain yourself, Ezekiel," Scarlet said. "Or I'll be forced to give your bollocks a squeeze until you start behaving."

"Double ouch," Ryan said.

"And I'll raise you a goddam," added Zeke as they walked to the woman.

She looked up and removed her earbuds. "You are the people who need information regarding a certain ring?"

"Only if you're Hiroko Adachi."

She nodded. "We should talk over here."

The small party sat in the shade under a cherry blossom tree far from any paths and Scarlet kicked things off. "Your father was Tōru Adachi, the famous treasure hunter?"

"Yes, he was."

"And he had one of these?" Scarlet turned to Ryan and snapped her fingers in his face. "Picture of the ring, boy."

Ryan frowned at her and then showed Hiroko his phone screen and a photo of the ring they had secured in Malaysia.

"Yes, but ours is different."

"They're all different," Ryan said.

Lexi leaned back on the grass. "Where did your father find it?"

Hiroko smiled. "I knew you would ask this, but he did not find the ring."

"What the hell does that mean?" Scarlet asked. "You just said he did."

The Japanese woman looked at her with a frown. "No, he did not find the ring – the ring found him."

"You'll have to explain that," Zeke said. "I ain't the fastest horse in the stable but I'm no dummy either."

"He was not searching for the ring when he found it. Normally, his treasure-hunting missions are meticulously planned down to the last detail, but on this occasion, he was simply on holiday in India. He was in a junk shop in Shimla in the north and there it was, sitting in a box of other rings. He knew at once he had something special. How long had it sat in the box among all that other comparatively worthless gold and silver? I do not know, and neither did he."

"It has some kind of engraving on its face," Lexi said, hope rising in her voice. "Can you remember what it looked like?"

"Etched into the gold was a very complex pattern, yes. Lots of lines and shapes. It was very beautiful. My father loved all of his treasures and treated them with reverence."

"If he loved them so much, then how come he sold the ring?"

"He did not sell the ring. Categorically not."

Hiroko was silent for a long time as she watched a man in a surgical mask slowly cycle toward them on the path. For a few seconds, Scarlet wondered if she had even heard the question. Then she said, "Have you heard of the Japanese concepts of *giri* and *ninjo*?"

"Can't say I have, darling," Scarlet said.

Hiroko gave a sage nod. "Loosely translated they mean *obligation* and *human feeling*, and they are very important in Japanese culture. Together they create a force of feeling that means debts of treachery or kindness to one must always be repaid, no matter the cost." She paused a beat and the gentle smile fell from her face. "And particularly important to the Yakuza."

"Not liking where this is going," Lexi said.

"Quite. I am very ashamed to say that my father got into some financial trouble with the Yakuza and caused a lot of trouble for our family."

"I see."

"He became heavily in debt in the pachinko parlors and then made things much worse by trying to recover his money playing mah-jong in an illegal casino in Susukino. Unfortunately, the casino was owned by the Yakuza. They were very clear about what they were going to do to him if he did not pay them back what he owed."

Lexi knew all about the pachinko parlors. A two hundred billion dollar a year national obsession, half of Tokyo was full of the places. The sound of the ball-bearings crashing about inside the machines could be heard up and down many streets in every Japanese city.

"I thought you said he never sold the ring?" Lexi asked.

"He didn't."

"So what happened?"

She sighed and started plucking at the grass near her knees. "The Yakuza demanded the ring as part of my father's *giri* – the obligation he owed them for waving his debts. They did this because they knew he was a treasure hunter and something more valuable may come along in the future."

"A lifelong debt?"

Hiroko nodded.

"It wasn't so bad. He had many more items he coveted more. But the ring was the single most expensive piece he owned. His choice was to give the ring to the Yakuza and clear the debts, or he would be forced to choose from several items he held much more dearly. Now you know the story of Tōru Adachi and his daughter Hiroko."

"He paid his debts," Lexi said. "Why didn't he use his skills to get the ring back?"

"He was a treasure hunter," Hiroko said quietly. "Mostly he dived into wrecks but he wasn't above digging holes in the dirt. What he didn't do was break into the private residences of Yakuza bosses to steal back relics they had taken from him."

Scarlet got the picture. Hiroko's father had been a treasure hunter of some repute during his salad days, but had fallen on hard times and turned to gambling in his desperation to improve his life. A brief encounter with the Yakuza had ended with him handing over much of his life's work to keep them at bay.

Including the Ring of Cyrus the Great.

"What was this Yakuza man's name?"

"A man? I never said it was a man."

Scarlet frowned. "I thought Yakuza were always men?"

"Then you thought wrongly. Most are men, but there have been women leaders in its history."

"In that case," Lexi said. "What is the woman's name?"

"Her name is Makiko Jojima, and I would think very carefully about crossing her if I were you. She inherited her empire from her father when he died in a gangland shooting. She is bitter and impulsive. Ruthless. If she finds you in her home trying to steal the ring, she will kill you, and it will not be fast or painless."

Hiroko paused to watch as a couple walked along the path with a little girl. She was holding a pink balloon and singing a song as her mother unwrapped an ice cream for her. "Only if this ring is of greater value than all of your lives should you pursue it."

"It is," Ryan said bluntly. "Where does this woman live?"

"The answer to that is, wherever she desires. All I can tell you is that the last I heard she lives at a luxury address here in Tokyo – Izumi Garden Tower in Roppongi."

"And you know where this is?"

Hiroko nodded. "Do any of you speak Japanese?"

"I do," Lexi said.

"Then you don't need me."

"When we get what we want," Scarlet said, "we're out of here, no looking back. It's always that way with us. If you want any of your father's relics for yourself then your only chance is to come with us."

Hiroko thought about it for a while. She drew in a deep breath and then blew it out. "There is only one item I would like back. A jewelry box that belonged to my mother. It has a tiger carved on the front. They took that too."

"It's yours if we find it."

"Then I will come. I will take you to the address in Roppongi."

CHAPTER FOURTEEN

They stepped up into the helicopter and quickly took their seats. They all seemed to know where to go so she guessed they usually sat in the same places. The Texan smacked his shovel hand down in the seat next to her and smiled. "You can sit here!"

She struggled to understand his accent but she knew what he meant so she sat down beside him and returned his smile. Buckled her seatbelt. Above them, the engine was already spooling up and the co-pilot was closing the door. They jerked upward and started lifting off the helipad.

Below her, to the right, she saw one of the new JAL A350s lining up ready for take-off. Seconds later they were screeching up into the Tokyo skyscape, ripping through a bank of pink clouds and banking hard into the sunset. She stared out of the window in amazement as the tiny aircraft seemed to tip almost on its side as it made the sharp turn to the left.

She had grown up in a good neighborhood, and both her parents had earned very good money. She had traveled a great deal, particularly to countries rich in historical artifacts and relics as her father dragged her around his excavations.

But she had never flown in a helicopter before.

She was determined not to show her excitement to the foreigners. She kept a calm, neutral face and pretended for all the world this was just like any old day in the life of Hiro Adachi.

Below, the neon streets she knew so well were soon

behind her and when she turned back to face the cabin, she saw the rest of the team were paying no mind to the take-off. Instead, they were busily engaged in the business of retrieving her father's mysterious ring.

Lexi turned to her. "Hiro, how long does it take to get from here to Izumi Tower?"

"I'm not sure, I have never flown by helicopter before. Maybe fifteen minutes."

Scarlet looked at her watch. "Good, we have a quarter of an hour."

Again, she thought about what they were saying. They were talking about attacking the heart of Makiko Jojima's Yakuza empire, and they were talking about it *casually*. She wondered if any of them truly knew what taking on a woman like that would mean. This was the head of a criminal empire that consumed massive police resources every day of the year and it still operated with virtual impunity wherever it wanted.

She didn't know anything about the people she was sitting with right now, but she knew enough about the Yakuza that even if they were successful in their mission to retrieve the ring, it would not end there. In stealing something from Makiko Jojima they would be giving her *giri*, or the obligation to pay them back for their deeds. It would never stop until that debt was repaid, and the only currency a person in her position would accept was blood and flesh.

As they crossed the city, Hiroko was amazed by just how vast metropolitan Tokyo was. Bigger than New York, Miami, Washington DC, Chicago, Las Vegas, and many other US cities put together, it was a monster of concrete and glass stretching to every horizon and offering endless possibilities wherever she looked.

She had been born here. Raised here. She went to elementary school in Hiroo and then they moved to

Azabu where she completed her junior high and high school years. She had gone out on the town with her friends and attended university here, gaining her degree in marine exploration. She knew Tokyo like the back of her hand and yet she had never flown over her hometown in a helicopter before. Flying so low and so fast, it lifted the curtain on what an enormous metropolis it truly was.

Without drawing attention to herself, she glanced at the foreigners sitting with her in the back of the chopper. Their leader was cool and distant. Tough, tall, and with raven black hair, she seemed distracted. She turned and poked the younger man in the ribs and flicked his ear. The young man pretended to be annoyed but seemed to enjoy the attention nonetheless.

The Chinese woman was harder to read. She seemed quieter than the rest and spent much of the journey with her eyes closed. For some reason, the fingernails on her left hand were artificial – some sort of prosthetic replacement. They looked metallic and she had never seen anything like it before in her life. Some sort of accident, no doubt. Or torture, maybe. She shuddered to think.

The last of them was the squarest, chunkiest man she had ever seen. He reminded her of a Hollywood movie star with his toned body, chiseled jaw, and sparkling, serious eyes. Upturned cowboy hat on the seat beside him with his shades inside it. A tough, determined face, and yet hiding behind the façade of merciless steel he had cultivated was another kind of man, a man with a good sense of humor.

"Right, we're here," Scarlet said. "This is the building you're talking about, yes?"

Hiroko nodded. "Jojima is on the top floor."

"Of course, she is," Lexi said. "They always are."

The chopper lost altitude and lined up with a helipad

on the roof of a skyscraper two blocks to the south. "All right, let's get on with it," Scarlet said. "We land, take the lift down to the ground floor, and then walk the two blocks to the Izumi Tower. Then we ask nicely and get the ring."

Hiroko raised an eyebrow. It wasn't going to be that easy, was it?

*

They stepped out of the elevator and hit the streets of Tokyo, surrounded by flashing neon signs and commercial advertisements. In a way, Lexi felt lost here, just as she felt lost everywhere. Since the murder of her parents by the Zodiacs, the only family she had left were her friends in the ECHO team, but was that enough?

She still had feelings for Hawke, and she knew Alex did, but now he was engaged to Lea. They would be married soon. Another happy couple and she guessed kids would be next. Scarlet seemed happy enough with Jack Camacho. Reaper's on-again-off-again relationship with his wife in Provence was funny to hear about, but they still saw each other even after all these years and they had their twins to think about.

Ryan was destroyed after Maria's murder but he had come back stronger and now he had started to talk about women again. He would be next. All of them were happy except her.

She recollected the memory back on the Duncan of Lea's engagement ring twinkling on her finger like a little star. Looking down at her hand she saw nothing but the hideous, ugly prosthetic fingernails shining dully in the neon night. She had never felt so low, and it was at this moment that her betrayal of Joe Hawke reared its grotesque head and pushed her other thoughts far away.

It was a long time ago, but he would never forgive her if he found out.

Maybe it would be better for everyone if the sniper's next bullet had my name on it.

Beside her, Ryan ran a hand over the tattoo on his upper arm.

Маша.

Masha. That was what he called Maria.

When he thought about her now it hurt much less. Time had passed. It had healed the terrible wound caused by her murder. Now he could remember the good times and laugh along with the memories. Only now could he consider moving on, and he knew it was time to do it, too. Nothing forced. Just opening his heart to future possibilities and seeing what happened, letting fate take the tiller and steer him where it wanted.

There was someone else out there for him, he knew it in his heart. He was young and wanted to live again but he was a different man now. Killing Dirk Kruger in Miami Beach had finished his long apprenticeship to become a warrior like his friends. Punching the South African arms dealer out of the airship and watching him fall to his death in shark-infested waters had been the last rite of passage. No one could doubt his will or capability now, and whoever he found to be with would have to accept this new man.

Lexi saw him rubbing the tattoo. "All good?"

He gave a sturdy nod. "Yes. All good."

"She was an amazing woman, Ryan."

"I know."

"But you will find someone else."

"I know that, too."

"We've been through a lot together, this team."

He huffed out a quiet, weary laugh. "You could say that."

"And you've changed more than any of us. I'm proud of you."

He turned. "Wow… I'm… Thanks."

They walked faster to catch up with the others, but before either could say a word, Hiroko's young voice broke the tense silence. "We're here."

CHAPTER FIFTEEN

Hawke smashed into the dirt and rolled three times until he was underneath the rear axles of a parked truck. He was smacking a fresh magazine into the grip of his Glock when he saw someone running over to him, bullets nipping at his heels with every pace.

"Get a move on, Reap!"

Reaper dived to the ground and rolled next to him. "Merde, that was close!"

"You move any slower than that and you may as well paint a target on your back."

"When you said we were going to Hawaii I visualized some surfing and a chilled out luau or two, not having some bastard using my bollocks for target practice."

"I see your colloquial English is coming on in leaps and bounds… Incoming!" The tire closest to them exploded in a cloud of rubber and the truck sank fast on its right side. "Move over!"

Reaper rolled over and Hawke followed him just in time to stop getting crushed by the collapsing truck.

"That was fun."

Like many of the other islands in the Hawaiian archipelago, Oahu was once covered in miles of sugar cane plantations. Established in the US Civil War when the Confederacy cut off supplies to the North, it soon grew to become one of the biggest crops in the islands. When the tourist trade took off after the second world war, landowners found their properties were more valuable if they sold them to developers wanting to build hotels and complexes, and today the industry is all but gone.

According to the research they had done on the plane journey, Jarrett McKenna's cane plantation was in the same boat, except he had turned down the offer of millions from leisure center developers. He made more money growing and selling cannabis on his land. His medical marijuana business was booming since several US states started legalizing it.

The authorities didn't have to know about the cannabis plantation hidden away in the jungles on his land and they doubted it kept him up at night.

In attacking the plantation, the Oracle was growing more reckless and dangerous by the minute. What was ostensibly a sugarcane plantation was a cover not only for cannabis but also for an illegal coca crop, and much of it had been torched and set on fire just before the arrival of ECHO, annihilated by the Athanatoi's brutal scorched earth policy. Hawke scanned the yard for any sign of the enemy. "This is their work, all right."

"But where the hell are they?"

"They're on the move." Hawke craned his head around to look through the wheel now collapsed and covered in shredded rubber.

"Where?"

"Over there behind the barn, and there are still some in what I guess is an office in the main property, next to that portacabin."

Lea's voice crackled over the comms. She and Nikolai were backup on a rise to the south. "I can see them from here. Looks like there are two of the bastards."

"Two verses two," Reaper said. "That's very considerate of them."

"One of them is on the move again," said Nikolai's low Russian grumble.

Lea said, "Looks like he's trying to get around to the

other side of the truck."

"We can't stay here," Hawke said. "Can't defend a position like this from an attack on two fronts."

"Where are you now, Lea?"

"We're still up on the rise to the south, about a hundred meters from the car."

"Can you take out the guy trying to get around to the other side of the truck?"

"He's using that big shed for cover."

"I see it."

"Me too."

A line of bullets ripped through the dirt and blew out the truck's right-hand rear tire.

"Fuck!"

The truck slumped down further.

Reaper scanned what he could see of the landscape from under the lop-sided truck. "They take out the other tires and we're squashed flatter than crêpes!"

The comms crackled again. "Yeah don't let that happen, Josiah. I got big plans for ya."

"Not planning on it."

"What if they hit the petrol tank?" the Frenchman said.

Hawke shook his head. "It's a diesel. Highly unlikely they'll be able to ignite it with gunfire."

"The problem I have with that statement, mon ami, is the *highly unlikely* bit. I'd have preferred *completely impossible*."

"Sorry, can't promise that, Reap. It's possible to ignite a diesel tank with high-velocity full metal jackets if you're committed enough to the task."

"Great, crushed, and burned alive."

"Tank's on the other side of the truck, mate. First thing I checked. Problems start when our runner leaves the cover of the barn and gets on our left-hand side."

"Which looks like now!" Lea said.

"Can you take him?"

"I don't know."

Hawke tried to point the gun down toward the direction his feet were pointing in but he couldn't raise his head enough under the truck to aim. "I can't do it."

"He's still out of sight."

"Time's running out."

A massive wave of automatic gunfire now raked up against the shredded tires on their right, blasting chunks of brown dirt and rock chips all over them. Hawke tucked his head down into his chest and leaned to his right to keep the debris from going into his eyes.

"Things are hotting up!"

"They're getting braver!"

Hawke twisted onto his back again and pulled his gun arm over his chest. Pointing the muzzle through the holes in between the spokes of the wrecked wheel, he let rip another few shots at the men hiding in the office. The angle was tough but he managed to shoot out another of the windows and then blow up a gas cylinder at the side of the portacabin.

The explosion was small but enough to stop the men firing on them as they ducked for cover.

"Nice shootin' Reap!" Lea said.

"Thanks."

"That was *me*," Hawke said.

"I knew that, ya eejit,"

"Hey!"

"Your little running man has got himself to the end of the barn, Josiah."

More gunfire from the men in the office, which was now even more obscured by the smoke from the coca fields. "Die you fucking freaks!"

"Hey, you don't even know me!" Lea shouted.

Reaper snorted as he reloaded his gun. "I don't think

they like us very much."

Hawke furrowed his brow. "Weird thing to shout in a gunfight. As you said, Lea – they don't even know us."

"You're going to die for what you're doing to us, you sons of bitches!"

Bullets pelted an upturned disc harrow and ricocheted at every angle, terrifyingly close to their heads, but Reaper scrambled to his feet and sprinted at full speed toward the main house. He only got halfway before a savage fusillade of defensive fire forced him to take cover behind one of the sugarcane planters, still on fire at the side of the yard.

"They're not giving in!" Hawke yelled.

"They think we're Athanatoi," Nikolai said. "They saw what the cult did to their friends here at this property and they'd rather die than go through torture like that."

Hawke returned fire from behind the burning truck while Reaper and Lea made their way over to the house from their positions on the flanks. It was a long and bitter fire fight. Nikolai gave Hawke some cover fire and the Englishman managed to reach the house. Standing on one side of the blown-out entrance, with Reaper on the other and Lea and Nikolai now closing in behind them, he burst inside and started the grim task of room-to-room clearance.

Reaper piled in behind him and the two of them took out the last surviving gunmen before Lea and Nikolai even made it into the house.

"What now?" Lea said.

"There's got to be a computer around here somewhere," Hawke said, ripping a fresh piece of his shirt from the hem and tying it around his face as a makeshift smoke filter. The others copied his example to protect themselves from the fumes, but they all knew it was a temporary solution at best.

"We don't have much time," Lea said.

"Here!" Reaper said from the end of the corridor. "A desktop."

Hawke turned desperate eyes on the Russian. "You said you knew computers, is that right?"

"Yes."

"Then get to work on that computer, Kolya. I hope your computer skills are as good as your combat skills."

"They are, but I must have time!"

Nikolai tapped away on the desktop as the room slowly filled with smoke. "Shit, I'm going to get as high as a kite on this stuff."

"That's why we need to hurry," Hawke said. "Jokes aside, this is a serious situation and if we let this smoke smash our judgment we're going to get killed."

"Got anything yet?"

"Just bypassing the password screen. Easy as pie."

Hawke scanned the area out the front of the office for any sign of McKenna's men, but there was nothing but smoke from the fire that had now jumped from the coca field to the barn. "Hurry it up, mate."

"Got it," Nikolai said. "Looks like our man McKenna had a deal with a guy called Bryce Cobb who owns a shipping cargo company based in Honolulu Harbor."

"I like the sound of this."

"Looks like he uses this man to smuggle his cocaine into various countries around the world, including the US West Coast. I'm on an email chain between them right now."

"And?"

"And McKenna's still alive. He just sent Cobb an email a few seconds ago telling him to get a ship ready to leave Hawaii at once. Says his life's in danger and that he owes him bigtime, as he puts it."

"Name of the ship?"

The Russian shook his head. “Doesn’t say.”

Lea sighed. “So the Athanatoi came here looking for the ring, which presumably is in McKenna’s possession. If they found it, they’re long gone, but if they didn’t their next stop is going to be that ship.”

“We need to get down to the harbor quick-smart,” Hawke said, blinking his red eyes in the smoke. “We’re out of here.”

CHAPTER SIXTEEN

Ezekiel Jones had never traveled to Japan before and he guessed this wasn't a typical experience. A lot of the guys in the Navy often swung through the place, most often with the Seventh Fleet in Yokosuka, but no one in the Pentagon had ever thought of sending a tank commander to downtown Tokyo. He knew that much.

He thought most of it looked kind of crazy – so much neon, so many wires. Not much like his part of East Texas, he knew that much too, but as crazy as it seemed, it was nowhere near as crazy as the new friends he'd made back on that Greek island. Now, watching the Englishwoman as she stared up at the top of the Izumi Garden Tower skyscraper with a Spartan night vision monocular, he started to realize just how boring his life had become until he'd met these nutcases.

Ryan Bale dragged on his cigarette. "What have you got, Cairo?"

"It's not good, boy," came the absent-minded reply. "At least half a dozen men armed with handguns on the upper floor and even more downstairs. I'm guessing Jojima is nicely tucked away in her bed somewhere on the top floor of the penthouse."

"But where's the third ring?" Lexi said.

"That's what we're here to find out, I guess," said Zeke.

"He's game," Scarlet said. "I'll give him that much."

"Bless you, sweetheart," Zeke said with a broad toothy smile, "but I'm always more than game."

"Good to know, darling."

"She might wear it," Hiroko said.

"Saves breaking into a safe," said Ryan.

"Always looking on the bright side," Lexi said, rolling her eyes. "But I guess with a face like that there's no other option."

Ryan slowly raised his middle finger at her. "Hey, you keep rolling those eyes, and one day you might find a brain somewhere back there."

"I doubt she wears it," Scarlet said. "At least, she wouldn't wear it if she knew its true value and we can't presume she's ignorant of that. We'll check the safe first. Hiroko, I want you to stay here. We'll bring back whatever we can of your father's, but I want you somewhere safe. This could easily get violent."

"As you wish," she said quietly.

Traveling up the Izumi Garden Tower in one of the external elevators, Ezekiel Jones stared out across the stormy neon city. He smiled at Scarlet, and she replied by giving him her backup weapon. The gun felt good in his hand. He'd grown up with handguns and hunting rifles and a gun in his hand felt as natural as holding a cup of coffee. By the time he hit basic training in the US Army, he could shoot straighter than the highway to hell and fast with it too. Now, he gripped the Glock and waited for hell to be unleashed.

Beside him, he saw Scarlet's mind was now focused on the mission like a golden eagle closing in on a running rabbit. She sure was an impressive sight and he idly wondered if there was someone special in her life. Exactly what sort of man could handle a woman like this he had no idea and started to doubt he would be up to the job.

The elevator pinged and the doors opened. They stepped into a plush marble lobby area with a few discreet signs on the walls covered in Japanese characters.

Lexi scanned the signs. "That way," she said. That's

the corridor that leads to the private apartments, and the penthouse too."

They crossed the lobby and followed Lexi down the peach marble corridor. The walls were smooth and polished and there was no noise except for the sound of their boots and shoes on the floor tiles.

"This is it," Lexi said. "The sign says Jojima. This is her apartment."

The wooden door was painted dark green, polished to perfection with a matte black iron handle and a tastefully unobtrusive video doorbell fitted almost out of sight.

"Push that button and it's game over," Lexi said.

"So how do we get in?" asked Ryan.

"The old-fashioned way, I guess," Zeke said. "Right, Cairo?"

Her gun was already out of the holster. She aimed it at the door and fired three times, blasting the handle and lock to smithereens.

Zeke yelled out. "Hell yeah! I like your style, Cairo Sloane!"

"I'm an old-fashioned kinda gal," she said and kicked the door open.

They smashed through the door and found themselves in a coral pink-painted hallway lined with ornate screen prints and antique tables covered in orchids. A man who had been asleep on a chair at the foot of some stairs was now awake and staring wide-eyed at the intruders with horror on his face.

Reaching for the gun under his jacket, Lexi fired on him, three times with her muffled pistol and blasted him back over the back of his chair. He slumped down dead on the bottom step while Scarlet leaped over his body and made her way up the stairs toward the upper level.

Moving quickly and taking the steps three at a time, she was at the top in no time. Lexi, Ryan, and Zeke were right behind her, weapons drawn and raised and ready for more action.

Scarlet scanned what she could see of the upper floor. "This way."

They followed her along a corridor of polished hardwood floorboards and bespoke furniture until they reached what resembled a T-junction, each leading to different wings of the enormous penthouse suite.

"Zeke and Lexi down there," Scarlet whispered. "Ryan, you're with me."

It didn't take the Texan soldier long to learn the pecking order, and he followed the Chinese assassin down the corridor which led into the west wing. Ahead of her, Lexi saw a large *daimon* or family crest on the wall outside a door at the end of the corridor.

"I think this is HQ," she said, explaining briefly the significance of the coats of arms that represented the various Yakuza groups. "So, in we go. Ready?"

"Hell yeah."

They booted the door open and charged into the room with their guns raised, but there was no one there. A speedy room-to-room clearance revealed that the entire wing was empty, and they holstered their guns. "All clear here, Cairo," Lexi said into her palm mic. "You?"

*

"We're clear here too, and in the world's biggest closet," Scarlet said. "We're into the safe but still searching for the ring. Maybe she's wearing it after all."

"Fine, we're on our way back to you," Lexi said.

Ryan stared down at the tray of jewelry. "Who knew the Yakuza loved their gold so much? There must be over a million bucks' worth of stuff here."

Scarlet kept one eye on the door as she spoke in

hurried, hushed tones. "But what about the ring we're looking for?"

"I'm looking for it!"

"Well hurry the hell up."

"Give me a chance! There must be two hundred rings in here. What about this one?"

She turned to see Ryan on his knees in front of the safe, holding a diamond and ruby ring up to her.

"I'm flattered Ryan, but I see you more like a pet than a future husband."

Ryan gave her a look. "I meant it must be worth at least a quarter of a million. Maybe a little something for ECHO's treasury?"

"We're not thieves, put it back and find the sodding ring."

He tossed it back into the pile and continued his search, mumbling something about pets and bad attitudes. "A-ha!"

"You got it?"

"No, but I got Hiroko's mother's jewelry box." He showed her the tiny jewel-encrusted box with the intricate carving of a tiger on it. "This has to be it, right?"

"I guess so. Put it in your pocket and find the sodding ring!"

"Got it."

Lexi and Zeke appeared at the door to the walk-in closet. "Any luck yet?"

"Not yet, but Ryan took a few seconds out to propose."

"Seriously?" Zeke said. "I'm so excited for you guys."

Lexi rolled her eyes. "They're not getting engaged, Zeke. I mean, talk about different leagues."

"Hey!" Ryan said. "I'm literally right here."

"You have the ring yet?" Scarlet asked anxiously.

"As a matter of fact I do not, and…"

Then everything changed fast. A Yakuza throwing

knife flashed past Ryan's head and slammed into the closet's wooden wall less than two inches from his head.

"Holy crap!" he yelled.

Scarlet spun around and raised her gun. "Take cover!"

CHAPTER SEVENTEEN

Ryan jumped away from the knife, lost his balance, and fell on his back while the others spun around to see Makiko Jojima standing in the bedroom, flanked on either side by a bodyguard. Scarlet immediately saw the ring they were searching for, tightly wedged onto her left ring finger.

Jojima ordered the men forward to attack the thieves. "Hashimoto! Mori!"

The two men drew their weapons and fired on the team, blasting the closet door to shreds and forcing them to take cover on either side of the marble mull posts. Bullets traced everywhere, smashing the stained glass panel out of the transom and spraying splinters and shards all over the interior of the closet.

"Holy crap!" Zeke yelled, covering his head from the flying glass. "This shit is real."

"We're sitting ducks!" Ryan called back.

Scarlet and Lexi returned fire, raking the bedroom with defensive fire and forcing the Yakuza to flee back into the central hallway.

"They're retreating!" Ryan said.

"Great work!" said Zeke.

"Not great at all," Scarlet said. "The buggering ring's on Jojima's left hand! We have to get after them!"

They got to their feet and exited the trashed closet, giving chase down the central corridor with their guns raised and their hearts beating at a million miles per hour.

"They're not in the apartment!" Lexi called out.

Scarlet knew where they were going. "We need to get

to the elevator. They're trying to get Jojima to safety before they regroup and hit us back."

They sprinted from the penthouse and back out into the peach marble lobby area where they saw the fleeing party of Yakuza standing outside one of the external elevators. Running up and down on the outside of the skyscraper, the famous elevators offered a breathtaking view of the city, but tonight no one cared about the vista.

The ECHO teammates fired on them and the bodyguards reacted in a heartbeat. Hashimoto pushed Jojima into the elevator while Mori blocked their bodies with his own and raised his gun into the aim, squeezing off half a dozen rounds to provide cover fire as Hashimoto reloaded and pushed the button for the basement parking lot.

Scarlet and Ryan were sitting ducks, exposed in the marble lobby area to the front of the elevator doors. The only cover was two substantial potted palms placed on either side of the penthouse suite entrance. They each took one and dived to the floor behind the heavy sleek black porcelain pots as Hashimoto and Mori retreated in a backward crouch walk, firing off defensive shots until safely inside the elevator.

"Damn it, Ryan! They're getting away."

Lexi and Zeke had reached the fight and were taking cover behind the doorposts on either side of the penthouse suite.

"What's happening?" the Chinese assassin said.

"They're in the sodding elevator already," Scarlet said, ducking as one of Hashimoto's last rounds struck the thick rim of the pot and blasted a chunk of porcelain into a dozen razor-sharp slivers.

Up ahead, the elevator doors were closing fast.

"We need some cover fire!" she shouted.

"Leave that to me," Lexi said.

Zeke gave a firm nod of approval as he slid a round into the chamber of his gun. "Hell, I don't need to be asked twice."

"We go in three, got it, boy?"

Ryan gave her a double-take. "You can't be serious?"

She sighed. "When am I not serious?"

He raised his eyebrows. "Point taken, but I still think we don't have a chance of making that lift."

"We're not going to get in that lift."

"Eh?"

"Three, two, one!"

Without further warning, Scarlet scrambled out from behind the cover of the potted palm and sprinted to the elevator shaft. Watching through the smoke glass doors, she saw the Yakuza's elevator slowly slip out of sight as it made its way down to the basement. Turning to the right she hit the button on the other elevator and the doors slid open.

"Get in!"

Ryan darted into the second elevator as Scarlet hit the basement button, and the doors slid shut as they too started descending to the ground.

"We'll never catch them!" Ryan said. "They're ten seconds ahead of us."

Scarlet wasn't listening but had craned her neck up to the ceiling of the elevator. "Give me a leg up."

"Eh?"

"A leg up, boy!"

Ryan's face was a picture of mock horror. "This is hardly the place, Cairo… besides I never knew you felt that way about me."

"That's a leg *over*, you silly sod, not a leg up."

Ryan grinned. He had already linked his hands to form a cradle for her to use for her leg up. "I know what you meant, Cairo, and I'm not going to argue with anyone who can consider doing what you're about to do."

Using his hands, she reached the elevator ceiling panel and swung open the maintenance hatch. Grasping either side of the hatch's rim, she pulled herself out of the elevator car and climbed up onto the roof.

The warmth and stillness of the car were instantly replaced with the rushing air and lashing rain of the outside world. As the elevator screeched at high speed down the outside of the building's western aspect, Scarlet clung to a support post to stop the wind from blowing her off the roof. At around thirty floors up, she didn't much like the idea of tumbling down to earth and hitting the plaza below at terminal velocity.

Think of the mess, you silly cow.

She moved to the northern end of the car's roof and peered down at the other elevator as it raced ahead of her on its journey to the basement level. The few seconds' head start had created a distance of about twenty feet. Not too bad but not easy either. She could make the jump but one error in judgment and she could break an ankle or miss it altogether and fall right off the edge.

"You don't have to do this!"

Rain in her eyes, she swept her hair back and peered down through the hatch into the cozy, warm little world Ryan was inhabiting. What he didn't know was that she *did* have to do it. She'd had to do things like this since she was a little kid. She had always taken the risky road, reached for the highest apple on the tree. A shrink would tell her it had something to do with her parents' murder, but true or not, it didn't change the fact that taking risks like this was a deep part of her personality, what made her the woman she truly was.

"I'm doing it, Ryan," she called back, and flipped the hatch shut with the toe of her boot.

The ground rushed up toward her. The plaza below

was sliding into rainy focus, as were the headlights of the cars driving in and out of the parking lot in front of Izumi Garden Tower still impossibly far below. One of those cars was a chunky black SUV heading toward the parking bay out the front of the elevators. "That's their ride," she said.

They're not going to the basement lot, she thought. Jojima must have called for a car to pick them up in front of the building. Getting panicky. Worried about a shootout in the basement. Either way, she still had a chance. She watched the SUV's headlights sweep up the side of the green glass wall of the elevator shaft. Behind it, a stretch limo honked its horn to get the SUV to move forward. A man leaned out of the SUV and waved a gun at the limo driver who instantly backed down and wound his window up.

"That's definitely their ride."

She took a step closer to the edge of the elevator car, still clinging to the steel support post for balance as it raced toward the ground. Halfway down now, but still over twenty stories to go. She blew out a breath, aimed for the Yakuza elevator, and leaped into the darkness of the night.

CHAPTER EIGHTEEN

When they got to the harbor, Bryce Cobb was easy enough to find. Way past midnight now and heading into the early hours and there was only one small area of activity down on Pier 38. A man was illuminated by a couple of lights, unloading some boxes from the back of a Hilux and walking down to a boat moored at the end of the pier. High above the craggy ridge of Mount Tantalus in the east, the first signs of dawn were appearing as a peach-colored ribbon in the Hawaiian sky.

They walked casually down the pier, knowing the man had nowhere to run and approached him with a cheery wave and smile.

"Who the fuck are you?"

"We're your worst nightmare." Hawke piled a fist into his face and knocked him down hard on the wooden pier. "Help me pick him up, Vincent."

"It's Reaper," he said with a knowing smile. "We're on a mission."

"This is an in-joke, am I right?" Nikolai said.

"You could say that," Lea said as Hawke and Reaper picked up the unconscious man and walked him down the pier. They dragged him over the gangway and into the wheelhouse of the boat. Nikolai scanned the marina for any signs of trouble while Lea opened the hatch leading to below decks.

Hawke, who was holding the man by his arms, went first. Reaper had the man by his knees and he followed him down the stairs. When they were down below decks, Lea and Nikolai killed the lights up top and joined them as Hawke and Reaper tied him to a pillar with some nylon winch rope.

Hawke saw a cup of cold coffee sitting on the side of the cabin. He picked it up and hurled the contents into Cobb's face. In response, the man gasped and coughed and blinked his eyes wildly as he tried to work out where he was and what the hell had just happened.

"Wakey wakey, asshole," Lea said.

Another gasp and more confused blinking as he slowly got his bearings. "What the hell's going on? Are you those freaks?"

"Who do you mean?"

"The dudes in the black suits!"

"Do we look like them?"

"I guess not." His voice was hesitant and confused. "So if you're not them, then who are you and what do you want?"

"We want McKenna," Lea said. "Or more accurately, we want something McKenna has."

"If this is about the coke, I swear to God he's blackmailing me. He threatened to kill me if I didn't ship it for him."

"Spare us, dickhead," Hawke said. "We've already read all your emails. He's not blackmailing you. You're the best of friends."

"True story," Lea said. "I'd say the two of you are practically sleeping together."

"Cosy, eh?" Hawke said.

Cobb got nasty and lashed out with his leg, almost hitting Lea with his boot.

Hawke leaned in and gripped his throat. "Try that again and I'll beat you black and blue, got it?"

Cobb snarled but backed down. "All right man… who the fuck *are* you?"

"My name's Hawke and I'm with the British

Government," he lied.

"Shit."

"Right. And you're a coke smuggler looking at life in prison in any one of a dozen countries unless you cooperate with us."

"Okay, okay… you got me real good, man."

Lea crossed her arms. "You bet your arse we did, you friggin' gobdaw. Now just tell us what we want to know and we'll be on our way."

A defeated and broken man, he gave a sullen nod and slumped down against the pillar.

"Where's McKenna?" Hawke asked.

"I swear I don't know. He was supposed to be here a half-hour ago."

"You're lying."

"I swear…"

Hawke punched him in the head and split his nose open.

Cobb screamed with rage and spat a wad of blood on the wheelhouse floor. "Fuck!"

"There's much more where that came from, wanker," Hawke said. "See, I'm in a bit of a rush, and my commando training emphasized power over finesse." Another punch and a dislocated jaw.

Cobb tried to scream but it came out as a garbled moan.

"C'mon, friend," Lea said. "Where's McKenna? I can't guarantee Joe here's going to get any nicer."

Hawke pulled back his arm and clenched his fist.

"Wait! Wait dammit!"

They turned to the voice behind them and saw McKenna climbing up the steps from a lower deck. "Jesus, just stop beating him. I'm here."

"McKenna, how nice of you to show yourself."

He jutted his chin over at the broken Bryce Cobb. "How did you know that wasn't me?"

"Simple," Lea said. "All the pictures of you back at your place. Unless you keep cheesy soft-focus photos of ship captains in your house, the conclusion wasn't hard to reach."

"You went to my house?"

"Sure."

"Then you saw what those freaks did." The drug baron approached them sheepishly. "What do you want with us?"

"What do you think?" Reaper said.

McKenna took a deep breath and slipped his hand in his pocket.

Hawke drew his Glock and aimed it two-handed in the center of the man's face. It took less than half a second. "Careful what you bring out of the pocket, son."

"You want the fucking ring, no?"

"When I see it, I'll believe it. Now, easy does it."

McKenna pulled his hand out slowly to reveal he was holding the third ring. "Happy now?"

Hawke lowered the gun and slipped it back in his holster. "I'm always happy, mate. Guess I'm just an optimist." He took the ring from the man and held it up to the light. "How about you?"

"Not any fucking more."

Hawke tossed the ring to Lea who caught it with one hand.

"The real thing?"

She gave it a quick study and took Razak's and Alexander's rings from his pocket. "Fake as a Hong Kong Seamaster."

Hawke raised his gun. "Last chance, friend. Where is the ring?"

"All right, all right! Lower your gun. They took it. The freaks."

"Why lie about it?"

"I just wanted you off my back so I could work out a way to get my ring back. My old man got that ring back in Vietnam. Guy who sold it to him said it came from Egypt. Belonged to some dude called Akhenaten. It's important to me."

Lea tossed the ring back to Hawke. "We're not getting the map with this thing."

Cobb looked up, sharp eyes squinting. "What map?"

Hawke elbowed him in the face. "When I want you to talk I'll rattle your cage."

McKenna's eyes widened. "Who the fuck are you guys?"

Cobb spat more blood and a tooth came out. "They say they're from the British Government."

Hawke shook his head. "What did I *literally* just say to you?"

"Sorry."

"Apology accepted." He turned to McKenna. "How many guys came to your plantation earlier today?"

McKenna paused before answering. He was searching for a way to speak without giving anything away, and they all knew it.

"How many?"

"Around twenty."

Hawke and the others shared a glance. "Quite a force."

"But it felt like a hell of a lot more, man. They move like frigging ninjas."

"And they wanted the ring, am I right?" Reaper said.

McKenna nodded. "They were supposed to be buying it, man. I swear it. They turned up like a goddam army and tell us the deal's off and if we valued our asses then we'd better just turn the goddam ring over. I told them to fuck off. I told them no one messes with me like that."

Hawke crossed his arms and leaned back on the galley cabinet. "And how did *that* work out for you?"

"You know how – you saw my property. They went crazy and killed all the men in the room except me. They put a gun to my head, took the ring, and then they set fire to the entire plantation. I only got away because I knew about a secret escape tunnel that my grandfather built into the property years ago in case the Japanese invaded during the war."

"A charming story," Lea said, "but it doesn't help us get the ring back. Do you know where these guys are now?"

"The terms of the deal were they paid me half a million bucks for the one poxy ring and then got out of my life, but in my line of work, you have to be suspicious to survive so I checked them out. I can tell you that they have a private jet fueled up at the airport. I guess they're planning on getting out of here as fast as they can, especially now they have what they came looking for, goddam thieves."

Hawke glanced at his watch. "When are the first flights out of the airport?"

"Just after five a.m."

"Shit," he said. "that's less than twenty minutes away. We'd better get running."

CHAPTER NINETEEN

"This is a zero-sum game, gentlemen," Vice President Davis Faulkner told the faces staring back at him over his opulent mahogany desk. "Either we get what's inside this ancient city or our enemies do." He leaned back in his leather captain's chair and deftly sliced off the tip of a cigar. "Get that son of a bitch Packard on video conference right now."

Josh Muston leaped from his seat and hurried across the room to one of the plasma screens situated on the far wall. When he turned it on, George Packard, the head of the NSA was chewing his lower lip and waiting nervously to speak with the Vice President.

When silence filled the room, Faulkner began. "As you all know, we've been working alongside a non-governmental force for some time now in a bid to secure some relics from the ancient world." He settled back into his chair once again and puffed on the thick musky cigar. "In fact, many of these treasures and weapons originate from a time a good deal older than the ancient world."

Muston and Mayhew, the Deputy COS exchanged a fraught glance. Was the old man finally bringing them inside the inner circle? They'd heard rumors about a man named Wolff who wasn't what he appeared to be, a man who had harnessed the power of immortality. Some were saying he was dead now, finally, after thousands of years. It all seemed too insane to be true.

Mayhew was first to speak. "The problems we had in Greece and Miami were brought on us by the ECHO team. They got hold of the Sword of Fire which led them to the King's Tomb well ahead of us, and they stopped the chaos we had planned for the Five Eyes conference, delaying our plans Stateside."

"And now our intel guys are telling us they're closer than ever to reaching the Citadel."

"What's our response?" Packard said.

"It comes in two stages," Faulkner said. He looked like he was starting to perk up. "First, we go all out to capture this pre-Sumerian city known as the Citadel. We need their knowledge, technology, and weapons. The second phase involves us eradicating the ECHO team, and I mean the full package."

"The full package?" Mayhew said, turning slightly pale. "Are we certain that's necessary?"

Faulkner leaned forward in his chair and jammed his cigar stub down hard in the glass ashtray. "You're not going weak at the knees are you, Brian?"

"Well, no, but…"

"There are no buts when it comes to ECHO, Mr. Mayhew. The full package will not only eliminate them physically from this world but also remove any trace of their ever having existed from all paper and digital records… and the same for all their friends and relatives. It will be as if they had never existed."

"Seems like we're using a sledgehammer to crack a walnut, Sir."

"You want me to use that sledgehammer to crack your walnuts instead, Mayhew?"

"No, Sir."

"Good, then get on board, man. I can't use someone who pees their pants every time a tough decision has to be taken."

"Sorry, Sir."

"But what about President Brooke?"

Faulkner looked at him with cold, steady eyes. "Never

mind about President Brooke. You just leave him to me."

*

The assassin known throughout the world's grimy underbelly as Cougar opened her apartment door and stepped into the lonely half-light of the hallway. Her recent journey to Greece to kill Magnus Lund had gone without a hitch, as her missions always did, but she was glad to be home and see her boy.

"Matty?"

No reply. She checked the answerphone and saw one message. She lowered her bag to the floor and hit the play button.

Hey Jess, it's Justin. I guess you're out at work or something. I tried your cell but no answer there either. I called to say that I found a great place here in Los Cabos. It's perfect for us, but only if we can find the money because it's mucho dinero. Anyway, take it easy babe, and call me when you're in. Hope Matty's doing better these days. Call me.

He signed off with a kiss and then the machine bleeped as it reached the end of the message. The tinny electronic note echoed around the silent apartment for a second or two.

"Matty?"

She stepped into his bedroom but no sign of him. The bedsheets were all over the floor alongside the pillows and his alarm clock. She felt her heart quicken. Had something happened to him? Why wasn't he answering her? Turning, she slipped her Glock from her holster in a lightning-fast fluid motion and raised it into the aim. Pushing the bathroom door open with the toe of her boot she checked the room was clear and moved back into the hall.

If there was anyone here, then they knew she was back – calling out to her son had given that game away – but she still had the advantage of knowing the apartment better.

And of being her.

She spun around the doorway of her bedroom with the gun raised and found her son.

He was sleeping in her bed, sheets twisted and tangled around his ankles and head resting on a sweat-soaked pillow. Several inhalers were strewn on the carpet and the ceiling fan whirred gently above the whole sorry scene. He had come into her bed to sleep, maybe in the middle of the night.

She sighed a breath of relief and slipped the gun back into the holster. Taking care not to wake him, she rested her palm on his forehead and checked his temperature. A little high but nothing to worry about. The sound of his intermittent, rattling wheeze as he struggled to breathe made her feel a mix of anger and pity.

She walked back through to the kitchen and prepared some coffee. Sipping the strong, black brew she perched on the edge of her sofa and flicked through her cell phone messages. Nothing from Garcetti, which was good. She finished the drink and stretched out on the soft leather couch. Yawned and closed her eyes.

Two down and nine to go. As she slipped into sleep, her mind leaped from visions of the new house in Los Cabos to the pack of marked bullets she had in her bag. The next hit would require another chartered government flight and more time away from Matty. She felt her shoulders tense and worked hard to stretch the muscles in her neck and try and relax.

She saw the name of the next hit on the bullet. A neat engraving for sure, but another grim task ahead of her. Another family told of a loved one's death and another funeral full of bitter tears. Daniel Devlin and Magnus Lund both gone now, and a third to follow very soon. None of them deserved to die, but she had no choice. She shook the thought from her mind and imagined diving into the pool in Mexico. Justin sipping a beer and Matty fixed up and laughing.

And then she was asleep.

CHAPTER TWENTY

Scarlet fell through the Tokyo night. The northern elevator car raced toward her as she neared her target. She slammed down onto the steel roof, slick with rainwater, and skidded to the edge at high speed. It happened like in a nightmare – slow and deliberate as she toppled over the edge. She thrust out her left hand and grabbed one of the car's support posts, arresting her fall and spinning back around toward the center of the roof in one fluid motion.

Drawing her weapon, she fired on the hatch and blasted open the lock. Kicking it open she dropped inside and landed like a panther in the center of the elevator. The two startled guards stood like lemons for a second too long. Their shock at what they had just seen gave her all the time she needed to aim her gun at Jojima's forehead. "Hands up! All of you!"

Hashimoto and Mori obeyed, raising their hands into the air

"Rings, now."

Jojima looked confused. "You want my *rings*?"

"And I said now."

"All of this for a common robbery?"

Scarlet remained perfectly still, the gun still pointing in the woman's face. The elevator raced toward the ground. She pulled back the hammer, just for the psychological effect. "Now."

Jojima scowled and started to slide off her rings one by one. She took her time, as cool as black ice. Never show the enemy you're rattled. "You realize, you will be executed for this."

"Just hand over the gold, sister."

Jojima looked at her like she was an insect. "Here."

Without a direct order, Hashimoto stepped forward and took the rings with a respectful bow of his head. He turned to Scarlet and stretched his arm fully out.

In his palm, she counted five rings, including Cyrus the Great's ring – just as their intel had informed them. She took only this ring and slipped it into her pocket, leaving the diamonds and rubies and emeralds and opals for Jojima's bony, withered fingers.

The Japanese woman's brow furrowed. "I don't understand. These gems are worth ten times more than that old junk."

"Shows what you know."

The elevator reached the parking lot level and stopped. A gentle *ping* alerted them all to their arrival and the brushed steel and smoked glass doors gently swept open. "Turn around, and keep your hands pointing at the sky."

They obeyed, but she could see Jojima bristling at the humiliating nature of the whole robbery.

She ran out into the rain just as Ryan's elevator reached the floor. The doors slid open and Zeke and Lexi jogged across the lobby and joined them outside the enormous skyscraper. "We took the regular elevators," Zeke said.

"Yeah," said Lexi. "We're not heroes like you."

Scarlet looked at Hiroko and handed her the jewelry box. "This is yours, I think."

Hiroko fought back an unexpected wave of emotion. "Yes, thank you."

"We need to get out of here in a hurry," Ryan said. "Look over there."

He pointed to the underground parking lot where the black Merc SUV Scarlet had seen earlier was racing up the ramp.

"They're going to pick up Jojima and her goons and then we're the main course," Ryan said.

"We can't outrun them!" Lexi said.

"We don't have to outrun them," Zeke said. "Not when we can ride in style!"

He nudged his square chin over their shoulders as the black Merc squealed to a stop outside the lobby and Jojima and her guards who were now drawing their weapons.

"You can't be serious?" Lexi said.

"Sure, why the hell not?" he said, pumped to the max with his idea and a childish grin on his face. "Looks like our prayers just got answered, right?"

Scarlet gave in. "All right, everyone into the limo."

As the limo idled outside the lobby, a group of businessmen and geishas were stepping out of the lobby and heading over to the car. The small party shuffled quickly through the rain, starched two-piece suits, polished shoes, kimonos, and oil-paper umbrellas, but Zeke was first to the driver's door. To the vocal protests of the driver, the towering Texan swung open the heavy door and grabbed him by the shirt collar. "Out you get, man."

One of the geishas gasped, and a businessman began shouting and pointing at him.

Zeke paid no mind and pulled the driver out and threw him to the ground, raising more than one eyebrow among the ECHO teammates, then he climbed in and adjusted the seat to allow more legroom. "It's now or never!"

He fired the engine up and revved it a few times while the others piled into the back of the Cadillac DTS Stretch Limo. Sleek, black with tinted windows and a full sixteen feet long, the whole car growled when Zeke stamped on the throttle. The 4.7 liter beast under the hood responded with another roar and the limo surged forward, crashing through some decorative shrubbery and swerving out into the street.

"Great wheels!" Ryan said.

"Sure is," Zeke called back. "What a beauty!"

The car powered forward, windshield wipers working hard to clear the rain. A specially adapted version of the car was used by George W. Bush as his presidential limousine, but apparently, it was not so popular with the leading lights in the Yakuza firmament who were now firing on it with all they had. Now, with little regard for the car's care, Zeke drove the enormous vehicle around the corner at the end of the street and hit the throttle to gain some speed on the straight.

Pumped to the eyeballs with adrenaline, Scarlet Sloane opened the electric sunroof and stood up to her full height so the upper part of her body was sticking out of the top of the limo. "Weapon!"

Ryan pulled an MP5 from his bag and passed it up to her.

With a little effort, she squeezed the MP5 machine pistol up through the gap and aimed it at the pursuing Yakuza in the Merc.

Wildly raking their car with bullets, they swerved and skidded in response. A panicked driver struggled to keep the car on the road as she peppered the windshield with rounds and punched a dozen holes through it, killing both him and the other man in the front passenger seat. The Merc lurched wildly to the right and careened off the road. Mounting the curb with an axle-busting crunch, it plowed through the front window of a busy sushi bar and sent the patrons screaming and running for safety in every direction.

Lexi saw it all through her open window.

Hiroko looked like she was going to be sick.

"Did we lose them?" Zeke yelled.

"Nuh-uh." Lexi pulled her head back in from the window and moved down the limo toward the driving compartment. "They're reversing back out, and there's another load of goons just turned the corner, right Cairo?"

"Right," Scarlet called back through the open sunroof. "Silver Honda SUV fifty meters behind us is Yakuza too, and they're much more heavily armed."

"Great," Ryan said. "All we need now is for the sodding sniper to be hiding around here somewhere and then we may as well just kill ourselves and save all these arseholes the bother."

Racing west along the Metropolitan Expressway, the gangsters in the Honda opened fire. Bullets chased after them, chewing into the tarmac as Zeke swerved to avoid having their rear tires blown out. The Yakuza's aim got better, and now the bullets ripped into the angled trunk panel on the very rear of the limo. One of the rounds hit the lock and the trunk's lid popped open, obscuring Zeke's rearview mirror.

Turning to the side mirrors, he saw the Honda was closing in, and two of the gangsters were hanging out of the windows. It was almost comical, except for the fact one of them was holding a submachine gun and he was aiming it right at them.

He heard Scarlet firing back and saw sparks spitting up all over the hood of their car as her rounds hit their mark. The Honda swerved hard to the right, pulling the man with the submachine gun back inside.

The limo screeched its way around another corner and they found themselves racing toward the notorious Shibuya scramble crossing. Tens of thousands of people were all over the street with a sea of neon signs and traffic lights hanging above them like a stormy electric sky.

What looked to Scarlet like a Minebea machine pistol made short work of the limo's back end, blowing out the window and punching holes in the metal trunk rim and side panels. Bullets shattered the glass and plastic housing of the brake lights, but the real trouble started when Hashimoto took out the rear tires from the battered Merc behind them.

Scarlet fired back. Ripping the Honda's front tires out, the wrecked SUV swerved off the road and crashed into a noodle bar. Celebrating the destruction of the Honda lasted a few seconds before Zeke cried out from the front.

"We're going down!"

Already under stress by the speed, Zeke was punishing the Limo with, the tires now exploded like bombs and sprayed shredded vulcanized rubber all over the street. Zeke struggled to control the long vehicle, whose ass was now swaying all over the place.

Without the rubber tires, the steel wheels scraped and scratched on the asphalt, spitting orange and white sparks from the wheel arches like fireworks.

Zeke checked the speedometer and then his mirror. "We're slowing down and the bad guys are closing in. We need a new plan."

All eyes swiveled to Scarlet Sloane.

"Just keep driving, Tex," she said, loading her weapon. "We'll keep them off for as long as possible."

"And what then?" Lexi said. "They'll be on the phones, Cairo! They'll have a dozen other cars all over us in minutes."

"I'd have thought of something by then."

Ryan shook his head. "I am not paid enough for this."

The Merc containing Hashimoto and Mori pulled alongside them. Mori aimed the Minebea at them and raked a mag's worth of rounds up the side of the limo.

Zeke saw it coming and swerved wildly to the left but with the rear tires blown out the car quickly spun out of control and tipped over. Scarlet only just managed to crawl inside before it crashed into its roof and skidded in a hail of sparks for fifty meters down the road before finally coming to a stop a few hundred meters short of the Shibuya scramble crossing.

The impact of the flip had banged Scarlet's head on the door pillar and knocked her out, and now Ryan and the others struggled with their belt buckles.

Ryan was free first and was upside down as he strained to unbuckle Scarlet's belt when someone pushed the muzzle of a nine mil handgun through the open window and into his face. He strained up to see Hashimoto's grinning face. Mori was behind him but no sign of Jojima. He guessed she had been whisked away to a safe house while the threat was still real.

"Ring."

Ryan punched the back of the seat and crawled across the limo's long ceiling. Gently slipping the ring off Scarlet's finger, he handed it to the man. There was no need to tell him he had two others in his pocket.

"And now, *die*."

Hashimoto pulled the hammer back but at that second a police siren wailed in the distance. The Yakuza man cursed, kicked the limo door, and folded his hand around the ring. He and Mori spoke in rapid Japanese and then fled into the crowd.

Scarlet came to and saw the ring was gone. "What the hell happened?"

"Hashimoto got the ring," Ryan said.

Behind him, Zeke was gently trying to bring Hiroko around while Lexi smashed her shattered window out and crawled into the street. "We have to get going, guys. Police on our six."

The rest of the team followed Scarlet out of the car. Zeke was last, with a barely conscious Hiroko in his arms. "I can't leave her like this."

"And we need a diversion," Scarlet said. "Lexi and Ryan wait till the police see you and then do a runner over there. Zeke, you get the job of handling all this shit."

"What the..?"

"Deal with it. That's life in ECHO."

"Bless you, sweetheart, but I ain't even *in* ECHO!"

"Think of it as a temporary secondment."

"What about you?" Ryan asked.

Scarlet turned and watched Hashimoto and Mori as they made their way deeper into the growing crowd of shocked commuters now gathering on the scramble crossing. Somewhere overhead she heard the familiar sound of helicopter rotors and presumed either TV news or police.

"I'm going to get that ring back."

CHAPTER TWENTY-ONE

Amidst the chaotic tinny racket of a nearby pachinko parlor, Scarlet heard the sound of car horns blaring and the screams of confused, scared people. She turned the corner and saw the Yakuza fighting their way through the scramble crossing, flick knives in their hands, and snarls on their faces. Some of the men and women noticed the tell-tale signs of *yubitsume* – the finger-shortening punishment used by the infamous gangsters – and made themselves scarce as fast as possible.

Scarlet struggled to follow the thugs as they pushed deeper into the world-famous crossing. Neatly placed outside the busy Shibuya railroad station, the crossing was one of the busiest in the world and had featured in countless movies from *Lost in Translation* to *Retribution*. Now, the Englishwoman was standing on tiptoes in a bid to keep her eye on the gangsters as they slipped into the insane crowd.

Neon flashed and car horns honked. The rainstorm had retreated to a light Tokyo drizzle which now fell from the electric sky like ash. It was a scene she would remember forever, but business was business and the Yakuza and the ring were getting away. She blew out a breath and slowed her breathing as she scanned the scene.

And then she saw them.

They were running into Shibuya station and planning on getting onto a train to make good their escape with the ring. She was sure they had no idea of the value of the thing, but she was damned sure they were going to keep hold of it now.

Above everything.

She sprinted over the crossing, raising a warning hand to stop taxis as they drove toward her in the night. Pedestrians gasped and stepped away from her. Many filmed her on their phones. Some presumed she was a famous actor making a movie and looked around for a film crew while others scanned the air for a police chopper. Chaos reigned, but Scarlet Sloane didn't care a damn. She had to get the ring back at all costs.

Gone again. The place teemed with people moving in a dozen directions. The smell of dashi emanated through the extractor fan of a nearby restaurant as she climbed onto the hood of a parked car and scanned the area once again for any sign of the fleeing men. She saw them again, much closer to the station's entrance, but a thick cloud of smoke billowed out the door of a yakitori restaurant and obscured them. When the drizzly breeze cleared the smoke, they were gone.

Damn it.

A policeman called out to her from the other side of the crossing and started to weave his way through the crowd toward her. She leaped down from the hood and hurriedly pushed a strand of wet hair away from her eyes, tucking it behind her ear as her heart quickened. The cop drew closer and was now on his radio.

Damn it again.

Did they go into Shibuya Station or not? She tossed a coin in her head and went with the trains. They'd made the effort to get to the station's entrance after all, and why bother doing that only to change direction in the last few steps?

She went with her gut and ran down the underground steps two at a time. Her gun was holstered but her hand was never more than a few inches away from the grip. Like all professionally trained soldiers, she knew exactly how many rounds were in it and that there was one in the chamber. She would use it if she had to, but the general idea was to protect the public, not start a firefight in the middle of countless innocent people. There were children here, holding hands with their mums and dads as they went about their evening. The gun would stay out of sight for as long as possible.

She made the platform just as the doors on an eastbound train were starting to close. She saw the two men split up. Hashimoto ran for the train while Mori moved further along the platform toward another exit.

Clever.

Which one had the ring?

She tossed another coin in her head. From the exchange in the elevator, she believed Hashimoto was the senior man. Unlikely he would have given the job of protecting the ring to his junior.

With Mori long gone and Hashimoto well out of sight somewhere on the train, she darted across to the train and slipped through the sliding doors with half a second to spare.

Eyes peeled and hand on the gun grip, she walked slowly through the packed train as it raced along the Ginza line eastwards out of Shibuya, carefully scanning the faces of the commuters until she found Hashimoto. With one hand under her jacket, resting on the grip of her weapon, she moved from the rear of the train toward the front, expecting a lethal firefight at any moment.

The train pulled into Shimbashi Station as she was reaching the last carriage. Up ahead she saw him now, in his black jacket and his slicked-back hair. He was weaving through the people on the train like a salamander, one eye on her and one on the exit door at the end of the carriage.

The train reached its automatic stopping place and the

doors lined up with the corresponding marks on the platform. A sigh of hydraulics as the doors swished open, and then Hashimoto was off the train and heading for an exit at the southern end of the busy platform.

Scarlet stepped off the train. People waited patiently in perfect queues to board the train but she pushed into them to get closer to the fleeing gangster before he slipped out of sight. She had followed him halfway across the heart of Tokyo and she was sure as hell she wasn't going to let him get away now.

Hashimoto glanced over his shoulder and smirked just as he slipped out of sight behind the tiled exit, but Scarlet was only a second behind, hand still gripping the gun in her shoulder holster. She turned the corner to see him bounding up the steps three at a time and instantly gave chase.

She reached the ground level. Another world of cream-colored tiles and bright white strip lights all around her. Ahead of her Hashimoto walked past a vending machine and headed for the station's exit.

She followed him outside.

Back in the rain. Hashimoto was jogging away from the station, dwarfed by yet more towering skyscrapers and flashing neon. This city must go to the end of the world, she thought as she watched the man turn right at a busy junction.

When she reached the intersection it was just in time to see him running toward the entrance of Yurikamome Station. He was leading her to the end of the world, or more likely into a terrible trap but she had no choice but to follow. Like a bolt of lightning, he darted onto the next train just as it was pulling away from the platform.

By the time Scarlet reached the platform the computer controlling the line had locked the doors and started to pull the train out of the station. She sprinted hard, rain in her face and her lungs aching with pain as she powered herself to catch up with it, just grabbing the rear of the final carriage in time.

The Yurikamome automated guideway is a computer-controlled transit service running on an elevated rail a hundred feet above the streets of the city; Scarlet Sloane took her life in her hands and clung to the back as it gained speed and headed out into the stormy night.

Wiping the rain from her face, she climbed onto the top of the train and made her way along the carriage's roof as the world-famous train jerked forward. Rapidly gaining speed on the elevated guideway now, Scarlet took a second to take the situation in and consider her game plan. She knew there was no way to avoid creating a panic if she wanted to take back the ring.

They were racing out of the station now and entering the heavily built-up area around the waterfront of Tokyo Bay. Theaters and palaces and shrines flashed past them in a blur of other buildings – schools, hospitals, and parks but there was no time to admire the view.

She had one goal in mind and that was the retrieval of the third ring before either the Yakuza or the Oracle or Razak could get it. With careful footfall to avoid slipping on the slick stainless steel roof, she made her way slowly to the front where she had seen Hashimoto entering the train.

She took a breath and pulled her gun. Either side of her the immense metropolitan sprawl of Tokyo receded to the horizon like something out of science-fiction dystopia. The carriage rocked gently from side to side in the wind as its rubber tires moved along the raised concrete bridge. The streets far below teemed with life. Lines of cars belched exhaust fumes and an A380 groaned and whined above her on its way to Haneda International, flashing in and out of the rainclouds almost low enough to touch.

She climbed down in between the first two carriages and pulled her gun. Swinging the weapon up to the window at the end of the carriage, she emptied her magazine into it. The thick, safety Perspex took a hell of a beating from the nine mil rounds but stayed in place. People inside screamed and ran to the far end of the carriage while she hammered on the Perspex with the grip of her gun.

Making a hole big enough to reach into, she operated the safety release and the door slid open to reveal the faces of dozens of terrified people looking back at her.

Where was Hashimoto?

Movement behind them, and she fought her way through the passengers just in time to see the Yakuza man struggling to open the other door.

"Hold it right there!" she yelled.

He froze like a statue, then twisted his head slowly toward her. He was calm, but there was a rage in his eyes and a fiendish grin on his face. "Looks like you got me at last. I'm impressed."

"I'm not trying to impress anyone, Hashimoto. Just give me the ring."

He was wearing it on one of his fingers and now he craned his neck forward and looked at it. "What's so special about it?"

"That's my business. Hand it over."

"It's good quality gold, but it has no other value," he purred. "Or maybe it does?"

She refreshed her grip on the gun and raised it from his chest to his face. "No more talking. Give me the ring."

The Japanese gangster turned to her, face to face, and pulled himself up to his full height with a steely determination on his scarred face. He wanted to reach for the gun in his holster, or maybe there was a switchblade tucked away on him somewhere. She wouldn't be surprised, but if he made a move for either of them she would bury a bullet in his head before his hand moved half an inch, and it looked like he knew it.

He was sweating now, and Scarlet noticed a woman move behind her. She took a step back and to the left so she could keep the woman and Hashimoto in her sights at the same time. The woman was reaching for the emergency stop button.

"Get away from it," she said sharply, gesturing with her gun to make the woman understand she should back off. She obeyed instantly, babbling a terrified apology and raising her hands as she stepped away from the button.

The train trundled on through the night, high above the city.

"The ring, Hashimoto. Throw it over to me, now."

"And what if I refuse?"

"You know what happens next."

The grin widened. "Tell me."

"I'll shoot you dead and take the ring off your finger."

His eyes glinted dully in the artificial lighting of the carriage. "You must want this ring pretty badly, foreigner."

"You'll find out how badly in less than three seconds. Last warning. Three…"

"You think you can threaten Yakuza?"

"Two…"

"And get away with it?"

"One…" she pulled the hammer back and squinted down the sights.

"Wait!"

She blew out the breath she had been holding to steady her aim and her nerve. She had won. She had beaten him, and now he was pulling the ring off his finger. He moved calmly and coolly, gently slipping the ring from his finger and then holding it up between them as if it were the world's most precious object.

And maybe it was.

"Good boy," she said quietly, keeping one eye on the other passengers. She could tell from the lighting outside the train that the next station was approaching. "Now throw it to me. Any funny business and I'll shoot you dead first and ask the funeral director the questions."

"What is this ring all about?" he asked as he tossed it at her. "Why have you crossed the Yakuza tonight?"

Scarlet caught the ring in one hand just as the train came to a stop and the doors opened.

"Why do you want to know?"

"Because tonight you have made an enemy – one that will never stop hunting you until you are dead and this dishonor is avenged. I must know why."

"The devil made me do it, Hashimoto, so take it up with him."

And then she was gone.

CHAPTER TWENTY-TWO

Honolulu International Airport is the biggest airport on Oahu and one of the busiest in the entire United States. The first properly built airport in the whole state of Hawaii, travelers to the island had to use landing strips or cleared fields before its construction in 1927, but when the ECHO team arrived it was a small city of runways and shops and departure lounges powering up for another busy day.

They approached from the north, cruising through Pearl Harbor on the Kamehameha Highway. Reaper was at the wheel and Lea and Nikolai were sleeping in the back. Hawke looked out across the harbor and saw the monuments on the east coast of Ford Island.

As a former military man with serious combat experience, he felt a deep sense of loss and respect as the USS Arizona Memorial came into view, and then the USS Missouri Memorial where the Japanese surrendered, ending the bloodiest war in history. It loomed out of the darkness almost as distant as 1945 itself, but it was there, all the same, and Hawke gave a silent salute before turning back to face the road.

"We're here," Reaper said, gently turning McKenna's stolen pickup truck off the highway and into the airport. "Let's just hope the Athanatoi are still here, too."

Hawke looked at his watch. "Should be. Lea checked what McKenna said about the flights and the first ones aren't until just after five. Must be some noise abatement law like they have in London Heathrow."

"You think anyone found Cobb and McKenna tied up

on their boat yet?"

"I'll check the news," Lea said. "Much later." She yawned and stretched her arms. "I don't know about you guys, but I could sleep for a hundred years."

"I hear you loud and clear," Hawke said. "But *they* never sleep, or so it seems."

"Et ça, c'est le problème," the former legionnaire followed the signs to the short stay parking lot. "We must win before we sleep."

Lea glanced at Nikolai who was snoring quietly beside her. "Well, this one sleeps, that's for sure."

They cruised past various car rental companies until finally pulling into the parking lot and killing the engine. The new silence woke Nikolai in the back. He yawned, checked his watch, and peered out the window. "At last," he growled. "We get closer to the prize."

Hawke watched the former Athanatoi man carefully in the mirror. The seed of doubt was still in his mind. Could he trust this weird monk? This man whose early life in Moscow had been a baptism of fire? The man who had been closer to the Oracle than anyone else they knew – the man who had come closer than anyone to the holy grail of immortality?

Maybe he had made a mistake by letting him join them. Maybe saving Lea's life was nothing more than a piece of theater aimed at hooking them and reeling them in. Had Nikolai been honest with them, or was it all nothing more than a piece of bait designed to lull them into a false sense of security before the Oracle made his last, devastating move against them?

Hawke felt the suspension rock as Reaper shifted his not inconsiderate bulk out of the truck and slammed the door. The sun was nearing the horizon now, and the temperature was already over twenty degrees Celsius. The airport parking lot lights shone down on them like

LED stage lights, turning everything a ghostly arctic blue color.

"Let's get this over with," Hawke said, popping his belt buckle. "Where are the gates for private planes?"

Lea was already on it, phone in hand as she climbed out of the back of the truck. "Looks like it's just over there. Quickest way is through the main terminal and then hang a right."

They walked into the bright lights of the terminal and followed Lea's directions, heading into the west where the private aprons were situated. En route, Reaper had to be pulled away from the welcoming mint and chocolate brown glow of the Honolulu Cookie Company store.

"Never come between a Frenchman and his stomach," he growled.

"We're sort of pressed for time, Reap," Lea said with a smile.

"Oui, mais…" He rubbed his stomach and sighed. "All right, but *later*."

"Yes, later," Lea said.

Walking through the air-conditioned calm of the airport they started scanning for any sign of the men who had raided the plantation and snatched the ring. To their right, three men dressed in black were walking into the mall section of the airport where vendors were opening up their stores for the day.

"There!" Nikolai raised his arm and pointed across the vast airport mall. "I know that man. His name is Benedict. He is a senior acolyte. The men on either side of him are his students. The man with one eye is Stefanus, and the man with the ponytail is Boaz."

"Not the sort of chaps you want to meet on a dark night," Lea said.

Hawke led the way, speeding up his walk while being careful not to draw any attention to himself as he moved closer to the Athanatoi warriors.

But then things changed fast. Walking with her parents, a child dropped a cookie and screamed. Benedict and the other cultists turned instinctively and instantly saw Hawke and the rest of the team closing in on them.

There was no hesitation. In one fluid movement, Benedict drew a Marlin BFR from his shoulder holster and spun around as he lifted it into the aim.

Hawke immediately recognized the powerful handgun. Chambered in .450 and capable of firing colossal 350-grain rounds at nearly two thousand feet per second, a direct hit would mean losing a massive percentage of your bodyweight followed by instant death. "Get down!" he yelled.

"Buggering fuck!" Lea said. "That's a handheld cannon!"

He fired and the round struck the façade of a water vending machine, blasting the front window to pieces and exploding most of the bottles inside it.

Hawke slammed down behind the counter of a nearby KFC and told the workers to get out the back to safety as fast as possible. Lea and Reaper piled in after him as the fast-food restaurant emptied in a hurry but Nikolai was still running for cover.

Then the lead flew. The Russian's heart pounded in his chest and his mouth was as dry as sandpaper. Making it behind the cover with seconds to spare, he made his arms into a cradle and tucked his head in them to avoid eye damage from the flying splinters and pulverized plastic and smoke. The airport was now a battlefield and the cult he had sworn allegiance to but betrayed were winning the fight.

They threw grenades and raked security guards with automatic fire.

Hell was unleashing all around them.

Peering back over the bullet-shredded frontage of the cookie store he saw something that made his skin crawl. Benedict had grabbed a small, lost child of no more than ten and was dragging her back into the cover of the escalator with a gun to her head. Her terrified face was obscured in his black clothes as he pulled her away from her mother and father with a warning to stay away. Behind him, Stefanus and Boaz were giving the motherload of all cover fires as their compatriot finally reached the safety of the escalator with a final warning: let us leave this place or the child will die.

CCTV cameras swiveled and security guards broke off from their attack and Nikolai knew that all hell wouldn't stop the cultists now they had the child.

Hawke wiped the sweat from his forehead and blew out a sharp, controlled breath. "Will they hurt her, Kolya?"

Nikolai knew from the Englishman's face that he already knew the answer, but he answered out of respect. "Yes, my new friend. They *will* kill her if we don't do as they say."

The child's parents were inconsolable with grief. The father's face an unforgettable twisted rictus that only a once-in-a-lifetime terror could inflict; the mother a sobbing mess of red eyes and tears streaking down her burning cheeks.

Instantly shepherded behind an improvised security barricade by security guards, they called out to their girl not to worry – that they wouldn't let anything hurt her – but everyone who heard it knew it was just raw instinct.

Everyone but the child, who believed every word she heard her desperate parents call out.

Nikolai felt an unquenchable rage burning inside him like lava. He thought of his own childhood and the hideous scars seared into his mind by the slaying of his own family – his mother's screams as the bullets tore through his heart, the look on his sister's dead, sightless eyes as her body lay out in the blood-soaked snow.

Never again.

Like a volcano, his own turmoil reached the point of no return and then burst through the surface at the weakest point. Leaping to his feet, he screamed at his former associate with anger burned on his face. "Put the child down, Benedict!"

CHAPTER TWENTY-THREE

"Silence, traitor!"

"I said let her go!"

Stefanus and Boaz watched their boss for his response. Above them all, a giant plasma screen now played live footage of an anti-terror team arriving at the airport. The ticker racing along the bottom of the screen read: ONE CHILD TAKEN HOSTAGE AT AIRPORT TERROR ATTACK.

"You will die for this treachery, Kolya…"

Flanked by Stefanus and Boaz, Benedict now made his escape bid. He walked backward, still gripping the frightened, sobbing child. The gun pushed into her young temple. Everyone felt the same mix of abject disgust and fear. Push this man too far and he might just do it, they all thought.

There was no *might* in Nikolai's mind. He knew Benedict better than anyone and he knew not only would he do it but the act would be committed with zero guilt or conscience. He would simply perform his rituals before sleep tonight and then the murderous matter would be settled in his mind forever.

He also knew he would almost certainly kill the child as soon as he no longer had a use for her but that use would involve taking her on board the aircraft as insurance. No fighter jet would shoot them down while they had her on board. He guessed that when the cultists were safely at their destination, they would kill her and dump her body.

He had to act now. If they got her onto the plane she

was a dead girl walking.

"I'm going after her, Hawke."

"We all are," Hawke said.

"Form an orderly line, gents," said Lea.

Guns now drawn, they followed the acolytes outside. The sun was higher now, but still low on the horizon. A 777 roared in from the east, probably Los Angeles International, and screeched down on the asphalt. Puffs of white smoke burst up from the undercarriage and the reverse thrusters growled in the dawn.

To their left, the three cultists and the sobbing child were almost at the private plane.

As expected, Benedict was dragging the girl up the airstair. He pushed her roughly inside the plane as Stefanus and Boaz darted in behind them and closed the door. The engines were already spooling and the plane turned to the taxiway.

"If we try and stop the plane, they'll kill her," Nikolai said. "I just know it."

"And they have the goddam ring too," said Lea.

"Call off your attack or we kill the girl!"

Reaper's gun was raised. "I've got the shot, Hawke."

"No! She's too close."

"What then?"

Hawke glanced over his shoulder at the FedEx car park. "I'm going after the girl."

He made an instant calculation that he could make it, and burst into a full-speed sprint in the direction of the FedEx building.

"Are you crazy?" Nikolai said.

"You be the judge," Lea said. "Watch."

Hawke's boots pounded on the tarmac as he drew closer to the FedEx building and straddled the motorcycle. Turning the key, he revved the machine before steering it in a tight arc and heading out of the car park.

He twisted the throttle and quickly shifted up to full speed, fast approaching nearly one hundred miles per hour. Looking ahead he saw the Gulfstream. The sleek white aircraft was turning from the final taxiway to the runway now, the early sun glinting on the metal of its smooth rounded hull.

The engines spooled up and created a mirage behind the aircraft as the heat from the twin turbofans blasted out into the atmosphere. The pilot increased power again, building thrust ready for the take-off, and the jet responded instantly, speeding even faster along the runway.

Hawke knew his only hope was to cut across the large grass area in between the two runways and meet it before it gained too much speed. Turning the bike, he scrambled across the dusty grass.

Looks like you're going to make it, but what are you going to do when you get there, idiot?

More power to the aircraft as he pulled alongside it, just keeping up as it raced along the runway. He steered closer to the wing, so near now he could see the shocked faces of the Athanatoi on board the plane.

No time for niceties, he said, forgoing a cheery wave, and leaped from the bike onto the aircraft's port wing.

Harder than he thought.

The speed of the jet was faster now, and the air resistance immediately knocked him backward and blew him down to the trailing edge of the wing where his boots crunched down into the slot created by the extended flaps.

Behind him at the rear of the jet, the engines roared like hell itself but there was no going back now. Falling off an aircraft going at this speed and hitting solid asphalt would mean death, and if not death then a year in traction.

No thanks.

Gripping onto the leading edge of the wing, he watched the end of the runway as it rapidly approached. No more than twenty seconds before this thing was at V1 and lifting off into the great blue yonder.

Maybe this was a mistake?

No time for regrets. He pulled himself along the short wing and reached the fuselage just beside the external door release. With one hand gripping onto the leading edge of the wing, he reached his other hand out to the door release and pulled it down like a fruit machine lever with all his might.

Snapping his hand back to his body, he grabbed for his gun as the door rolled back into the jet's fuselage. He fired on the men who had raced to the door to shoot him.

He struck one in the chest and blasted him back inside the cabin just as the plane hit V2 and the pilot started to rotate the aircraft ready for the climb. The nose pitched up and knocked him off his balance. As he tumbled to the trailing edge of the wing, he threw his hands out and grabbed onto a hydraulics line in the gap between the main body of the wing and the flaps.

Another cultist appeared in the door but knew better than to fire a gun at a wing full of kerosene. The Englishman clung on nervously as the aircraft roared into the sky, the twenty-degree pitch flinging his legs off the back of the wing from which he now dangled like a dying man.

A loud whine of hydraulics and the flaps started to retract. Hawke knew they would crush his hands if he didn't get out and back onto the wing in time, and managed to pull his right leg up and use the moving flap as a purchase to push himself up out of the cavity and back onto the wing.

The wind whipped at his hair as he crawled closer to the door, which was now closing again. Hawke fired on the man and killed him, just managing to reach the external lever and open the door a second time before the plane banked to the left.

Grabbing the seal running around the door he pulled himself inside just before the plane banked hard to the left. No time to think about how he would have tumbled to his death during the turn had he not been inside the jet, he raised his gun and fired on another man who was running toward the girl.

He took him out before he reached her, leaving him and the terrified child alone in the cabin. He closed the door and ran to her. "Listen, I'm here to save you." As he spoke, he lifted her into one of the luxury white leather seats and buckled her in. "You're going to be okay. I can fly this thing, but I just need a word with the pilot first, all right?"

She nodded but said nothing. She was frightened out of her wits, but he knew what he had to do.

Padding up the cabin, he slid a round into the chamber and fired on the cockpit door's lock five times before blasting it to pieces. Booting the door open he slammed his body against the side of the cabin just before bullets raked up the jet's ceiling.

"Okay," he muttered. "So that's how you feel."

He spun around and emptied his magazine into the two pilots, instantly killing both men who now slumped forward in their harnesses.

He stuffed his gun into his holster and released the pilot from his harness. Dragging him out of the way, he jumped down into the seat and checked the gauges. None damaged thanks to his accurate shooting, and he quickly gained control of the aircraft and radioed in to the airport to tell them he was bringing it back in.

"How's the girl?" the woman on the ATC said.

Twisting his head, he craned his neck around and saw

the kid still buckled into the seat back in the main cabin. "In shock, but safe."

"Understood. You have priority on Runway 8."

He reduced power and leveled the aircraft, turning to port as he prepared to make the landing. "Priority on Runway 8, over."

The Ring of Akhenaten was theirs, and he had saved the child's life.

CHAPTER TWENTY-FOUR

Jack Camacho and Kim Taylor landed at Washington Dulles Airport and hailed a cab. There was supposed to be a government car waiting for them but when they finally got outside the airport it was nowhere in sight. They walked out to where the cabs parked up, and Kim was unnerved by the absence of the official car.

"I don't like it, Jack."

"It's just a cab," he said deadpan. "The poor travel in them all the time."

She rolled her eyes. "You know what I mean. Stop being an asshole."

"So they forgot our car! It doesn't mean anything."

"Ordinarily I'd agree with you, but not with all the shit that's going down in DC right now. It's frightening me."

He turned to her, more serious now he could see how rattled she was. "What are you saying? That there's been some kind of coup already and we're on a blacklist?"

She looked back, her face straightening with a new fear. She bit her lip as she thought about his words. "Maybe that's exactly what I am saying, yeah. Things are getting crazy right now, Jack! Alex was very clear about the threat the President is under."

"And we're here to help her and work everything out. No one's going to harm the President or Alex on our watch, right?"

She nodded, but his words hadn't steadied her nerves at all. Alex had been more than clear when they had spoken earlier. The young woman had sounded scared out of her mind, and they both knew she was the last person who would exaggerate a threat or let herself get spooked by something that wasn't real.

Kim wasn't sure exactly what was going on in the city tonight but she knew it wasn't good. She had a bad feeling that something very dangerous was unfolding all around them and she had to work hard to stop feeling like a bug in a Venus flytrap, struggling to escape as the leaves slowly crushed her down and trapped her forever.

"Listen." Camacho's voice was smooth and relaxed. "You'll feel better when we get to the White House. Alex is waiting for us there and we can grab a shower and get something to eat in the Residency. We'll get a full briefing from Agent McGee and maybe even get five minutes with the President. After you've seen how normal and boring everything is you'll be fine. Alex is probably just worrying too much about her father. You know how she is."

Kim's eyes widened. "Yeah, I *do*, and that's why I think we could be in danger."

The cab cruised through the Washington suburbs – Highland Park, Cherrydale, Colonial Village – and then crossed the Potomac on the Theodore Roosevelt Bridge. The ride was smooth and slow, traffic building up as they drew closer to the city's beating heart.

After a long silence, Camacho spoke up. "As I say, let's just wait till we speak with Alex and Brandon, and then we'll decide what sort of danger we're in."

*

Davis Faulkner wasn't ashamed to feel nervous as he sat at the top of the long table and watched the members of the US cabinet enter the room. After years of planning, he was almost ready to make his move and show the Oracle what he was capable of, and yet for the first time, he had started to look beyond the cult leader. No one was untouchable, right?

After a preamble and some coffee, he went straight to business.

"The evidence is clear, ladies and gentlemen. President Brooke used his position as our Commander in Chief to abuse the Constitution and use his powers to give our enemies aid and comfort." He leaned forward in his chair and jabbed at the papers on the table in front of him for emphasis. "It's all right here!"

The Secretary of Defense sucked air in through his teeth and shook his head. "I don't know about this. I can see the evidence, and I admit that it's compelling enough, but *treason* seems to be taking things too far. The President has such wide-ranging powers in foreign policy that I think you've got a hell of a job cut out trying to prove this charge."

A murmur of agreement filled the air and Faulkner could see he was losing the room.

"We have the power under the Constitution to remove him from office for doing what he has done. Dammit, Kelvin… he's supplied foreign terrorists with weapons and intel, and well…"

The Secretary of State leaned forward. "Is there something else, Mr. Vice President?"

"Yes, Sarah, there is." He gave a heavy sigh and signaled for Josh Muston to activate the overhead projector and pull the drapes. As darkness settled over the secure room, Faulkner watched with veiled pleasure as his Chief of Staff started the slide show.

"What the hell is this?" Sarah Montague said.

"What you are looking at is the scene of a crime."

"Looks more like a bloodbath," the Secretary of the Treasury said, disgusted.

Faulkner grimaced and put on his most horrified face

to mirror those around him. "These pictures were taken in the Caribbean very recently. They show the bodies of two units of Navy Seals. All of them killed by the ECHO team using US weapons and intel provided by President Brooke."

A rush of shocked gasps filled the room. "Good God…"

The Attorney General watched in horrified silence as Muston casually flicked through the images of the slaughtered Special Forces. Corpses everywhere. Blood on the sand. Gaping bullet wounds. Missing limbs. It looked hot and desolate.

"This is no way for loyal American soldiers to die," the AG said.

Faulkner looked at him with his most serious face. "Like dogs, Jeff. They died like dogs on that beach!"

The Secretary of Labor now joined in the new chorus of revulsion. "And you're saying Brooke ordered the deaths of these men?"

"I'm sorry, Erika, but yes… he did."

"Oh my *God!*" The Secretary of Homeland Security chimed in, shaking his head in denial at what he was seeing and hearing. "Why the hell would he do such a thing?"

Faulkner shrugged. It looked like they were buying the little package he and Josh had put together. Now wasn't the time to say the wrong thing and blow all their hard work. "That's what we intend to find out."

The AG tapped his pen on the hardwood table, his face now a picture of solemn fear and anxiety. "If this gets out it's bringing the whole damned administration down."

They'd just figured out their jobs were in the balance.

Now they were cooking with gas.

"And we all know that son of a bitch Bill Peterson will be all over this like fleas on a stray dog."

So turn the heat up.

"Damn straight, he will," Faulkner said. "And with the mid-terms coming up this will cause a lot of trouble for us. We'll be walking on hot coals right up to an election we have no hope of winning… not after *this* gets out."

"What the hell?"

"You're looking at images of the recent terror attack in Hawaii."

The AG turned to the Secretary of Homeland Security. "I thought that was already being connected with ISIS?"

"We have nothing yet."

"Yes we do," Faulkner said.

Everyone in the room stared up at the pictures of the devastating attack on the shopping mall inside the airport in Honolulu. Twisted metal. Shattered glass. Crumbling concrete and splintered wood. Paper and food and blood and screaming kids. Ruined bodies blown apart and sown over a scene of destruction.

And ECHO.

"You're looking at pictures of the ECHO team leaving the scene of the attack. As you can see, they're heavily armed with the weapons supplied to them by President Brooke. As of yet, we have no idea why they committed this atrocity on these American citizens but we know they did it, and we know they did it with the approval of Jack Brooke."

He was moving things up a gear. Would they buy it? ECHO had been in Hawaii in the last few hours in pursuit of the rings but the explosion and murder in the airport had been carried out by men working for the Oracle and had nothing to do with Brooke or ECHO.

"This is *appalling*."

"But why would President Brooke do such a terrible thing?"

Faulkner got serious. He could smell the end. "We

don't know yet, Sarah, but there's only one way we can find out and that's by initiating a full and proper investigation."

"And don't forget about Peterson," the AG threw in. "He'll roast our goddam nuts for a decade with this."

"I think the Vice President is right."

"I would agree."

"And... and," Faulkner took off his glasses and rubbed his tired eyes. It was so *tiring* having to deal with such a terrible mess. "The only way we get on top of this is by getting out in front of it, and fast. How long before the press gets a hold of this?"

Not long, if he and Muston had anything to do with it.

Letting that sink in, he continued. "This is highly classified material, ladies and gentlemen, but these things always get out sooner or later. How many iPhones caught ECHO at that crime scene? How many internet nerds can connect them to Brooke? To this administration? We need to move on this and we need to do it fast."

"I agree."

"But the Twenty-Fifth?"

A wholesome, nonchalant shrug from poor hard-done-by Davis Faulkner. "I've been struggling with this for days now but I can't see any other way. We cannot conduct any serious investigation into Brooke while he's President because a sitting president is immune from prosecution."

"Unless he's impeached by the House and convicted by the Senate first."

"Right," Faulkner said. "And how long will that take? You all saw the evidence. Not only is he involved with a foreign terrorist network and the murder of American soldiers, but via his links to these people his fingerprints are all over the recent Honolulu airport terror incident. When it gets out we knew about this and did *nothing*, we'll be burned on both sides and thrown in the trash." He fixed his eyes on everyone around the table one by one. "Every single one of us."

And now to bring her home.

"With the Twenty-Fifth we can end the danger to our nation right now. Then we'll have all the time we need to mount a full investigation against him and see to it that he faces justice for the abuses he's committed in that most glorious of offices, the Presidency of the United States. But it needs cabinet approval."

This time, it was a murmur of assent.

"I'll vote for it."

"Count me in."

Josh flicked back through the images and left one of the screaming children in Honolulu up on the giant screen.

"Me too."

"If this is real, then he has to go."

"We can't delay," Faulkner said. "We can't risk any more innocent deaths."

"Then let's do it," the AG said. "We'll invoke the Twenty-Fifth Amendment and get the son of a bitch out of that office."

"If you're all sure," Faulkner said, suppressing the smile of his life. "I don't want anyone to think they're being pushed into this."

"No one's pushing me into anything," the AG said, once again looking at the images on the screen. "It's time to get Brooke out of the Oval Office."

CHAPTER TWENTY-FIVE

The first thing Scarlet did when she got back to the hotel in Roppongi was to grab a shower, and the second thing she did was check her calls. There were a dozen messages from various friends and acquaintances but only one from Lea Donovan, and it was hours old. She opened the message and read it. Short and to the point: Hawke's team were still in pursuit of the fourth ring, and had a lead involving a man named McKenna. That was that.

She tossed the phone onto a table and crashed down onto one of the two double beds, exhausted, A life spent burning the candle at both ends and chasing the most dangerous men and women in the world took its toll, and that toll seemed to get higher the older she got.

"Any word from Joe?" Ryan asked.

"They still don't have it," she replied. Ryan was next to her on the bed, and Lexi and Nikolai were next to one another on the bed beside them. Not too long ago the smutty jokes would have been flying thick and fast but not tonight. They all felt drained and hungry and dying for a drink.

Ryan read her mind and reached for the telephone between the two beds. He ordered some food and cold beers to be brought up to the room, and then he dropped the receiver down into the cradle with a bitter laugh and rolled back onto the bed. "At least we got *our* ring," he said, chortling into the pillow.

The phone rang.

Scarlet flicked it onto the speaker and set it on the bed so everyone could hear it. "It's Lea, everyone."

"How goes it, Cairo?" the Irish accent said.

Scarlet sighed as she ran a hand through her hair. It needed a wash and she felt like shit. Watching the flashing neon signs outside their hotel room, she reported the news back to Lea. "We have the Ring of Cyrus."

Lea blew out a breath. "Thank God, and great work guys."

Some high fives in the Japanese hotel room, and then Scarlet said, "What about you?"

*

"We got the Ring of Akhenaten," Lea said, watching the surf crash along the coast. She was leaning on the back of their pickup truck in a parking lot overlooking Waikiki Beach. Dawn surfers were climbing out of their trucks and getting ready for a morning of action, but she was more interested in ECHO's latest possessions. "So that makes four, right?"

Hawke gave a thumbs-up as Lea told her about the mission in Hawaii, and Scarlet reported in return the news about the Tokyo mission. He felt a massive relief that Scarlet's crew had successfully secured their ring. Along with Alexander the Great's ring, plus the ones they had taken from Razak and Jojima, that made four of the eight ancient gods' rings – halfway there, but their actions had enraged many dangerous forces along the way, not only the Oracle but now the Yakuza and Razak.

"Where's number five?' Scarlet asked.

"We don't know yet," Lea said quietly. "Rich is getting back to me. He thinks we'll have a destination within the next few hours but he wants you to bring the jet to Hawaii in the meantime."

"Easily done," she said.

When she hung up, they watched in silence as the

rising sun lit the waters of Māmala Bay a bright copper blue. Hawke was the first to end the moment.

"Wherever we go we have an uncanny habit of making enemies," he said, holding Akhenaten's ring up to the light of the rising sun. Holding the ring's shank, he gently twirled it around and studied it more closely. After exchanging photos of the rings they had all tried to be the first to make sense of the ancient map engraved on the flat gold surfaces. The markings were clear enough, but with only half the rings it was like trying to guess the combination to a six-figure lock on a safe. A million combinations and no hope of success.

The lines and dots and tiny carved symbols were as clear as day, but how to fit them together so they made sense and formed a map they could use to find the Citadel was the big mystery and there was only one way to solve it – secure the other four rings. And they had to do it before the Oracle or anyone else got their hands on them if they wanted to be first to the greatest treasure of them all.

Lea's phone rang. She answered it and put it on speaker. "It's Eden."

"Back so soon?" Reaper asked.

"We have new information," Eden said, dispensing with any small talk. "When will Cairo and her crew be in Hawaii?"

"She's leaving right now, so in around six hours."

Eden was mulling something over. "Good. As soon as they land, I want you back in the air and on your way to the US without a second's delay."

"America?"

"We'll talk when you're in the air."

CHAPTER TWENTY-SIX

As the ECHO jet raced away from Hawaii and across the Pacific sky on its way to the United States, the reunited team were all crashed out in their seats. Scarlet was nursing a chilled vodka and trying to forget about the last few hours. Like everyone else, they felt exhausted, battle-worn, and shell-shocked.

When she told the Hawaii team that she had narrowly avoided being killed by the Yakuza on the bullet train, the battle-worn former SAS officer reminded them all of just how perilous their lives were. Then, when they discovered Hawke's team had secured the Ring of Akhenaten, they breathed a sigh of relief and shared a moment of celebration before leaving Tokyo.

The joy was brought to a swift end when they heard that Kim and Camacho had landed safely in Washington DC and were on their way to the White House. This shook them all back to the reality of what was happening in the American capital and raised a lot of worrying questions about Alex Reeve and her father, President Brooke.

Having access to the highest levels of US Government was not something they took for granted, but along with Eden's Westminster contacts it sure as hell made life a lot easier, plus Jack Brooke was a friend as well as a president. So was Alex. If Faulkner was moving against them with some kind of insane plan to take over the Executive Branch, they could both be in a lot of danger.

And so could ECHO.

With an enemy in the Oval Office things could get very difficult for them, if not impossible. There was no way they could engage in a firefight on US territory like they had done tonight at the cane plantation and later the airport without the support of the president himself. If the man sitting behind the Resolute Desk wasn't their friend things would be very different. Not only would they not be able to get away with it, but Hawke was also certain they would quickly be arrested, separated, and locked away somewhere.

She sighed with the stress of it all but closed her eyes and thought of her island. A fantasy now, but long sought after and one day a reality. Her daydream was broken by a bustling of excitement in the cabin. When she opened her eyes, she saw the grim face of Sir Richard Eden on the partition wall's plasma screen.

"Good work on the rings." Straight to business, but the former Paras officer was tired and he looked it. "It's great news that we now have the third and fourth rings. Now we have four of them and that makes half the map."

"I'm sensing that something's on your mind," Lea said.

Eden sighed. "The Oracle and the Athanatoi were in Hawaii because they've read the Codex. They know what we know about the rings and they're working out the locations. This puts us on a collision course with them on this mission."

"We can handle a bunch of idiots that look like undertakers," Scarlet said.

Now Hawke spoke up. "True, but it puts us on an elevated threat warning for the entire mission, plus the emergency in Washington has taken two of our team members away so we're weaker than usual."

Eden nodded. "There's nothing to be done about any of that, Hawke. You just have to get through it and secure the eight rings."

"A piece of piss." In old-style, Scarlet cracked a

miniature bottle of chilled vodka and downed it in one. "That's much better."

Ryan shook his head. "Now she's cooking with gas."

"Burn, baby…burn," she said. "It's four in the morning and I just spent today riding an external elevator in a thunderstorm and almost got killed by a Yakuza torturer on a speeding train. If I want a drink, I'll have one." She turned to him, glowering. "Unless of course, you want to try and stop me?"

Ryan shifted uneasily in his seat. "No, you're all right."

"Thought as much."

Lexi opened up her sandwich and took a big bite. "I'm so hungry."

After passing food around, Scarlet asked the obvious question. "So where are we flying? We've been on board the plane an hour and I haven't even asked where we're going."

"Las Vegas," Eden said bluntly.

"Woo-hoo!" she said. "It's party time, baby."

"It is not *party time*," he said with a smirk.

She slumped. "More bloody work then?"

"Afraid so, yes. My research has come up with a man named George Kozlov as the owner of the Ring of Ramesses the Great."

Zeke's eyes narrowed. "I've heard that name."

"He was the third pharaoh of the nineteenth dynasty and the mightiest of all the New Kingdom rulers."

Zeke was confused. "Huh? No, the other dude."

"Kozlov?" Eden said.

"That's the fella."

"George Kozlov is one of the most famous gambling tycoons in the world. He owns the Castillo."

"That's the biggest casino in Vegas," Scarlet said.

They all turned to her.

"What? Jack and I go there all the time."

Eden raised an eyebrow. "I hope you and Mr. Camacho make these junkets on your own dime?"

Scarlet sniffed. "Well…"

"What else do we know about this Kozlov?" Lea asked.

"As Cairo rightly says, he owns the Castillo. It's the largest casino and hotel complex in Las Vegas situated right bang smack in the heart of the city on Las Vegas Boulevard. He has a certain reputation for protecting himself and his assets, and he is also well-known for dealing with his enemies with, how shall I put it… extreme prejudice."

Nikolai sniffed. "I cannot wait to meet this man."

"I think I read about this guy," Ryan said. "They tried to put him on trial about a million times but he has so much money he just buys his way out of it every time."

"That's him," Eden said. "The last occasion was for massive tax fraud and salting millions away offshore, and the time before that was the Big M."

Lexi's eyes widened. "Murder?"

"No," Scarlet said sarcastically. "He refused to pay for a Big Mac."

"Very funny."

"Murder, yes," Eden said. "One of his poker buddies was a man named Cash Lombard and although details are sketchy, it's thought he'd racked up a big gambling debt with Kozlov and then refused to pay it back. I can't speak for the rest of him but they found his head and hands in a storm drain."

"Yikes," Zeke said.

Nikolai lowered his eyes and shook his head.

Lexi put her sandwich on the seat next to her. "Maybe I'll finish that later."

"So what makes an animal like that have an interest in

ancient jewelry?" Lea asked.

"He doesn't," Eden said. "But he has a very big interest in money, and according to our research here, he bought the ring at an auction in New York City twenty years ago along with a whole heap of other ancient relics, mostly gold, and mostly from a treasure trove excavated in Upper Egypt. He's had all of it, including the ring, ever since."

"Good work, Rich."

"Thanks."

"Where does he keep the ring?" Hawke asked.

Eden grimaced. "This is where it gets tricky. As I already said, George Kozlov owns the Castillo, and along with owning it and managing it he also calls it home. The entire top floor is his private residence."

"Ah."

"It's top floor time!" Lexi said.

"Right," Eden said. "If you want a quick way to think of it, then visualize a sort of private military compound with its own security force of heavily armed men, mostly former Special Forces. Accessed by key-code activated executive lifts and guarded twenty-four-seven, the inner sanctum of Mr. Kozlov is probably one of the most secure locations in the United States."

"Excellent news," Ryan said. "At least we all know now how and when we're all going to die."

Lexi play slapped his shoulder and smiled. "Idiot."

"I aim to please."

"You said it's the entire top floor," Lea said. "Helipad?"

Eden nodded. "Not one but two, one at either end of the roof. Both guarded around the clock by former Green Berets."

"This joker doesn't take any chances," Hawke said. "But do we know where exactly he keeps the ring?"

"We certainly do," Eden said. "The same place he's

kept it since the day he bought it – on his ring finger."

Hawke exchanged a look with the rest of the team and saw they were all thinking the same thing he was. "I think when I speak for everyone when I say, oh bugger."

"Exactly."

"Just like Jojima," Zeke said.

Hawke watched the faces of the other team members. They looked tired and the usual energy that crackled in any room they filled seemed weaker now. They were closer than ever to their goal of finding the Citadel, but they all knew that a man like Kozlov was hardly going to roll over and hand them the ring.

And worse than that, they didn't even know where the other rings were.

The Rings of Romulus, Remus, and King Sudas in India were still out there somewhere.

Even if they got the ring from Kozlov, the Oracle could be securing them right now. It was a difficult time full of uncertainty for the team but they had no choice but to keep on keeping on. Never give up, never give in. He repeated the words to himself, muttering them under his breath like a mantra.

Never give up, never give in.

If he showed weakness now the whole team could crumble.

Since Eden's injury, they had all started to look up to him more and more as their leader. He had leadership experience in both the Royal Marines as an officer and later as a sergeant in the SBS so he knew what was expected of him, but this was different. ECHO was different – it was more like a family than anything he had ever known.

Lea was his fiancée now, for one thing, and Eden had become a sort of father figure sitting at the top of the family tree. Ryan sometimes felt like a son to him or at the very least a wayward younger brother. And if Ryan was the younger brother then Reaper was like an older brother, gnarled and cynical but with a heart of pure gold. He'd slept with both Scarlet and Lexi but there was no awkwardness – both women were too strong and confident for anything like that. Maybe one day even Zeke and Nikolai would feel like family – if they chose to stick around after all this craziness.

And if they survived the terrible bloodshed he knew was racing toward them all.

"All right," he said firmly. "We put together a plan and we get the ring from Kozlov."

He stretched his neck and looked out the porthole. Bright sunshine glittered on the endless Pacific and to the east, Sin City beckoned them like the sexiest, dangerous siren in the whole damned and jaded world.

*

The Oracle did not know how long he had been staring at the flame. Beneath a tendril of gray smoke, its iridescent curves bent and twisted in the otherwise darkened room. When the door opened and Salazar stepped into the inner sanctum, the flame flickered for a few seconds, fighting for its life against the breeze from the hall.

A deep breath in, and a longer, slower exhalation. Count to ten. Never let the rage rise.

"What do you want, my loyal servant?"

"They got the ring."

He felt his eyes close. "Which one?"

"The one in Hawaii."

Never let the rage rise.

"So now they have four of the rings and we have none?"

Salazar swallowed hard. "Yes, sir."

They both heard the attempt to quell the rage in the Oracle's long, heavy sigh. "How did this happen?"

"He climbed on board a moving aircraft as it rolled down the runway, opened the door with the emergency external lever, and then shot his way inside the cockpit during its take-off."

"And by *he*," he growled, "you mean Josiah Hawke?"

"Of course. Benedict, Stefanus, and Boaz are all dead."

He opened his eyes and turned his wrinkled face to the nervous acolyte at his side. "Maybe I should induct him into the Order and get rid of the rest of you useless fools?"

"With all respect, sir…"

Everyone in the Order knew what the raised hand of the Oracle meant, and it meant immediate silence. To challenge the command would be suicide and both men in the room knew it.

"I like you, Salazar. You are a good acolyte, a good, loyal servant. My loyal apprentice."

"Yes, sir."

"But don't bring me any more news of failure or I will be forced to reconsider my evaluation of you."

"Yes sir. I'm arranging more acolytes to pursue the rings as we speak."

"Who?"

"Ignatius."

"And his number two?"

"Absalom."

"A good choice. Yin and yang, black and white. The ruthless, surgical cruelty and depraved genius of Ignatius, and the wild animal madness of Absalom. I am certain this combined force cannot fail me again."

"No, sir. I am confident they will secure the location of the Citadel."

The flame burned hard, now more than halfway through the thick, black candle on the desk. The old man felt his shoulders tighten a little as the tension in his muscles increased.

"Your words do not fill me with confidence, considering how poor your men have been at locating and securing the rings for us so far."

"I will not fail you again, Oracle."

"If you do, it will be your last failure."

Salazar felt the temperature in the room drop as his leader delivered the icy reprimand. His skin crawled and his mouth dried up like deadwood as he fought to contain the terrible fear so easily struck into his heart by the monstrous man whose eyes he was avoiding at all costs.

The Oracle was not concerned by the prosaic concerns of his underling. Rising to his level in the Order came with many rewards, but also with many risks, and upsetting the boss was chief among them.

He blew out the candle and the room plunged into semi-darkness with only a streak of moonlight on the far wall for illumination.

"This is my destiny, Salazar."

"Closer than ever, sir."

"Closer than ever, indeed. Those our people worshipped as gods lived in the Citadel for millennia and it is in that place that we will find our destiny. Their knowledge, their technology, their weapons… All so far ahead of us today it would look like black magic to the greatest scientists of our time."

"I have waited an entire lifetime to witness it, sir."

"As have I, Salazar," the old man croaked. "Many, many years."

CHAPTER TWENTY-SEVEN

An hour after landing in Las Vegas, Hawke watched Scarlet win her third hand of blackjack. She slid her chips into the tray, winked at the croupier, and strolled over to him with a cold beer in her hand. Lea and Reaper were at the bar and Lexi and Ryan had gone back outside for another walk around the block and then back to the getaway car. After causing much interest at the security checkpoint, the robed Russian monk Nikolai and his Texan tank commander friend Zeke had gone to check out the roulette tables.

"Not bad for five minutes," Scarlet said. "Won a thousand bucks."

Hawke couldn't resist a smile. "But can you keep it up?"

"Yes," she said, glancing at his crotch with a withering sigh. "And just as well one of us can, too."

"Funny."

"Tell me, you spend half your life in these places – how long till they come and throw you out?"

She considered for a moment. "Depends on the casino, but it's not like you see in the movies. I've watched people bet a quarter of a million dollars on a hand of baccarat and win and not get cut off."

Hawke's eyes widened like two full moons. "Bloody hell, I'm in the wrong game!"

"That's nothing, darling. I once played a shoe of baccarat where someone won twenty million dollars."

"And the casino let him keep playing?"

She gave him her best *aww* look. "You don't keep

playing after winning twenty million bucks, Joe."

"I guess not." His eyes were now glazed over and dreamy as he thought about winning that much money in one day.

Or in one lifetime.

"Money like that, crazy..."

Scarlet twirled the unlit cigarette in her fingers. "But that's just how the whales live."

"Whales?"

"High rollers – people who always make large bets. Jesus – you really are green. I could tell you stories that would blow you away."

"I'm all ears."

She shook her head and laughed. "My favorite is when the Australian tycoon Kerry Packer was playing at a table right here in Vegas. A Texan walked up to him and asked if he could join him at the table and Packer said no. The Texan got pissed off with him and told him he was worth a hundred million dollars. So Packer, who was a billionaire back when it meant something, turns, takes a coin out of his pocket, and casually says to him, *I'll toss you for it.* The Texan guy disappeared in a hurry," She laughed and shook her head. "Oh, I love that one."

Hawke laughed. "Yes, it does seem very *you*."

"And what's that supposed to mean?"

"Nothing, just don't tell Zeke. He might not like it, coming from Texas and all."

"Time to go back to work," she said. "If we're still sure the best way is for me to get caught cheating, right?"

"It is."

"I want it on the record I don't need to cheat to win."

Another smile. "Noted, but you *do* need to cheat to attract the attention of the security and cause a diversion. I'm guessing a man like Kozlov has a fairly low threshold for tolerating losses, so it won't be long, and then me,

Reap, Lea and Kolya are going up to the penthouse."

He recalled Nikolai from the roulette tables and told Zeke to get ready for his walk-on part as he watched Scarlet go back to the blackjack table. Walking over to the bar, he met Lea, Reaper, and Nikolai and ordered some bottled water, and waited again. Even he could see Scarlet was counting cards now, and pretty soon the security started to respond.

There were only two of them, which Scarlet had already told him was standard for throwing a card counter out. They were big guys who looked like they'd been inflated with bicycle pumps, shoe-horned into tight-fitting suits and all dressed up in shades and earpieces and crew cuts.

They spoke into their palm mics for a few seconds as they loitered behind a wall of fruit machines and then they got the order to throw her out and started to saunter over to the blackjack tables.

"Everyone check their packs?"

They all had done, and now he, Lea, Reaper, and Nikolai slipped the slim packs onto their backs. Hawke stepped away from the bar and casually raised his wrist to his mouth. "They're on their way over to you, Cairo."

She gave the signal that she had understood him by tucking her hair behind her ears, and moments later the security guards were all over her. "Ma'am, we're going to have to ask you to leave."

"What for!?"

"You know why. You're counting cards."

"Time to heat things up," Hawke said. "Zeke, you're on…"

Zeke set his glass down and walked over to Scarlet and the guards. "What the hell's going on here?"

"Who are you?"

"I'm her husband!" Zeke said.

As soon as he said the words, Scarlet slapped Zeke's face as hard as she could.

Genuinely shocked by the power of the blow, the Texan rubbed his bright red cheek and looked at her with a sly sideways glance. "Son of a bitch!"

"And if you think that's all you're getting, you cheating bastard then you can think again!"

He raised his palms. "I'm so sorry, baby!" he said in his Texan drawl. "I never meant to hurt you!"

"You're a lying, cheating bastard!"

Hawke and the others kept their distance, just close enough to help them if needed but far enough away so no one guessed they were together.

A crowd gathered around the fighting couple.

The guards sighed. "I don't care about your personal life. You were cheating the casino and you're out."

"And on our honeymoon, too!" Scarlet yelled.

Zeke gave her a look, not expecting such good improv from the Englishwoman.

The crowd booed and started shouting insults at him.

"He cheated on you on your *honeymoon*?" one woman asked.

Scarlet gave a sad nod. "With twins."

Jaws dropped and a wave of disgusted gasps and groans rippled around the fruit machine area. "That is just *gross*," someone called out.

Zeke gave her a look. *Thanks*, he thought, but he knew he had to play along. "Hey, I never meant nothing by it!"

A man in a black cowboy hat stepped out of the crowd, arms crossed over his bulging chest. "You disgust me, man."

The show was working. Several of the security officers from the penthouse elevator now wandered over to see what the fuss was about. There was a lot of talking on palm mics and above their heads, CCTV cameras swiveled and zoomed into the fracas.

"And I'm pregnant, too."

"Woah!"

"You need a lesson on how to treat women, boy," said the man in the black cowboy hat. He stepped closer and smacked one fist into his palm to demonstrate what he had in store for him.

"There's not going to be any of that in here," one of the security guards said firmly. "You're both banned for life from the Castillo."

Another more senior security guard walked over. "What's going on? Clear this area!"

"My wife's gone fricking *insane*," Zeke said.

"I just found out he cheated on me!"

"I don't give a rat's ass," the guard said. "You're taking this shit outside right now or I'm calling the cops."

He grabbed Scarlet's arm, and she pretended to struggle. "I'm pregnant!"

The man softened his grip and slowed down, but continued to steer her toward the door as the other two security guards took hold of Zeke, an arm each, and drag him out of the fruit machine area. "You're outta here, boy."

Scarlet swiveled as far as she could and was just in time to see Hawke and his team slipping into the penthouse elevator.

Job done.

Now they had to pray they could finish the job and get the ring off Kozlov's chubby finger and bust out of here before he sent an army of Russian Mafia after them.

Finally, they reached the main entrance and the man pushed Scarlet out of the front doors and off of the casino's property. "As I said, you're banned for life."

"Suits me."

The other two guards hurled Zeke out into the street

with less finesse. "You too, man. I see your sorry ass in here again and it's cop time… if you're lucky. You hear me?"

"Yes, sir I do!" Zeke said with a two-fingered salute.

Scarlet looked through the open doors and watched as the penthouse elevator doors slid smoothly shut. They were in.

CHAPTER TWENTY-EIGHT

Hawke and the rest of the team stepped into the private elevator and ordered it up to the penthouse suite on the top floor. Kozlov's ring was the fifth part of the puzzle, but the ancient gods weren't going to give up all their secrets without a fight. Even with all five rings put together in various combinations, they doubted any of the lines and other markings would make any sense at all until the whole set of eight was together.

When the elevator reached the top floor and the doors pinged open, Hawke led the small team along a plush, carpeted corridor until they reached the main living area. Guns drawn into the aim, Lea, Reaper, and Nikolai were at his side as he swung around into the formal living room.

Empty.

He beheld a hideous place of tiger hide rugs complete with head mounts and snarling jaws, pink diamond chandeliers, a Porsche pool table, and a full-size roulette wheel. The faint smell of cannabis drifted in the air, and a bottle of flat, warm undrunk champagne was on top of a table near the window.

Seeing one of the tiger rugs, Nikolai looked at the beast's dead face with disgust. "These things are an abomination."

Lea nodded. "I'm with you on that one."

"Moi aussi," Reaper said, cracking his knuckles. "I don't think I'm going to like this Kozlov."

Hawke gave an absent-minded nod as they progressed

deeper into the suite. He was pretty certain he wasn't going to like him either, but they had to meet him first and there was still no sign of the big boss or any of his goons. Moving into the study and still no luck. He noticed a paneled door behind the desk. It was ajar. Stepping closer, he opened it and they found themselves inside the tycoon's study. Tastelessly furnished in brightly colored leather and with a long bookcase on one wall, an open sliding door led out to a deep balcony.

"He's not hiding out in here either."

"I'm not hiding anywhere."

They all heard the thick Russian accent, and then they saw the man himself. Kozlov stepped into the study from the balcony. Two men with guns stepped in after him. As calm and casual as if he were ordering from a wine list, the tycoon started speaking. "Who are you and what do you want?"

"Drop your guns!" Hawke said.

"I think not."

"You're outnumbered."

"Again, I think not." As he spoke, the bookcase slid open to reveal two more men, both armed with submachine guns. "It is *you* who is outnumbered. Drop your guns."

Like the others, Hawke knew their handguns were no match for the two Makarov PP-90s staring them in the face. They lowered their guns to the floor and kicked them over to the Russians.

"Da," Kozlov said. "Now we make progress. Before I have you drilled with bullets, you will tell me who you are and what you want."

"We'd like to buy into your Gold Star Membership plan," Hawke said.

One of the men clubbed him with the stock of the Makarov and he tumbled down to the thick white plush pile.

Lea leaped down to him. "Joe!"

"Last time I ask," Kozlov drawled. "Who are you and why are you in my home?"

It happened faster than anyone expected. Lea disarmed one of the men holding the Makarov and took hold of his hand, rapidly twisting it sharply in the wrong direction. The brutal rotation of the hand shattered the wrist bones and the goon howled in pain as his wrist hung down from his arm like a dead fish.

"My hand!"

"It's your balls you should be more worried about."

He looked at her confused. "Huh?"

The ax kick landed like a cruise missile between his legs. Reaper and Nikolai both winced in pain as they watched him crash to the ground, clutching his most prized possessions and howling like a baby.

The other man with the Makarov took a step back and prepared to fire, but Hawke jumped to his feet and tackled the man back down to the ground. He punched him in the face and stole the Makarov away from him, turning it on the other two goons armed with handguns standing on either side of Kozlov.

"Stop them!" the tycoon yelled.

One of Kozlov's other guards took a step back and raised his gun. He was about to fire his weapon but fumbled at the last hurdle. It was enough for Nikolai to jump into action, flying through the air like a ninja, arms in a martial arts readiness pose and tough as hardened steel.

As Reaper punched Kozlov back against the bookcase, Nikolai landed in front of the goon and spun around in a three-sixty circle, pivoting on his waist to deliver a taekwondo round kick in the side of his face, which crumpled on impact as his head smashed away with the power of the blow.

The gun spun in the air and landed with a metallic clatter on the asphalt surface of the alley and skidded to a stop behind some trash bins. Facing him now, Nikolai pummelled him with a merciless barrage of hook punches and hammer fists until he gave up the fight and fell to the ground like a sack of rotten potatoes.

Momentarily distracted by the sight of the brawl, Kozlov lowered his guard. Reaper took instant advantage, striking the Russian tycoon on the jaw and knocking him out in one blow. He collapsed to the floor, and Hawke slid the Ring of Ramesses off his finger in half a second. Lifting his palm mic to his mouth, he spoke rapidly and clearly to the whole team. "We've got the ring. Get the car ready, Lex."

"Incoming, Joe!" Lea cried out.

She pointed into the apartment where at least half a dozen men armed with Makarovs were sprinting toward them.

"Time to leave, I think," Hawke said. "Care to join me?"

They followed him out into the balcony, where he climbed up over the railing and looked down at the seven hundred-foot drop to the ground. Lea peered over too and gave an appreciative nod. "I love my job."

The goons were bursting through into the study. "Hold it right there!"

Hawke made sure the slim BASE jump container on his back was comfortable and in the right place and leaped from the balcony. Lea, Reaper, and Nikolai followed him over, instantly tumbling away from the top floor and rapidly approaching the terminal velocity.

The goons fired on them, but they were too far away. Carried off to the east by a strong westerly, they opened their canopies and soon found themselves drifting over the Las Vegas cityscape. To their west, the setting sun turned the glittering boulevards and hotels a warm amber, and at their backs, a very angry Russian mafia tycoon.

CHAPTER TWENTY-NINE

The sun was well below the horizon when they checked into the Desert Sky Motel in Paradise and tossed their bags onto the carpet. Their room was up on the first floor in the corner of a horseshoe-shaped complex and from their room, they had a good view of the city skyline to the north. A modest swimming pool below their balcony reflected the stars but no other lights were lit and there was no sign of life in any of the other rooms.

Hawke peered through the drapes to make sure the coast was clear, and then Ryan opened his bag to reveal Kozlov's ring. Holding it up to the low light of the flickering TV, his face turned into a wide grin. "That's five down and three to go."

"We can do it," Lexi said.

"Nothing on the news," Zeke said.

"Not surprising," Scarlet said. "A man like Kozlov settles his own score."

Lea's phone rang. "Rich," she told the room and switched to the speaker. "Hey."

"Anything to report?"

"We got the ring from Kozlov," she said. "But we're tired. This is just relentless, Rich. I don't think we've ever had to work this hard before."

"This is great news," he said, "but there's no time to relax because I have more news. Since Magnus's murder, people in high places have been moving heaven and earth to help us, including a member of NESA, the UAE's internal state security agency."

"Oh?" Lea said. "I never knew you had any contacts

there."

He shrugged calmly. "I love you like a daughter, Lea, but there's an awful lot you don't know about me."

"What's the info?" Hawke said, cracking a cold bottle of sparkling water they'd picked up in a gas station on their way out of the city.

"I take it you've never heard of a man named Mokrani?"

Blank looks filled the room.

"Exactly as I thought. Known simply as Mr. Mokrani, he's a shadowy figure in the Gulf region, but one of the richest men in the world. A serious player and a big-time collector of jewelry. According to my source at NESA, a ring matching the description I gave him was sold at an auction not long ago, and it was bought by Mokrani."

"Does he know anything about it?"

"Hard to know. All my contact can tell me is that after I told him what we were looking for he got in touch with some auction houses in the region and one of them came up with the goods. He had no problem getting the name of the successful bidder, but the rest is up to us."

"Where does this dude hang out?" Zeke asked.

"On a yacht named the Seahorse, usually parked up off the coast of Dubai. There are several legal advantages for staying offshore, including tax, or so I'm led to believe. So that's why he lives out on it."

"An easy strike," Scarlet said, lighting a cigarette as she flicked through endless muted TV channels.

"And there's more," Eden continued. "A very old friend of mine has come forward in response to my request for information." He twisted his lips and everyone could see something was amusing him.

"I'm intrigued," Scarlet said. "Do go on."

"His name is Salim al-Hakim, a hustler and small-time smuggler based in Baghdad."

Lexi smirked. "You do hang around with the nicest people, Rich."

"Naturally," he fired back. "I know *you*, after all."

A whoop of laughter went up, the loudest being Reaper's deep belly growl, but things soon got back to business. "It turns out Hawke and Cairo share a mutual friend with Salim."

"And who might that be?"

"Ali al-Majid, from Baghdad, but these days he lives in Mosul."

Hawke and Scarlet shared an astonished glance. "You *are* joking, darling?"

"No joke and Salim tells me this Ali is ready and willing to help."

"Great!" Hawke said. "That old bastard, Ali… I can't believe it."

"But who is he?" Lea asked.

"Someone we met in Iraq during the war, a thief and a smuggler just like Salim."

Scarlet laughed "No wonder they know each other. It'll be good to see him again."

"There'll be time for that later," Eden said. "Getting back to business, Salim put the word out among his associates in the criminal fraternity in the city – which is how he collided with Ali – and it didn't take long for him to get the information he was looking for."

"So this Ali knows where one of the rings is?" Ryan asked.

"He knows where they *both* are," Eden said. "And he knows about Mokrani's ring too."

The team erupted in celebration, but Eden quickly poured cold water over the joy. "I said *he* knows where they are, but *we* still do not know. If we want to know, he's prepared to tell us, but for a massive price."

"That sounds like Ali." Hawke looked skeptical.

"What sort of price?"

"Yeah," Scarlet said. "What's he asking for?"

"Turns out your friend Ali drives a hard bargain," Eden continued. "He wants a million dollars in unmarked US currency."

"To be fair," Eden continued. "He said he'd throw in some transport as well as the name."

"That's very generous of him," Lea said.

"Sounds a bit steep to me," Scarlet said.

"I'll say," Ryan threw in. "That's your make-up budget gone for the next six months…ow, ow, sorry."

Scarlet's grip on Ryan's ear was tight and hard, and when she twisted it around, the young man had no choice but to allow his head to be dragged in the same direction. "What was that, boy?"

"I said your natural beauty is astonishing and you're so lucky that you don't require any make-up."

"Which is *exactly* what I thought you said." She released his ear.

"I mean for your significant age," he said, raising his middle finger and darting out of her reach. "Seriously though, you look all right. A bit of foxing around the edges but you're good to go in the right lighting conditions."

"Come here you little sod."

She jumped over the couch and grabbed at him but Eden cleared his throat and called the meeting back to order. "Can we get back to business, please? We are talking about the end of the world, after all."

"This time," Scarlet said with a scowl, "you live, but next time, your arse is mine, Bale."

"Please," Lexi said with a devilish grin. "What you two do in your spare time is your own business but don't pollute our minds with it."

"A million dollars, though?" Reaper said, breaking up

the laughter.

"And that's not all," said Eden. "He also wants in on the operation to find the Citadel."

A murmur of serious discontent moved around the room.

"Absolutely not," Hawke said. "I know Ali and he's not trained for this sort of thing."

Scarlet nodded. "I agree. He's a thief and a smuggler."

"So are you," Zeke said. The rest of the team turned to see him at the back, kicked back on the bed with a beer in his hand. They had almost forgotten the Texan was in the same room with them. Under their accusatory glare, he shrugged and sipped his beer. "Well, you kinda are."

"We are not thieves," Eden said.

"You took the idols."

Nikolai now opened one eye and watched the conversation with interest.

"And?" Lexi said.

"Why aren't they in a museum someplace?"

Eden took a deep, patient breath. "Because if we had given them to a museum, the Oracle would now have them all."

"This is true," the Russian monk said. "And to be honest, I am surprised he has not broken into the Bank of England yet to take them for himself. He simply cannot know they are there, or they would be gone already."

"Quite," Eden said flatly. "And you now have your marching orders."

"So it's Dubai and then Baghdad," Lea said.

Hawke caught her eye, and they shared a smile. "Time to get back on the road."

CHAPTER THIRTY

Kim Taylor and Jack Camacho passed security at the main Entrance Hall and soon found themselves walking through the busy corridors of the world's most famous residence. As her old friend had said on the way over, now she was here and saw that everything seemed to be normal, Kim started to relax.

"I'm not going to say I told you so," Camacho said, turning to her with a wide grin on his face. "But I told you so."

"I think I'll just wait until I speak with Alex. Then you can tell me so."

He laughed. "Have it your way. You going to see her now?"

"Sure – you?"

He nodded his head. "I was planning on going to see Frank, but I'll go later. He's still working on the President's security detail after all these years. He's an old friend from the CIA."

"Frank Trentino?"

"Uh-huh. You know Frank?"

"Not personally, but I've heard *of* him."

Another laugh. "Hasn't everyone?"

They continued to walk through the main building on their way to Alex, passing the portraits of several former presidents – Lincoln, Roosevelt, and Kennedy whose official portrait was unique because he was looking down at the ground and not at the viewer. Kim found it strange to imagine that one day Alex's father's portrait would be hanging in this place. Faulkner's was even harder to imagine.

They skipped up the steps to the second floor of the Residence. She'd been here a few times before and knew her way to Alex's suite. When she reached the top she saw a familiar face standing outside Alex's door.

"Kamala?"

The woman standing guard outside the door turned and looked at her with pleasant surprise on her face. "Kimmy, is that you?"

"In the flesh! I had no idea you were working here." Kim hadn't seen her old friend for at least two years. She and Kamala Banks had trained at the Secret Service Academy together and had become good friends before Kim's adventures with ECHO had taken her away from her life in Washington.

"Six months now."

"That's great."

"What are you doing here?"

Kim introduced Jack Camacho and they shook hands. "We know Alex. She's expecting us."

Kamala frowned. "No one said anything to me about it."

Before things got too awkward, the door swung open. "Kim! Jack! Thank God you're both here."

Kamala stepped away to let Alex push her chair out into the hallway. "What the hell's going on, Alex?"

"I asked Kim to come to see me, Kami."

Kamala watched as the three old friends hugged. "Please – come in."

Kim felt awkward leaving her old friend standing outside on security detail while they went into the room to talk with Alex, but that was her job. She said goodbye and closed the door as Alex wheeled herself back across the room and parked up beside her desk. "Thanks for coming, guys. I think shit's about to get real around here."

Kim looked at her and almost felt sorry for her. For the first time, she realized she was starting to doubt her friend's mind. Everyone knew Alex was a genius. Her mind was capable of thinking at speeds and across a breadth of subjects that would make most people's heads spin, but maybe she had finally reached her limit.

"Listen, Alex." Kim lowered her voice. "Things seem okay around here. No problems at security and Kamala was pretty chilled out too."

"You know her?"

"We go way back."

"She's nice."

"Yeah, she is."

"Scary, but nice."

Kim laughed. "No one ever messed with her, that's for damned sure. You're safe with her outside your door."

Alex sighed. "I'm not so sure."

Camacho said, "Where's this coming from?"

"Wait a second." Alex picked up her cell phone and made a quick call. "They're here. We'll wait for you."

Kim furrowed her brow. "Who was that?"

"An old friend."

"You're starting to scare me, Alex."

Kamala opened the door and Brandon McGee walked into the room. He thanked Kamala as she closed the door behind him.

"Hey Alex," Brandon said.

"Hey Brandon, This is Kim and Jack."

They made their introductions, and then Brandon said, "You're sure we can trust them?"

"I've trusted them a lot longer than I've trusted you."

Brandon weighed the no-nonsense response. "Fine. In that case, let's get down to business. I have it from an old friend of mine who works on the VP's security detail that he's planning some sort of attack on the President."

"Alex already told me that," Kim said. "That's why Jack Camacho and I flew straight back to the States, but from what I can see nothing's going down around here at all."

Brandon gave a heavy, weary sigh. "Suzie isn't sure when it's going down, Kim. All she knows is that it's happening and we have no way of knowing who's on whose side. Things could get very ugly very fast. That's why we needed you to be here. We need people we know we can trust. People who are above the VP's reach."

Kim's mind flooded with questions. "What sort of attack are you talking about?"

"Not military," Alex said.

"No, no military," Brandon repeated. "Suzie said it's a political attack."

"You mean a coup?"

"Not exactly," Alex said. "We think maybe they're trying to get the cabinet to invoke the Twenty-Fifth Amendment."

Kim was shocked. "You can't be serious?"

Brandon fixed his eyes on her. "Look at our faces, Kim."

Kim almost felt giddy. "Holy *crap*, this is big."

"You can say that again," Camacho said.

"And we have no idea how things are going to go down," Brandon added. "If the VP goes ahead with this and strikes against the President, it could spin out of control in about a million different ways. There's a real chance people could get killed if this gets out of hand."

"So what do we do now?" Kim asked.

"For now we wait," McGee said. "We can't risk letting anyone figure out that we know what's going on. For one thing, it would put Suzie in danger, and for another, it could make them panic and do something even crazier. The second we know it's going down, we get out of here as fast as we can."

"Doesn't sound like much of a plan," Kim said.

"It's the best we got," McGee. "Unless you have a better one?"

Kim and Camacho exchanged a glance. "Fine, we'll do it your way."

*

Josh Muston watched in a state of serene disbelief as General Vance and his men gathered in the Vice President's official residency at Observatory Circle. The disbelief was induced by the sight of the general ordering his men to arm themselves and prepare to board the SUVs waiting to take them across the city to the White House.

Faulkner himself seemed calm. From Muston's point of view, he was just a silhouette now, standing in the wide bay window with a smoking cigar in his right hand. What drove men like him to do the things they did, he had no idea. Muston was a backroom man, an advisor, nothing more than a state assistant behind the curtain and that was enough for him.

The idea of standing in the Rose Garden later today and explaining to a gaggle of dumbstruck TV crews why he had persuaded the Cabinet to invoke the Twenty-Fifth Amendment and arrest President Brooke didn't appeal to him one bit, but it seemed to excite Davis Faulkner beyond words. Not Muston, no sir. He would be the man inside the Oval Office, safely tucked away behind the drapes monitoring the polls and watching his boss's back.

"So, gentlemen..." Faulkner turned to face the room and twirled the cigar in his tanned fingers. "This is it. Today, with the approval of the Cabinet and the assistance of loyal patriots like General Vance and his men we will remove a corrupt, traitor from our greatest office and restore the greatness of the United States of America."

Vance gave a solemn nod but said nothing. His men followed his lead and maintained their composure.

"We might not be successful," Faulkner continued. "There's a good chance we may fail today. We may be arrested or even killed in our attempt to save our country on this day, but I know all of you men will not shy away from your duty. If we fail, we will answer to a higher power than the President of the United States."

"Amen to that," Vance said.

Muston wasn't entirely convinced his boss was referring to God. Faulkner's idea of a higher power wasn't exactly what most people had in mind, and visions of the mystical Oracle rose in his mind like Rougarou, the legendary monster lurking in the swamps of his childhood Bayou.

What exactly was the deal with that? Who was the Oracle, really? He had no idea. Faulkner talked about him from time to time, his words usually hushed and respectful – fearful, even. He talked about him as if he truly were a god, but one that could reach out and touch him and destroy his life.

But things were changing. Lately, the boss had started talking about the Oracle with a hint of resentment in his voice. He'd slipped up a few times, saying how the Oracle wouldn't be around forever and that when he was gone, things would be very different. He'd even overheard him calling the Oracle a freak after one particularly agitated phone call. What did the boss have in mind for this *Oracle*? Only time would tell.

"Well, Josh?"

He looked up and saw Faulkner and General Vance glaring down at him.

"Sir?"

"I said, is your staff team in place to run the White House after we take over today?"

Vance sighed. "We can't have any lapses in concentration today, Mr. Muston. If we do, then we screw up, and if we screw up we're going to the chair for treason."

"No, we're not," Muston said, standing to meet the general eye to eye and reassert his authority. Vance would be Chairman of the Joint Chiefs of Staff in a few hours, and the general needed to know he would be no push-over in his role as the President's Chief of Staff. "We have the legal authority to do what we are doing, as given to us by the Cabinet's official and unanimous invocation of the Twenty-Fifth Amendment."

"You don't know what the hell's going to happen when we try and pull this off."

"Yes, I do, General Vance. The Vice President is right when we say there is a chance of death. It may be the case that things go wrong and a firefight breaks out. A young marine overreacts or a gun goes off accidentally. Unlikely, but possible in an atmosphere as supercharged as the one we're about to create, but no one's going to the chair for treason. This is legal and it's going to happen. Legally. So just unbunch your panties and dial it down."

Vance narrowed his eyes and turned to Faulkner, but the Vice President was already chuckling. "Sir?"

"Josh is right, Richard. What we're doing today is a legal, political exercise. You and your men are essential back-ups, but also a touch of window dressing. When we get to the White House we do this my way and Brooke will be done and dusted before sunset."

Vance stepped down, glaring at Muston. "As you say, sir."

"All right then," Faulkner said, stubbing his cigar out in an ashtray on his desk. "Then we're almost ready to go.

Tell the men to make their final preparations and ensure everyone who is in on this knows it's on. Gentlemen, today we make history."

*

Jessica Clarke liked her coffee strong. She'd noticed that the older she got, the stronger the coffee got, and that was okay with her. She liked the deep, dark roast taste of the black gold as it rolled over her tongue and then the caffeine kick. It helped her think, and now she needed some serious thinking time.

With her son playing in the other room, she set the cup down on her kitchen table, closed her eyes, and went through the mission one more time. The next target had been selected and ECHO would be another member down in just a matter of hours. Devlin and Lund were already out of her mind, and she was focused on the next mark. Disciplined, vigilant. She was a trained killer whether she liked it or not, and now she used her skills to intricately plot the next assassination. Not one error could be permitted.

Another sip of coffee and a tense exhalation. On the table was the bullet. She had taken it from the box and was now reading the name engraved on its smooth metal jacket.

Another funeral.

Another wake.

More grieving friends and family.

She had no problems with her conscience. Her son's suffering grew worse with every sunrise, after all, and there was no other way to help him.

She thought of Justin down in Mexico. He'd gone on ahead and was working hard to find them someplace nice to live in. The pictures he emailed to her looked great.

Modest but like palaces compared to her apartment in LA. Villas with white stucco plaster walls and terracotta tiled rooves. Just like how the other half lived. Fan palms around the pool and a west-facing deck to watch the sunset over the Pacific with a beer in her hand and her son laughing and playing.

She *had* to have that. It wasn't something she was going to negotiate with the universe over, it was something that *must* happen if she and her son were going to survive.

More coffee, and she slipped the bullet back in the box.

Time to pack.

CHAPTER THIRTY-ONE

The journey on the luxury tender out to the yacht gave them all a few moments of peace and quiet. Skimming across the warm turquoise waters of the Persian Gulf, Hawke looked back to the impressive skyline of Dubai – the Marriot Marquis, the Princess Tower, and the Elite Residence all dwarfed by the monumental Burj Khalifa. The 835-meter building sparkled in the sun as it stretched up into the scorching Arabian sky. It was a far cry from the drizzle and gloom of his London childhood.

The rest of the team sat on the custom boat's wooden seats and shared the moment with a few laughs. Reaper and Scarlet smoked. Lea and Ryan were talking and Lexi was sitting with her head tipped back, eyes concealed by her mirrored sunglasses. From the look of things, Zeke and Nikolai were exchanging war stories and hand-to-hand combat moves.

It was good to see Kolya had finally ditched the robes and gotten himself some ordinary gear. Maybe he could fit in after all, or maybe he was lying to them. The darker half of the battle-worn and weary SBS sergeant wondered if their new Russian friend was a spy – a thousand-year-old Athanatoi warrior doing the Oracle's dirty work and biding his time until ordered to strike. The better half-remembered how he had saved Lea's life and risked his own life fighting alongside them since the battle at the monastery.

If he was a spy, then he was a good one.

The captain of the tender steered the small vessel to starboard to come about to the superyacht's stern. "We'll be docking in a few minutes. Get ready to disembark."

Hawke stretched his arms and yawned. Checked his gun and slid it back into the holster.

Lea walked over to him and slipped her arms around his waist. "It's beautiful here."

He smiled and kissed her. The boat rocked as it turned again and slowed down ready to approach the yacht. They clung together to stop from falling over. "You're beautiful."

"God, someone pass me a sick bucket," Scarlet said.

"Why, seasick?" Reaper asked.

"No, just too close to these two revoltingly smug people behind me."

Lea laughed. "Ah, you're just jealous, you miserable cow."

"Hey!"

"True story," Ryan said, lighting a cigarette and taking a long drag. He blew out the smoke and grinned mischievously. "She wants me but knows she can never have me."

Scarlet gave him a doubtful look. "You know where you can blow that smoke, boy."

"You haven't even bought me dinner," he said. "I feel used and dirty."

"You'll feel my boot up your arse in a minute."

Still staring up at the sky, Lexi said, "One kink at a time, Cairo or you'll frighten him away like a little sparrow."

"Don't *you* start," Scarlet said.

"Hey, I'm just saying."

The captain pulled up into the docking bay at the stern of the yacht and sailors on board the main vessel attached the tender to the Seahorse via the davit crane.

A man in a white bisht and keffiyeh was standing in the shade behind the crane, and now he stepped forward with a guarded smile and welcomed them on board. "I am Hafez. Please, Mr. Mokrani will receive you on the rear deck."

They followed the man up a series of staircases and down a polished teak deck stretching along the port side of the vessel before turning right at a shaded swimming pool and crossing over to the other side of the yacht. "Please," the man said, gently guiding them with his hand. "Mr. Mokrani is just through here."

Hawke turned the corner and saw an enormous man dressed similarly to Hafez, only his keffiyeh headdress was red and white checkers. He did not rise to meet them but gave a casual nod of his head. His eyes were obscured behind a pair of gold and river diamond Chopard sunglasses.

Ryan lowered his voice and leaned toward Lexi. "Why am I reminded of the sail barge scene in *Return of the Jedi*?"

"Keep it down, fool," she snapped. "Unless you want a light saber up your ass."

"I certainly do *not* want that," he said. "Despite vicious rumors spread by a certain former SAS officer of the female variety."

Lea turned and scowled, mouthing *zip it* to both of them, and Hawke approached the man and made the introductions.

"Please, sit. Hafez, mint tea for everyone, at once."

"Yes, sir."

Hafez slipped away into the shadows as they took their seats in the shaded deck area, grateful for the cool breeze whipping across the boat's deck.

"So, Sir Richard tells me he is in the market for a certain ring in my possession?"

"That's right," Lea said. "A very specific ring. It looks like this."

She handed him the one they had secured in Las Vegas from Kozlov. He took it in his chubby hand and twirled it around for a moment, never once lifting his sunglasses. He handed it back a few seconds later. "Yes. I have a ring like this, but the markings on the top are slightly different, I think."

Lea gave the team a look of hope before returning to Mokrani. "You know we're in the market to buy the ring, Mr. Mokrani, but are you in the market to sell it?"

Mokrani smiled as Hafez returned, hovering just out of sight in the shadows with a silver tray in his hands. The billionaire clicked his fingers and the servant stepped forward and poured a cup of mint tea for everyone at the table.

"And why would I want to sell it?"

"Because you implied you were interested in selling it."

"But perhaps I have changed my mind. Now I know some people are prepared to pay such a handsome price for it, I ask myself if perhaps I have undervalued it." His smile revealed a set of expensive, whitened teeth. "You must agree?"

"Supply and demand," Ryan said. "Simple economics."

"But what we're offering you is more than fair, Mr. Mokrani," Lea said. "The price is far more than the value of the gold and takes into account the historical significance of the ring as well."

"Yes," Mokrani said. "This is true. After Sir Richard contacted me I had my people research the ring more thoroughly, and what they discovered interested me a great deal, I must say."

"And what did they discover?" Scarlet asked.

Another sly grin. "My researchers tell me that they found several other rings in existence that very closely resemble the one in my possession. They looked into these rings and found nothing but speculation, but that speculation has piqued my interest very much." He leaned back and stretched his arms out along the back of the leather couch. "You see, there are rumors about these rings."

"What rumors?"

"Don't be coy," he said. "You know why you're here. My researchers tell me the rings may be a sort of map that will lead to some sort of ancient site."

"That's true," Lea said. "This is supposed to be confidential but I want to be honest with you. We're looking for the place you describe. We think it's called the Land of the Gods, and it was some kind of civilization before Sumer."

Mokrani sniffed and looked distracted for a few seconds. "This Land of the Gods must be a myth," Mokrani said. "There was no civilization before Sumer, not in this part of the world anyway."

"It's no myth," Hawke said. "The Land of the Gods was real, and we have to believe that at least some part of it still exists. Only the eight gods' rings can lead us there."

"Gods' rings?"

Lea explained what they knew, but Mokrani was unmoved.

"What you say is fantastic, but impossible to believe. Alexander the Great searching for an antediluvian civilization predating Sumer?" He waved the thought away and raised the cup of mint tea to his lips. Taking a sip, he tasted the fine liquid for a few moments before setting the china cup back down on the table. "Ridiculous."

"May we see the ring?" Lea said.

"Yeah," Scarlet piped up. "All this prattling is one thing but we don't even know you have the thing."

"Hafez, bring the item."

Hafez left them and returned with a golden cloche. He laid it on the table in front of Mokrani, who now lifted the lid and revealed the ring. It was sitting on a red velvet cushion in the center of a golden plate. Mokrani leaned forward slightly and lifted it off the tiny display cushion. "Yes, I remember this piece."

"You remember it?"

"After purchase, I rarely look at my jewelry. Many pieces I never see at all. I simply commission one of my people to bid on my behalf and then bring the pieces back to me here on my yacht."

As Mokrani stared at the golden ring, Ryan squinted at it for a moment and whispered to Hawke. "The Ring of Remus if I'm not mistaken."

"Good work, mate."

Lea said, "Will you sell it to us?"

"Very well," he said. "I am prepared to sell you this piece, but I don't think you will find the price within your range."

"Try us."

"Five million dollars."

"Five million?" Scarlet said. "That's ridiculous. The gold's worth no more than five thousand."

"But I am not selling you the gold," Mokrani said patiently. "I am selling you a ticket to your Land of the Gods and I am certain you would pay a much higher price to get there after all your travels and wars."

The Havoc approached low and fast, barely fifty feet off the surface of the gulf. Hawke saw the sun glinting on the rotor head as the Russian killing machine roared toward the yacht at two hundred miles per hour.

Mokrani rose from the couch and walked to the balcony rail. "What the hell is that?"

Lexi leaped from her seat and shielded her eyes from

the day's glare. "An attack chopper!"

Close enough now for Hawke to see the undernose barbette flash in the sunlight as the chin-mounted Shipunov cannon swiveled in their direction. Hanging from the stub wings on either side of the gunship were sixteen Ataka-V anti-tank missiles and ten S-8 rockets.

"It's death on wings," Hawke muttered, and we needed to be off this deck two minutes ago… run!"

It was too late. The gunship opened fire, unleashing two of the unguided rockets at the port side of the ship and tearing the deck to pieces with the dual feed autocannon. Grim Soviet power had arrived with a savage vengeance, the substantial thirty mil rounds from the Shipunov almost tearing Mokrani in two at the waist and blasting his guts all over the ivory white shade cloth above the decking.

"Hafez is taking it off Mokrani's finger and making a break for it!" Lea yelled.

"Leave it!" Hawke called back. "It's not worth dying for."

They ran for their lives across the transom just as the two rockets exploded under the waterline, striking the boat with a massive explosion and punching two car-sized holes in the hull. The entire vessel shook in the water as fire and smoke engulfed everything in sight.

"To the Helipad!" Lea yelled.

"No!" Hawke said. "That's the next target."

The chopper roared over the top of them now and spun around in a tight arc off the yacht's starboard bow.

"Where then?"

"Take cover inside the bridge!" Hawke said.

Now Ryan pointed at the bird of war. Worse than a nightmare, its hideous angular body covered in rockets and guns was bearing down on them all over again. "They're coming back for another run!"

CHAPTER THIRTY-TWO

"There's nowhere to go!" Lexi said.

Reaper pointed at the sky. "I see another chopper."

"I can take it out!" Ryan said, raising his gun and walking to the door.

"Bugger me, Ryan, get back inside!" Hawke said sharply. "You couldn't hit the floor if you fell on it!"

Ryan did as he was told and came back inside where Hawke now watched its progress. "Looks like a Kasatka, and he's slowing up."

"Kasatka?" Ryan asked.

"Russian-built military transport."

The chopper pulled into a hover above the top deck. Rappel lines tumbled out of the doors and then things got interesting fast. Smoke grenades provided instant cover as half a dozen men in black combat fatigues and gas masks slid down the ropes and hit the deck.

Scarlet loaded her gun. "The gunship's not here to destroy us but to provide a diversion while the Kasatka dumps its crap on us."

"Russians?" Lea asked.

"Not necessarily," said Hawke. "Looks like another Oracle purchase to me."

Reaper watched the men fan out, submachine guns gripped in their leather-gloved hands. "Kolya, are they Russians?"

"Hard to know, but I think not. They are better."

"If it *is* Athanatoi," said Ryan, "how the hell did they know we were here?"

Hawke knew what they were all thinking. Someone

was leaking information and all eyes swiveled to Nikolai. "We have no evidence."

"I would never do such a thing," Nikolai said. "And why would I put my own life at risk?"

Lexi frowned. "Kind of convenient that since you're on the team these guys know where to find us, though."

"We have *no* evidence," Hawke repeated. "And no time to think about it. Our new friends are cutting through Mokrani's security like a blowtorch through warm butter."

"Where the hell is Hafez?" Lea said. "He has the ring!"

"He went inside," Ryan said. "Once we have the ring we can try and get off this thing, but how?"

"The tender," Hawke said. "If we can get down to the davit without getting our heads blown off."

"So what do we do?" Scarlet asked. High above their heads on the top deck, the fighting between Mokrani's men and the invaders was intensifying.

"We get Hafez and the ring before they do!" Hawke said.

With sheer mayhem exploding all around them, they split into teams and started to search the boat for Hafez and the ring.

Leading the charge, Lea shot her way through the stern doors and was first inside the rear of the yacht's main deck. Safely behind the thick marine windows, the chaos unfolding on the outside decks was muffled to her now. Hawke jumped in behind her, gun drawn and eyes dilated wide as the adrenaline pumped through his body.

"You see him?"

"Nope."

"Hafez! Where are you?"

No reply.

The fighting increased. The men in combat fatigues had quickly eliminated Mokrani's yacht security and were now charging down the stairs on both sides of the bridge as they headed toward the lower decks, also in search of the ring.

"Where is everyone?" Hawke said into his palm mic. "Report."

Everyone called their locations in except Ryan.

"Ryan? Where are you mate?"

Silence.

Athanatoi burst through an internal door at the other end of the galley and charged toward them with handguns raised. Behind them, Lea now caught sight of Ryan being bundled into what she guessed was an escape route, but the view was blocked when the men opened fire and she and Hawke dived for cover behind some of the galley cabinets.

"I have Ryan, Joe!" Lea yelled. "They're taking him away, and they have Hafez too!"

Hawke spoke rapidly into his palm mic once again. "All teams, be advised they have Ryan and Hafez and the ring and they're on the run back to the helipad."

"Me and Reap are on it, Joe," Scarlet said.

Hawke and Lea were still pinned down.

"These guys are good," he said.

"Well, we sure as shite didn't come this far to give up, Josiah!"

"No, we didn't," he called back, bobbing his head back down to protect his eyes from more flying splinters. The fruit bowl on the side exploded in a shower of glass crystal and shredded bananas and mangos flew into the air, raining down over their heads. "Umm, yummy!"

She rolled her eyes. "Still a total eejit, I see."

"Always and forever."

She blew him a kiss as she reloaded her gun. "It's good to know some things in life don't change."

They both fired on the men again, this time with more

success. Lea took out the man on the port side and Hawke killed the other man, blasting him out of the starboard door where he crashed over the rail and tumbled down to the deck below.

Two more charged them, but Hawke fired on them and killed them both, emptying his magazine into them without mercy and covering the galley wall with blood as the rounds tore through their bodies and ripped out of their backs.

But it wasn't over yet.

A second later, Lea's worst fears came into sharp focus in a hurry. Another squall of violence ignited like a tinderbox with more Athanatoi streaming out of every door and hatch in sight.

"We have to get out of here!" Hawke yelled. "Follow me!"

They crawled out of the galley and got outside. Hawke slammed his body against the starboard gunwale and got busy warning Reaper's team about several men sprinting down the stainless steel staircase toward the foredeck. Beside him Lea reloaded her gun, her mind fixed on Ryan's kidnapping.

The mercs stopped playing and the real fighting started. A man operating a pintle-mounted machine gun spun the weapon's muzzle around and began laying serious fire down on Scarlet and Zeke as they attacked the starboard companionway toward the stern. Another team of mercs now bedded down near the starboard console and battered them with a brutal fusillade and forced a retreat.

Zeke tripped on one of the scuppers and fell flat on his face. His gun spun away along the deck, well out of reach. A sitting duck, Scarlet sprinted down the deck, raising her gun into the aim and firing on the men above them as she kicked the Texan's weapon back down to him.

"Thanks, Hun."

"Less of the Hun, Tex."

"Got it!"

He grabbed the gun, flipped over onto his back, and joined her in firing on the men on the top deck. With deadly accuracy in their aims, they killed two of the mercs and forced the rest of them back inside the yacht, giving them just enough time to run for the cover of the saloon a few yards to their right.

Hawke and Lea took advantage of the break in firing and moved from their position towards the saloon. Scarlet and Zeke had cleared the room and were running up a series of carpeted steps on the far side of the room. Broken glass and blood and dead mercs were scattered behind the Englishwoman and the Texan, shocking evidence of how savage the fighting had been in this part of the yacht.

Then, solemn words delivered in the chaos by a thick southern French accent brought everyone to a standstill.

"It's over, everyone."

Reaper's voice on the comms.

"Say again," Lea said.

"It's over, they killed Hafez, took the ring… and they have Ryan on board the transport chopper."

Hawke and Lea stared at each other in disbelief. For a moment there was no movement or sound, just the two ECHO friends surrounded by the cooling corpses of Mokrani's men and some of the snatch squad.

"I don't believe it," Lea said. "Not Ryan…"

Then they both saw movement and each spun around, guns raised.

One of the men in back combat fatigues was still alive, but barely. They moved over to him and took off his gas mask and riot helmet to reveal a man in his twenties. Hawke dragged him away from the dead bodies and out onto the deck where Reaper, Scarlet, and Lexi had gathered with grim expressions on their faces.

"We have one still alive, hein?" Reaper said.

Lea frowned. "Only just."

"What is your name?" Scarlet said.

No reply.

"Your friends are long gone, matey lad," Hawke said.

As the Kasatka flew away with his comrades and Ryan and with the gunship nowhere in sight, the mysterious mercenary knew the game was up and crashed back onto the deck visibly deflated. "Who do you work for?" Reaper said. "Is it the Oracle?"

The man tried to laugh, but his cackling quickly turned into a long coughing fit, and then he died right before their eyes.

"Dammit all to hell!" Lea said.

Then several of the team had the same thought at once. "Wait, didn't Ryan have the rings?"

"No, thank God," Lea said. "He gave them to me before we got on the tender."

A sigh of partial, qualified relief. They had Ryan but not the rings.

"They took him for a reason," Lea said. "They're not going to kill him… yet."

"When we find the Athanatoi, we find Ryan," Hawke said. "And we all know that means getting to the Citadel as fast as possible… *hang in there, mate.*"

"So what now?" Zeke asked.

Hawke's jaw tightened. "We need to get out of here and back to the hotel," he said at last. "We're no good to Ryan standing around a burning bloody boat."

CHAPTER THIRTY-THREE

From their room on the fiftieth floor of the Burj Al Arab hotel in the Umm Suqeim district of Dubai, the breathtaking view of the sunset over the Persian Gulf had weaved a spell over the exhausted team and given them a few moments of peace to gather their thoughts. Losing Mokrani's ring had laid them all low, but Ryan's violent kidnapping had hit them much harder and now they were licking their wounds and trying to work out the best way forward.

If there was a way forward, thought Hawke. Maybe this time they were just up against too many people who wanted them dead. On this mission, their enemy had included not only the Athanatoi but also Razak and his guerrillas, the Yakuza and Kozlov, and his Russian mafia thugs in Vegas. Worse, they had lost valuable friends and teammates in Danny Devlin and Magnus Lund at the lethal hands of the mystery sniper. Maybe this time, he thought darkly, they were doomed to fail. It was all starting to get to him in a way as previous missions had never done.

"The priority is getting Ryan back," he said, breaking the gloomy silence. "We've rescued friends before and we'll do it again. The risk of kidnap and death is part of our lives and we all knew that from the start, including Ryan."

"But we don't even know for sure who took him." Zeke scratched his neck and frowned.

"It was Athanatoi," Nikolai said. "I'm certain of it."

"And how could they know where we were?" Lexi

asked.

"Just a coincidence." Lea switched on the plasma screen and dialed Eden. "They're researching the rings' locations from their copy of the Codex and we got to Mokrani at the same time."

Scarlet lifted her eyes from the floor to Nikolai and back to Lea. "A hell of a coincidence."

"Enough speculation." Hawke crocked his neck and pulled a beer from the fridge. "We can't afford to waste the time. We have to look at what we *have* got, not what we haven't got."

"We still have five of the gods' rings." Eden's face loomed above them on the giant plasma screen on the hotel wall. "Those, plus the eight idols locked in the Bank of England's vaults still put us at a strong advantage over the Oracle. Remember he still only has two rings."

"With two more to get," Hawke said. "That gives us only seven of the rings even if we presume we're successful finding the two remaining ones, and no Ryan to help decipher them."

Eden nodded. "What are the chances of being able to use the seven rings to locate the Citadel? Anyone?"

"Ask Ryan," Reaper said.

The words hung in the air. Lea said, "Not great, Rich. Seven rings aren't even ninety percent of the puzzle… but you never know."

"What about the sniper?" Scarlet changed the subject. "Any news on that?"

Eden shook his head. "Sorry, but no. I've made contact with several good sources of intelligence information in France, Germany, Israel, and the United States. No one knows for sure. They only have theories."

"And what are these theories?" Hawke asked. "Because whoever this bastard is they've taken two of our own and we don't know when he'll strike again."

"So far, my Israeli colleague speculates that it could be Gideon Dayan, a former Mossad man gone rogue over a year ago, but he has his doubts due to the equipment being used. The French have a different theory."

He paused for a second too long.

"And?" Hawke said.

"You're not going to like this, Hawke, but Paris is telling me it could be the Spider."

Hawke felt his blood turn to ice. The Spider was the Cuban hitman behind his wife's murder in Vietnam, a man he had sworn to kill as soon as he had tracked him down. Finding out that he could be the killer behind the deaths of two more of his close friends and colleagues was a hammer blow, so he had to be sure. "You *are* talking about Alfredo Lazaro?"

"Yes, I am. They're not one hundred percent on it but it's possible. They can't be sure about the attack in Miami, but they have good intel placing him in Athens during the exact hour Magnus was murdered outside the Theatre of Dionysus."

"Bloody hell," Lea said. "This is too much."

"Just hang on," said Hawke. "This is just speculation from the French, right?"

"Right," Eden said.

"So let's not get carried away. The sniper could still be anyone, and we're making a massive mistake if we focus our attention on Lazaro."

Lea was not persuaded. "But don't you think that it's a hell of a coincidence that the hitman who killed Liz was in Athens the same hour that we were?"

"A coincidence, maybe," Hawke said. "Maybe the bastard is following me around again, maybe he wants me dead too. I want him dead, so that makes us equal, but we can't make a strategy based on speculation. Lazaro is a dead man one way or the other, and in the meantime, we go forward on the basis that the sniper is still unidentified."

"A sound plan," Eden said. "And I'll continue shining my torch in the darkest corners from this end to get a firmer ID on the mystery man with his finger on the trigger."

Hawke settled down again, but the sound of Lazaro's codename had unsettled him. The Spider was a ruthless assassin raised in the back streets of Havana. He was a predator, a killer without a conscience, and the man who had snuffed out his young wife's life without a hint of mercy or regret.

Up till this moment, he'd always planned on tracking Lazaro down and avenging Liz's murder the old-fashioned way, but now there was the possibility that the Spider was hunting *him* again. Is that why the team was being targeted? Could Lazaro have killed Danny and Magnus because of their association with him? The mere thought of it felt like a lead weight on his shoulders. Now, more than ever, he had to hunt the Spider down and end the threat.

"Moving on," Scarlet said, sensing the anguish her old friend must be feeling, "What's the skinny on the last two rings?"

Eden blew out a breath and smiled. He, too, was relieved to move away from Alfredo Lazaro. "Good news. Less than an hour ago I received a message from our old friend Ali al-Majid. He has kindly decided to accept our million dollars and in return has given us the locations of the two last rings. The first is what he believes to be the Ring of Romulus. He says it's in the private possession of an academic. His name is Professor Qasim al-Hashimi and he works in the Iraqi Museum in Baghdad."

"Sounds like we're getting warmer," Lea said.

"Not just warm but hot," said Eden. "We're almost there, team."

A shocked silence fell over the team as they each processed what Eden had just said.

"Is he going to cooperate?" Hawke asked. "Or do we need another million?"

Eden gave a firm nod as a smile broke out on his face. "He is, but only on the condition that he can go with you on the journey to the Citadel."

"I have no objections," Lea said.

Lexi shrugged. "Nor me. He's an archaeologist. He could be useful."

"Wait a minute," Hawke said. "What sort of man is he? Can we trust him? Is he fit enough to reach the Citadel?"

"Fit enough?" Zeke asked.

Scarlet rolled her eyes. "It's not going to be just lying around with a red bow tied on it, Zeke. It's going to be underground, or in a hidden mountain pass, or fuck knows how hard to find. If our Prof is a major league lardy then he could get seriously hurt, especially if someone's shooting at us."

"Major league lardy?" Zeke said. "That's not very nice."

She shrugged. "I'm not very nice."

Hawke sucked his gut in. "If he wants in then fine, but we tell him the risks first."

"Like Lex just said, he's an archaeologist," Lea said. "He's going to be used to visiting excavations all over the world, right?"

"Right," Eden said firmly.

"You said Ali had information about two rings?" Lea asked.

"Yes, the last ring should be even simpler to secure, or at least to borrow temporarily."

"How so?" Scarlet said.

"According to Ali, the Ring of Sudas is in the possession of the American military in Camp Angel, outside of Baghdad."

"I didn't think there were any US soldiers in Iraq anymore," Lexi said.

"Over five thousand of them," Zeke said immediately. "The Victory Base Complex near the airport was a major military camp until 2011 when we officially pulled out. Last I heard the Iraqi Government wanted to turn it into some kind of university."

"So the rumors go," Eden said.

"Near the airport, you say?" Lexi asked.

"Yes. It's inside the Al-Faw Palace," Eden said. "It's an enormous building in Baghdad built by Saddam Hussein in the nineties to commemorate an Iraqi victory during the Iran-Iraq war and as Zeke says, up until 2011 it was occupied by the US military as a logistics facility."

"And today?"

"It's very hard to get detailed information out of Iraq," Eden said. "But a trusted CIA contact has confirmed Ali's intel. He tells me that there is a small US contingent in the palace, unknown to the general public. They're probably working alongside the Iraqis as they establish the university there, but that's of no concern to us because also not available to the public is the neat little fact that Saddam had vaults built into its basement to stash various treasures for his own personal use. Thanks to Ali, and my CIA contact, I can tell you that the last ring is among those treasures."

"Getting hotter!" Lexi said, unable to conceal her excitement.

"You said borrow?" Lea rarely missed detail.

"I think it's unlikely General Tucker will allow any of the treasures off the site, and I would doubt appealing to the Iraqi Minister of the Interior will help either."

"Great."

"And we can't risk losing an easy opportunity to secure the ring because of frankly unimportant concerns. If we know about these rings, then so must the Oracle. From now on it's just a race against time to see who gets to them first, which is why you're all on a plane to Baghdad as of an hour ago, got it?"

"Why not get President Brooke to get us the ring?" Lexi asked. "It's in US custody after all."

"First, it's not in US custody – not officially. It's in Iraqi custody, and..." Eden paused, and they all saw something was on his mind. "I didn't want to brief you on this until this mission was over, but it looks like things are getting too serious across the pond to keep you in the dark anymore. I know you're aware of *vague* talk of a coup, but it's worse than we thought. I had a communiqué from Alex Reeve earlier today in which she outlined to me what looks like a full-scale coup against President Brooke."

"Holy shit," Lea said. "Who's behind this?"

"It's confirmed now. Vice President Davis Faulkner."

Hawke blinked, unable to believe what he had just heard. "So she wasn't being paranoid then?"

Eden shook his head. "It doesn't look like it. Agent Brandon McGee has become a trusted friend of hers and he briefed her on the coup after receiving intel on it from another trusted source, Agent Suzie Matsumoto."

Reaper twirled a cigarette paper in his calloused, nicotine-stained fingers. "Who is she?"

"Matsumoto is an agent with the US Secret Service attached to the Vice President's protection team."

"Mon Dieu..."

Zeke was sitting up now and dropped the empty beer bottle on the carpet as he slid off the bed and walked closer to the plasma screen. "Is this some sort of joke?"

"No joke," Eden said. "I'm sorry."

"I can't believe it," he wandered over to the window and stared blankly out at the setting sun. "A coup?"

"Technically not," Eden countered. "They're invoking a special amendment in the Constitution to force the President out of the Oval Office, but it adds up to the same thing because it's bogus. Brooke has done nothing wrong."

"Is this an episode of the Outer Limits?" Zeke said quietly.

"No," Lexi said. "Welcome to a day in the life of ECHO."

Nikolai had kept his counsel, but now his low Russian grumble filled the room. "Is this Faulkner operating alone?"

All eyes turned to him. Eden spoke first. "We don't know. What are you suggesting?"

The Russian monk shrugged. "Nothing. Just that the Oracle and Faulkner are… how shall I say – *acquainted* with one another."

His words shocked the entire team. "Davis Faulkner knows the Oracle?" Hawke asked. "How?"

"He is an acolyte, but other than this I know nothing more than what I have said. I was too low in the food chain."

Hawke, still blindsided by the revelation that Otmar Wolff and Davis Faulkner were associates, walked to the window and worked hard to consider the consequences. It explained the attack on Jack Brooke for one thing, and it meant the future was likely storing up even more trouble for the ECHO team. Now, more than ever, time was of the essence.

"We're getting closer now, Rich," Lea said. "I know it sounds callous but we have to focus on our mission here in the Middle East. We're going to need the idols."

"No problem," Eden said. "I'll have them flown out to you from London on a Royal Air Force transport plane at once."

With Eden's words hanging in the air, Hawke turned and faced his team. "All right then, it's time to cross the border. We're going to Iraq."

*

Jessica Clarke looked down at the screen of her iPhone and sighed when she saw the caller ID: PEGASUS, a.k.a. her pain-in-the-ass boss Tony Garcetti.

She took the call. "What is it?"

"You're flying to Iraq."

"Iraq?" Jessica asked. "What the hell are they doing in Iraq?"

"Don't ask me, Cougar," Garcetti said. "I'm just passing orders down from the organ grinder to the monkey. Brand new intel hot off the press."

"You're the monkey, Garcetti."

"I'm starting to believe it."

She cut the call and sighed. Looked at her bag, all packed with weapons and ammo and ready to go. Same old same old. A note for Mrs. Kowalczyk asking her to check on Matty. A drive to the airport. An unmarked government jet. Bland men in somber suits and earpieces checking her ID. A long, tiring flight and then a hunt in the desert for the next target on her list. Another new home for the next bullet in the box.

But then, Mexico.

CHAPTER THIRTY-FOUR

Baghdad was not as Hawke remembered it. During the war when he was last in the country, the city was a very different place. The place he had left behind was mostly a shelled ruin, broken down by artillery fire and bombing runs of over a thousand sorties per day. Citizens cowered in their homes and prayed to see another day, while he and the rest of his covert Special Forces unit moved through the city's underground searching for senior members of the Republican Guard.

Today, peace had just about reasserted itself on the beleaguered, ancient city. Luxury cars adorned many streets and he even saw a pleasure boat sailing up the Tigris. Young people laughed as they walked along the sidewalks, shaded by date palms and in no rush to go anywhere in particular.

The contrast between some of the horrors he had witnessed during the war and the apparent serenity of today could not have been starker. No more fear of kidnap for foreigners walking the streets, but instead a wide range of glittering shopping malls and nightclubs and smiling street vendors offering *masgouf* from carefully positioned food carts.

How people move on, he thought.

"What the hell is that?" Lexi asked, spying one of the carts.

"Grilled carp," Hawke said. "It's usually very good."

He checked the SUV's satnav was still correlating with the research he had done earlier on what he had called a *proper paper map*. Something no one could hack or track them on. All was good, and they were nearing their first destination in good time.

"Are we there yet?" Scarlet asked in the style of Bart Simpson.

Lea rolled her eyes. "Really?"

"Just trying to lighten the mood."

"The answer is yes," Hawke said, glancing at the satnav as he powered the SUV across another wide junction. "It's just up ahead a little on the right."

They turned onto Nasir Street and the Iraqi Museum loomed quickly into view. Heavily looted during the invasion of 2003, many of its ancient artifacts were never returned and the museum wasn't formally reopened to the public until twelve years later in 2015.

As they drew nearer, the impressive crenelated towers that formed the façade shone brightly in the Iraqi sun, obscured here and there by enormous palms placed on either side of the main entrance. They cruised past the impressive building as they drew closer to their destination, but as they drove deeper into the city, things began to change again.

Away from the richer central district, the outer regions began to resemble what Hawke had seen back during the war. Concrete blast walls covered in graffiti, wrecked cars jacked up on the side of the road, and trash cans rolling on their sides in the hot desert wind.

"So this is where Professor al-Hashimi hangs out." Lea's voice was full of uncertainty.

"According to Rich, yes," Hawke said, glancing once again at the satnav.

"Thought a university guy would earn more."

Hawke pulled the car up outside the house and turned to the rear. "Okay, this is where we split so have fun kids. Mum, Dad, and Uncle Reaper are going to speak to the nice General, while you guys have a chat with the prof.

We'll meet here in an hour."

"An hour?" Scarlet said.

"Things have to be even faster now because of Ryan."

"You took the words right out of my mouth," Reaper said, opening the door to let the others out. Scarlet, Lexi, Zeke, and Nikolai climbed out into the street and a rush of hot air blew into the SUV's interior, bringing a taste of dust and diesel fumes.

The burly Frenchman climbed back in and slammed the door. Leaning one elbow out of the window, he lit his cigarette as Scarlet turned, shades flashing in the sun's glare. "One hour, oui?"

"Last one back's a rotten egg, lads," she said.

*

General Braxton Tucker was a broad-chested, tall man with a tanned, rectangular face and a short scar running down from the corner of his left eye. Wearing his camouflaged US Army combat uniform, he tossed his pen down on the desk and rose to greet the visitors to Camp Angel.

Lea took her seat first, then Hawke and Reaper joined her. "Thanks for seeing us, sir."

"I was intrigued when I got the call from the DOD," he said. "You want access to the collection of relics we store here on site, is that right?"

"It is."

"Never been asked that before."

Still no hint of a smile.

"Is it something you'd consider?" she asked.

"I've already considered it, and I can't see any problem why you can't see the item in question and borrow it for one week. After that, I want it back on site or I'm coming to get you, no kidding around."

"We understand."

"You're all vets, is that right?"

Hawke nodded. "Former Royal Marines Commandos and SBS."

"And I'm former Irish Rangers."

"What about you?" he said to the silent Frenchman.

"Foreign Legion," was all he said.

He gave an appreciative nod. "One week, as I say."

"That's all we need."

"To find this archaeological site?"

Lea nodded. "That's right. We think it could be the archaeological find of the century."

"I couldn't care less about old pots and pans and fossils," he said bluntly. "I couldn't care less about this place, either. I'm not even supposed to be here. Hell, I'm *not* here officially. If I can help out a bunch of relic diggers then fine."

"Is the ring on public display?" Lea asked.

"No," Tucker said. "The relics, including the ring are not kept in the public section of the palace and never have been. Certain items, mostly those from the very distant past such as the Sumerian age, have always been kept under lock and key. First, by the British, then by Saddam Hussein and now by the new Iraqi Government."

"Why?" Lea asked.

"Because they would raise too many questions," Reaper said flatly. "That's why – right, General?"

Tucker nodded but was reluctant to go further. "Yes, I think our Legionnaire friend is right when he says this. Certain special antiquities raise more questions than they answer when it comes to understanding our history and where we all come from. It is always easier to crush the truth than to shine light upon it. Now, I'll make the call."

Less than a minute after he hung up, there was a knock on the door.

"Come!"

A stocky man in combat fatigues walked in and snapped to attention, giving the general a sharp salute.

"At ease, captain."

"Sir."

"This is Captain Benning. He'll take you to the secure area where our little hoard is retained on behalf of the Iraqi Government. As you heard from the phone call, Benning's been fully briefed on the situation and knows you're to have the item in question for one week only, and that's only happening because the Pentagon personally intervened on the President's orders."

Lea stood up. "Thank you, General Tucker. You'll have your relic back in Al-Faw in one week."

Hawke and Reaper stood up and shook hands with the general.

"Good luck," Tucker said.

*

Professor Qasim al-Hashimi was sitting on his balcony when Scarlet and the others walked up outside his house in the Kadhimya District. Just three miles from the city center, the area was rich in history with intricate shrines and ornate mosques lining its twisting, dusty streets.

"I was most interested when I received the call from your people," he said as he showed them inside his home. "The ring is one of my more recent discoveries. I found it in an excavation only a year or so ago in northern Iran and while it has intrigued me I have not spent much time on it. I am so busy with my research work at the university."

He stopped in his tracks and turned, slipping his hands out of his pockets and adjusting the wire-rim spectacles on his nose. "You mentioned something about it forming some sort of map?"

"So I'm told," she said.

"You don't know?"

"I'm just more of a hired hand."

He looked amused. "Well, it's just through here."

They followed him along the narrow corridor and into a small room at the back of the first floor. Frayed rug on the floor, tattered throw over a worn leather couch. Ceiling fan swirling above their heads. Black shadows from the sun streaking through an old plantation shutter on the open window and striping the wall above the desk.

Qasim walked into the room and tripped over a pile of journals on the floor. He stopped himself from going over by grabbing onto Scarlet's arm. "Sorry… I need to tidy, I know."

Lexi's eyes danced over the heaps of books and junk all over the small room. "You can find the ring, right?"

He opened an old coffee chest beside the desk and reached inside. Out in the heat, a long and powerful adhan drifted over the city, called by a muezzin from some distant minaret. Qasim turned to face them with a beaming smile on his face, and in his hand, he held what they had flown around the world for.

The Ring of Sedus.

"Is this what you seek, friends?"

"It sure as shit looks like it!" Zeke said.

Lexi frowned. "Excuse the help, Professor," she said.

The Texan laughed and slapped her on the back, almost bowling her over. "The help! I love it."

Nikolai said nothing but kept his eyes focused on the ring.

"That *is* what we're looking for, Professor," Scarlet said.

He sucked hard on a Pine cigarette before blowing out a thick cloud of smoke. "I'm glad it is what you are looking for, but from now on we travel together. If there is a Land of the Gods to be found, I must be there when it is discovered."

*

Deep in the Al-Faw Palace, Captain Benning ordered a soldier to unlock the vault door and switch on the light. The room was unremarkable and like any other storage space, they had seen – cool stone walls and electric strip lights painting everything the color of old lemons. Padlocked chests and crates were stacked in neat lines across the room, forming aisles they were able to walk down as they followed the young captain through to the long room.

After a few moments working out where he was, Benning stared at the paper in his hand and then glanced up at a number sprayed on the stone wall. "This is the section, right here. Looks like you're about to get what you're searching for."

Hawke and Lea caught each other's eye.

The quest was nearly over.

CHAPTER THIRTY-FIVE

"Stand down, marine!"

The US Marine sentry outside the Oval Office looked nervously at the Vice President of the United States and the men behind him. Faulkner held his ground, knowing what the young man must be thinking. Along with the Secret Service, he was charged with the responsibility of protecting the life of the President, and yet here was the Vice President and several members of the US Cabinet, and they were accompanied by their own Secret Service and other marines.

"You were told to stand down!" barked General Patterson.

In the face of an angry four-star general, the marine folded like a deck chair, standing down and lowering his weapon.

Without waiting for another second, Faulkner opened the door of the anteroom and marched through into the Oval Office. Flanked by Patterson and several other senior military personnel he made an awesome sight as he approached the President.

A startled Jack Brooke stood up behind the desk and fixed his eye on Faulkner. "What the hell is this?"

Patterson stepped forward. "Get away from the desk and raise your hands, sir!"

Special Agent Suzie Matsumoto was standing behind Brooke. She unholstered her gun in a flat second and pointed the muzzle at the general, simultaneously standing in front of him. "Drop your weapon and step away from the President!"

Brooke reached out and gently pulled her arm down. "It's okay, Agent Matsumoto. To say we're outgunned is the understatement of the year." Ignoring Patterson, he walked out from behind his desk and squared up to Faulkner. "Now, as I just asked, what the hell is this all about, Davis?"

Faulkner puffed his chest out and looked Brooke in the eye. "Mr. President, under the powers given by the Twenty-Fifth Amendment, I have assembled the members of the Cabinet and we are here today to remove you from the Office of the President of the United States."

Brooke was speechless. He stared up at the men and women gathered in the Oval Office and tried to judge just what the hell they were thinking. He knew these people well. He had personally appointed all of them to their cabinet positions, including the Attorney General. Hell, he'd even lifted Faulkner out of nowhere to be the Vice President, and yet here they all were in the middle of his morning talking about invoking the Twenty-Fifth? It had to be some kind of nightmare.

"I don't understand what's happening."

"All of that will be explained to you, sir," Faulkner said. "But as of this moment I'm invoking Section 4 of the Twenty-Fifth Amendment, and..."

"Section 4? What the hell? I'm not unable to discharge the powers and duties of this office! What game are you playing?"

Faulkner stood his ground. "I'm sorry, sir, but you are hereby removed from Office of the President of the United States under the powers given to us by the Twenty-Fifth Amendment, Section 4 and I am assuming the position of President in accordance with the Constitution. The cabinet and I have sent written notice to President pro tempore of the Senate and the Speaker of the House of Representatives. It's over. I'll inform the people in an address within the hour."

"This is insane!" Brooke marched around the desk and confronted Faulkner. "I don't know what the hell you think you're doing, Davis, but you're not going to get away with it."

"The members of the Cabinet are witness to this," Faulkner said, turning to the Attorney General. "Please proceed."

The AG stepped forward with the Bible he'd been holding throughout. "I will now administer the presidential oath. Are you ready, Mr. Vice President?"

Faulkner never took his eyes off Brooke. "Go ahead, please."

The AG held out the Bible. "Please put your left hand on the Bible and raise your right hand, sir."

Faulkner followed his instructions.

The grand prize was so close he could taste it. It rolled in his mouth like honey.

"Now, repeat after me…I, Davis Jefferson Faulkner do solemnly swear…"

"I, Davis Jefferson Faulkner do solemnly swear…"

"That I will faithfully execute the Office of President of the United States…"

Faulkner's voice was as cold and strong as steel. "That I will faithfully execute the Office of President of the United States…"

"And will to the best of my ability…"

He slowed his breathing. "And will to the best of my ability."

"Preserve, protect and defend the Constitution of the United States."

Faulkner felt a swell of pride and achievement. "Preserve, protect and defend the Constitution of the United States."

"So help me God."

"So help me God."

The AG removed the Bible, but there were no congratulations today because they all knew what was coming next.

President Faulkner squared up to Jack Brooke. Stripped of his office and all his political power, he looked smaller now. "Jack, I'm putting you under arrest for treason."

Brooke was aghast. "For *treason?* What the hell are you talking about, Davis?"

"You know damned well what I'm talking about, Jack." He glowered at Brooke, hate filling his eyes. "And it's Mr. President, not Davis."

Before Brooke could reply, Faulkner turned to the marine sentries. "Get him out of here and make sure you get his daughter too. She's got to be part of this outrage, this national *disgrace!*"

"What the hell?" Brooke struggled in the arms of the marines who moments ago had been protecting him. "You leave Alex alone, you son of a bitch!"

"How's the team doing over in the Residence?" Faulkner asked Muston.

"No word yet."

"I want Alex Reeve out of this place right along with her father."

"You'll pay for this, you bastard!" Brooke said.

"I think not."

General Patterson took off his peaked cap and tossed it on one of the couches. Ignoring Brooke completely, he turned to Davis Faulkner and watched as he walked over to the Resolute Desk. "Congratulations, Mr. President. You saved America today, sir."

Brooke struggled in the marines' arms.

Faulkner traced his fingers along the edge of the desk, almost in a dream as he thought about all the mighty figures who had sat right here and directed the fate of the world. Now it was his turn. Without a second thought, he turned to Patterson. "All right, General. Give the order to put the ECHO team on the Most Wanted list. I want them hunted down and arrested if possible. If they resist them take them out. Pay particular attention to Iraq."

"Iraq?" Patterson seemed shocked. "What the hell are they doing in Iraq?"

"Just do as I say, General. Tell your men in Iraq to be on the lookout for the ECHO team, and if they find them it's just as I said – arrest them or kill them."

"No!" Brooke said. "You can't do that!"

"I can do whatever I want, Jack. I'm the President of the United States. I've been planning to take over this office and throw your traitor ass out of here for years. Who do you think ordered ECHO's Caribbean headquarters to be smashed the year before last?"

Brooke's mind snapped back two years ago to when his daughter had been badly wounded in an aerial assault on ECHO's HQ building on the island of Elysium. "Oh my God! That was you? You nearly killed my girl you son of a bitch!"

"Cool it down, Jack... cool it down. We've had this in the pipeline for years, only you were too dumb to see it coming. You and your little friends in ECHO running your terror campaigns around the world!"

"This is insane! They're not *terrorists* – they fight against terrorists!"

"You would say that, but while your little friends were trying to set a nuke off on Alcatraz, who was trying to stop them? Me. When they were trying to destroy Atlantis, who tried to stop them by blowing up their island? Me. Without me who knows what they… and *you* would have gotten away with."

"This is crazy. I can't believe I'm hearing it."

"No, it's totally sane, and now I'm ending what I started all those years ago. You and ECHO are going to be arrested and tried for various offenses ranging from treason to terrorism and there's *nothing* you can do about it. I've waited a long time for this, Jacky boy – ever since you first made me VP all those years ago, and as the gods are my witness, I'm going to enjoy every second of it. Now, take him away, and *her* too!"

The soldiers grabbed Jack Brooke and Suzie Matsumoto and dragged them out of the Oval Office.

Brooke struggled to twist his neck and look over his shoulder at the new Commander in Chief. "You're making a big mistake, Davis!"

"Goodbye, Jack."

Faulkner watched his men bundling Jack Brooke and his loyal Secret Service agent out of the Oval Office and along the corridor outside. "The door, Josh."

Muston gently closed the door and blew out a deep breath. "My God, we did it."

*

The tired, weary general picked up his phone in a temper. "Tucker."

"General Braxton Tucker?"

Now he recognized the voice. Secretary of Defence Kelvin Beauregard. "Sir, yes sir!"

"Relax, General. Are you sitting down?"

Tucker furrowed his brow. "Sir?"

"You are hereby informed that there has been a change of leadership in the United States."

"A change of leadership? I don't understand."

"President Brooke has been removed from the Office of the President of the United States. The Cabinet invoked the Twenty-Fifth and took him out. Davis Faulkner is the

President now."

Tucker collapsed back in his chair. "What the hell happened? There's nothing on the news."

"About to break. Treason."

"My *God!*"

"Right, and it's going to be a serious shitshow when it all comes out."

Tucker scratched behind his ear. "This is one of those *where were you* moments, right Mr. Secretary?"

"Sure is."

"President Faulkner, huh?"

"Yeah, and you just got your first Presidential order direct from him, too."

"I don't get it."

"According to CIA records, the passports of three known fugitives just got swiped through your security."

"Three fugitives?"

"Josiah Hawke, a British citizen, Lea Donovan, an Irish citizen, and Vincent Reno, a French citizen. Am I right?"

Tucker was dumbfounded. "Yes, sir. They were here a few moments ago representing some sort of archaeological institute from England. We put them through the usual security protocols, fingerprints, and passport scans and they came up clear. The Pentagon ordered me to assist them."

"Not anymore," Beauregard said flatly. "President Faulkner personally put them on the Most Wanted list. They're terrorists and they are to be detained immediately – is that clear?"

Tucker felt his mouth dry up and his heart start to pound. "Yes, sir – just as you say."

"How long since they left you?"

"They left my office a few minutes ago. As far as I know, they're still on site. I guess they'll be about ready to leave any minute and then they'll be on their way."

"As I say, not anymore, General. You let them get away and the President will personally burn your commission and he'll use your pension papers to light it. Am I making myself clear?"

"Sir, yes sir!"

CHAPTER THIRTY-SIX

Hawke looked at the ring and smiled with satisfaction. "This is it, all right. Take a look."

Lea took it from him and held it to the light. "Sure is. We're not doing so bad, you know?" she said, blowing him a kiss.

Reaper smiled. "I hope Cairo's team have been as lucky. If so, we already have the seventh and eighth rings."

"Still missing number six, though," Lea said. "Poor Mr. Mokrani."

A soldier appeared at the door, leaning half into the room, sweat beading on his forehead as he spoke. "Captain Benning, sir?"

"What is it?"

"I need to speak with you, sir, urgently."

Benning followed the soldier out of the dingy vault.

"And we've got it for a week!" Lea said. "I'm going to call Cairo and let her know the good news. With some luck, they got the other ring from Professor al-Hashimi. They might be meaningless to anyone who doesn't know their true meaning, but to us, they're worth the weight of the world in gold."

"Hold it right there!"

Hawke turned to see Captain Benning had lifted his pistol and was aiming it at his head with a firm, solid grip as he marched over to him. "Hand over the ring and raise your hands, nice and slow."

"What the hell is this?" Lea said.

Hawke and Reaper exchanged a glance. "Yes, what's

going on, Captain?"

"I'm sorry Major Hawke, but General Tucker says these are orders direct from the Pentagon."

"What orders?"

"You're to be arrested at once and detained here until transfer off base."

"Arrested?" Lea said, shocked. "What the hell for?"

Hawke already knew. "Don't tell me, we're now the most dangerous people on the planet?"

Benning looked to the other soldiers with an awkward expression on his face. "That's what they tell me, sir. You're on the Most Wanted. You're terrorists. It comes right from the very top. The President."

"President Brooke would never call us terrorists!" Lea said.

Benning looked confused. "I guess you haven't heard then."

Lea felt her stomach turn over. "Heard what?"

"President Brooke was arrested today and charged with treason. He's been removed from office by the Cabinet. Davis Faulkner is the new President and the new Commander in Chief, and he says you're on the Most Wanted, so you are. Now, do as I say and raise your hands!"

"So it's happened," Reaper said.

The Englishman felt the cold steel of the Beretta's muzzle pushing into the base of his skull and realized with dread what must have happened back on Washington. He could hardly believe Faulkner had been successful in his bid to take over the White House and remove Brooke from the Presidency.

"You don't have to do this, Benning."

The young American captain paused before replying. It looked like he was thinking about what Hawke had said, which was a good sign.

No one else in the vault moved or spoke. A grim stillness had descended over the whole place as the gravity of the situation sank into everyone in its full horror.

"As I say, those are my orders." Benning's voice was calm and cool.

When Hawke replied, his words were also measured and level. "You're not a robot, Captain. You know what's happened. Your country has just suffered a coup d'état and your democratically elected Commander in Chief has been arrested by criminals and terrorists."

"General Tucker just described President Brooke with the same words."

Hawke felt the pressure of the gun lessen slightly on the back of his head. Maybe Benning was thinking the matter over, or maybe he was just being sloppy. He considered turning on the soldier and taking him out.

It was possible, but not without triggering a massive firefight inside the vault, and his team was too exposed. Maybe Reaper might make it to the cover of the crates behind them, but Lea was too exposed. She would be killed before she could start making a dent in Benning and his soldiers.

Plus he didn't want to kill any of them. These were US soldiers, allies in the cause. These men came from regiments he had trained with as a younger man in the commandos. The idea of firing on them to get out of this situation wasn't one he could live with unless they forced his hand.

"They're lying, Captain," he said at last. "You know in your heart that they're lying."

Behind Benning, his sergeant called over, "What are we doing here, sir? These people are our allies. You heard what General Tucker said – some of their team are US citizens!"

The US Army captain paused again and took a step back from Hawke, but kept the gun raised and aimed at his head. "I have to ask you to throw your weapons down."

"You're in charge here, Benning," Hawke said. "You're the OC. There's no one here to tell you what to do. Your new boss is all the way over in Washington. This is your decision, your call. If you arrest us and take us into custody, you're working with criminals and terrorists against a good man like Jack Brooke. Only you can make this call."

"Wrong, my boss is a few hundred feet away right inside this palace. Turn around."

Hawke followed his instructions and turned around, his hands still in the air and his gun still on his belt holster. "What's it going to be?"

Benning lowered his gun to his side and the rest of his unit breathed a collective sigh of relief. "I can't do this, it's not right."

"You made the right decision," Reaper said. "Faulkner might be the President right now, but trust me when I tell you his ass isn't going to be in the Oval Office very long."

"Stand aside, captain!"

Benning turned to see General Tucker standing in the door. Flanked by soldiers holding submachine guns, the old warrior stepped into the vault, a snarl on his face. "You were going to disobey a direct order from the Pentagon?"

"Sir, I…"

"You realize the implications of this?"

"It doesn't feel right, sir."

The general looked astonished. "It doesn't *feel,* right? Do you think this is some kind of Sunday School picnic? You're a captain in the US Army!"

Crestfallen and ashen with fear, Benning climbed

down. He lifted his gun and pointed it at Hawke again. “Lay down your weapons.”

Tucker nodded. “I’m going to overlook what you did, Benning, but don’t let me down again, you hear me?”

“No sir.”

“What now?” Lea said.

“Now you’re on a transport back to the States. Extraordinary rendition, go to jail and do not pass go. Now, move it!”

He waved the gun at the door, and they filed past the soldiers.

“And I’ll take that,” Tucker said, plucking the ring from Hawke’s fingers. “You won’t need it where you’re going.”

“And where’s that?” Lea asked.

“Tartarus.”

Lea darted a quick look at Hawke and then back to Tucker. “What?”

“You’ll have plenty of time to think about it on the flight.” He turned to Benning and handed him the ring. “See to it this gets to the Pentagon.”

“Yes, sir.”

“You’re making a big mistake, Tucker,” Hawke said.

“That’s enough, get them out of here. There’s a USAF transport plane waiting for them at the airfield.”

The soldiers pushed her out of the room and along the corridor leading up to the steps they had taken to reach the vault. Outside, Lea raised her hand to her mouth and pretended to cough as she spoke into her palm mic. “You there, Cairo?”

“Sure am, but where are you? You’re not at the rendezvous point.”

She glanced around at the guards and lowered her voice. “We’ve been put under arrest by the US Army.”

“What the actual fuck?”

"No time to explain," she said quietly. "They're flying us out on a transport from the airport right now. How fast can you be here?"

"We're a few minutes out. Hold tight, darling."

CHAPTER THIRTY-SEVEN

"I see them," Scarlet said. "Just as Lea said – they're marching them across the airfield now."

"How many guns?" Lexi asked.

"Three soldiers," she replied coolly. "Two with subs and an officer with a pistol in a belt holster. They're ordering them up into the back of the plane now."

Zeke whistled. "Not good."

"If they take off we're never going to see them again," Nikolai said.

"They're not taking off with them on board," Scarlet said. "Lea, still receiving, darling?"

Nothing.

"Lea?"

Some crackling, and then Lea's Irish accent weakly crackling through the comms. "I'm here, but I won't be for long. We're taking off in seconds."

"I know, I'm watching you from outside the airfield. When you're on the take-off roll, it would be mighty handy if someone accidentally opened the rear cargo door."

"Are you crazy?"

"Your ride will be waiting for you at the back of the plane."

"Yes," Lea said. "You really are crazy."

"It's your only hope. Do we have a date?"

"We'll be there, Cairo," Lea whispered. "Just make sure you are!"

"Hold on tight, darling."

Scarlet cut the comms and turned to Zeke. "You were

a tank commander, right?"

"Hell yeah."

"So you'll have no problem driving this Toyota along the runway under heavy fire and chasing that plane on its take-off roll?"

"Hell no."

"Smashing. Let's get on with it – they're powering up for take-off!"

Nikolai shook his head. "No wonder we always lost to you."

They climbed into the Land Cruiser and Zeke stamped on the gas. With nothing to lose, they piled through the perimeter fence and bounced along the scrub surrounding the airport. Hitting the runway, the Texan spun the wheel to the right and pulled up straight behind the C130 in a squeal of burning rubber.

"Faster, Zeke! I need more power!"

The laconic Texan turned to meet Nikolai's eyes. "I bet she talks like this to all the boys."

The Russian's lips never moved a millimeter, but Lexi rolled her eyes. "Boys."

Zeke stomped on the throttle and increased power.

"We're in place, Lea," Scarlet said. "I know you can't respond, but if you're going to open that cargo door then it's now or never!"

*

Lea hadn't even had the chance to tell Hawke or Reaper about Scarlet's communication, and now it was time to act. He was going to think she was insane, leaping out of her seat and trying to open the rear cargo door while the plane was rattling down the runway, but that was exactly what she did.

Jumping from her seat, she reached the lever before

Benning and his soldiers had a chance to react, and by the time they'd pulled their weapons and aimed at them the door was already halfway down.

"Holy crap!" Benning said, shocked by the sight of a Toyota Landcruiser right out the back of the transport aircraft. Scarlet Sloane was standing on the hood with her legs apart and a Heckler & Koch MP7 in her hands. On her face, a devilish grin appeared as the wind whipped her black hair around like a wild banshee.

"Sir?" one of the soldiers screamed. "Do we fire?"

It was too late. Reaper heaved his shackled hands up and elbowed the soldier in the face while Hawke reached down and disarmed him. With his hands also shackled, he held the gun at Benning's head. "Tell your men to lower their weapons, captain!"

Benning reluctantly complied, still taken aback by the sight of the woman in black on the hood of the Land Cruiser.

"The ring, captain!"

Benning handed the ring over to Hawke, who now turned to Lea and Reaper. "Go!"

"Not without you!"

"I'll go first and catch you when you jump over!" Reaper said.

He dived out of the back of the transport plane, crashing down on the hood of the Land Cruiser. Scrambling to his feet, he stood beside Scarlet and called out to Lea. "Your turn!"

The C130 reached V2 and its nose lifted into the air as it started to take off. Lea tumbled backward and slid down the cargo ramp.

Hawke reached out to grab her, missing by inches. "Lea!"

She clutched onto one of the hydraulic actuators to stop herself smashing into the tarmac and getting chewed up in the Land Cruiser's front wheel. "Shit!"

Benning took the moment to edge closer to Hawke, but the Englishman raised his gun higher into his face. "Don't even think about it!"

Lea scrambled to her feet and leaped across to the Toyota, almost slipping off the side of the hood. Reaper grabbed her and hauled her back to her feet, and then the two of them climbed inside the cab through the front passenger window. At the wheel, Zeke swerved and fought to keep the vehicle steady.

The C130 took off, rapidly climbing into the air. Twenty feet up and Hawke knew it was now or never. He leaped out of the back of the cargo door and crashed onto the Toyota's wide roof, leaving a shallow dent as he smacked down into the aluminum.

He flipped over onto his back to see a scowling Cairo, and behind her, the monstrous sight of the C130 roaring up into the air. "You get to have all the fun, Hawke."

"The sun shines on the righteous."

Scarlet and Hawke climbed into the SUV as Zeke spun the wheel and plowed the heavy vehicle into the sandy scrub at the side of the runway. The airport's perimeter fence approached rapidly, but Zeke never flinched as he smashed through it and thundered away from the airport.

"Anyone in pursuit?" Hawke said, hurriedly loading his gun.

Zeke checked his mirror. "Nothing. Some flashing lights but they're way over the other side of the airport. We'll be outta here before they get anywhere near us." He killed the lights and steered them off the road and out into the desert to the north. "They ain't gonna get their hands on us, no way baby."

*

Far to the north of Baghdad, the reunited team cut across the desert for an hour until they were certain Tucker and his men were out of their lives. When they were sure they were alone, Hawke ordered Zeke to pull up on the side of the road and kill the engine.

The silence of the desert is a unique experience. Anyone who has ventured out into these desolate parts of the world understands the deep sense of peace that washes over these endless stretches of sand and dunes.

Hawke had walked away from the vehicle for a few moments to contemplate the scale of what they were attempting in their bid to discover the Land of the Gods. He also considered the raft of new enemies the mission had thrown their way: Razak, Yakuza, McKenna, Kozlov, and now the entire United States military. They sure were in a big barrel of shit, and right at this moment, he had no idea how to get out of it.

When he returned to the Toyota, the rest of the team were gathered around desperately trying to configure the seven rings into an understandable map. It didn't look like they were getting very far.

"Any luck?"

Lea frowned. "Nope. "How the hell are we going to work this out without Ryan?"

"We send them to Washington," Hawke said. "Only Alex can do this."

"Aren't you forgetting that Mokrani's ring is in the hands of the Athanatoi?" Lea said. "I bet the bastard Oracle has already got it on his withered little finger."

"I'm not forgetting it," Hawke said. "I'm banking on Alex being able to do something with the seven rings that might be enough to give us the location, or at least close enough for us to extrapolate the Citadel's location without it."

Hawke laid the rings out on the Land Cruiser's hot

hood and Lea took photos of them from every angle.

"There," she said. "I'll email these to Alex. Fingers crossed she's still safe enough to do something with them."

"Then get onto Rich and update him." Hawke turned and stared out over the desert. "Wherever Alex says we need to go, we're going to need to get there as fast as we can so he needs to organize a transport chopper for us."

"On it."

"So now we wait," he said. "And we rotate sleep shifts with lookout duty."

"Fingers crossed indeed," Scarlet said, repeating Lea's words. Hot dry air rushed over the dunes and ruffled her hair. She lit a cigarette and blew the smoke out into the night. "After all, Life is an adventure, right? An adventure that has to be grabbed with both hands."

*

Alex Reeve looked at the HD images of the rings with a frown on her face. Seven golden rings, each one predating all current evidence of human civilization by countless millennia, and each one a piece of a puzzle that would reveal the Citadel. Strange carvings on smooth faces. Were these lines important or just scratches made by the passing of so many centuries?

"Looks like the team has been pretty damned busy," Kim said.

"I'll say," said Camacho. "But the question is, can you do anything with this information?"

Alex nodded. "Sure, but I have to work fast."

"Very fast," Camacho said.

"Beats sitting around here doing nothing waiting for Faulkner to get us," Kim said, agitated. She looked at her watch. "Where the hell is Brandon? He's been gone nearly fifteen minutes. He said he was going to talk to Frank about what was happening. Maybe he should have gone in a bit heavier."

"You catch more flies with molasses," Camacho said.

"I think I have it," Alex said, turning in her wheelchair. "It's actually not that difficult to work out. It's a variation of a very old way of X." She fired up Google Earth and then referred back to her notes. "If I'm right, it looks like the Citadel is somewhere in the Zagros Mountains on the Iraq-Iran border. On the southwestern side of them... somewhere around here." She pointed to the screen.

Kim frowned. "Doesn't look like anything's there."

"What did you expect?" Alex said. "A giant neon sign?"

"I guess not. Are you sure this is right?"

"It's not *exactly* right because I only have seven of the rings. The eighth would give us the exact location, but this is as close as we're going to get. From there on, it's all down to the guys in the field."

Camacho patted her on the back. "Great work, Alex."

"Just give me a second to write down these coordinates and I'll email them over to Lea."

Brandon burst in through the door, a terrified Kamala Banks at his side. "It's happened."

She looked at him with fear shading her face. "What do you mean?"

"Faulkner's stormed the Oval Office and removed your father from power. They arrested Suzie Matsumoto and took her away someplace else, and there's a team of soldiers on their way here right now to arrest me and you."

He crossed the room and stared down at the images on the phone. "Are they the rings?"

"Yeah."

"Woah," he said. "Any luck?"

"Yeah," she said hurriedly. "I'm just emailing Lea the coordinates." She hit send and dropped her phone. "We have to get out of here, Brandon!"

"We sure do," Kim said.

Brandon picked up the phone and slipped it into his jacket pocket.

"What about the panic room?" Camacho said.

Brandon shook his head. "I know it seems safe, but they'll have a dozen ways of overriding the system and getting you out."

Alex wasn't convinced. "Are you sure?"

She looked longingly at the panic room and felt immediately safe when she saw its heavy eight hundred-pound steel door with its fifteen deadbolts. Specially designed ballistic walls and floors meant no one could fire bullets at them and a high-tech self-defense system consisting of knock-out gas and a direct line to the outside world. There was even a CCTV system and a small bank of monitors from which she could monitor the world, including anyone trying to get into the panic room.

"Trust me," he said. "We have to get out of this place completely, not lock ourselves up inside it."

"Okay," Alex said nervously. "I'm in your hands."

Brandon jumped in behind her and started pushing. "We need to split up."

"Agreed," Camacho said.

"Is your spare wheelchair in here, Alex?"

She nodded. "Sure, why?"

Brandon checked over his shoulder as he wheeled Alex to the door. "Kim, you get into Alex's spare chair and have Kamala and Camacho wheel you to the north exit. Make plenty of noise and get their attention. Meanwhile, I'll take Alex to the south. I know a way out of here. We'll coordinate a rendezvous later.

"Sounds like a plan," Kim said, climbing into the other

wheelchair.

Camacho grabbed the push handles while Kamala drew her gun. "Let's go!"

Brandon gave a proud nod of his head. "Good luck, everyone."

CHAPTER THIRTY-EIGHT

Alex Reeve fought hard to slow her breathing and Brandon McGee pushed her along the corridors on the first floor of the Residence. He wasn't exactly running, but she knew she'd never been this fast in her wheelchair before and part of her was more scared of falling out than what would happen if Faulkner's soldiers caught up with them.

Almost.

"We're nearly there, Brandon. Take it easy."

"Sorry, Alex, but we can't let them catch up with us. They already have the President and we have no idea if Kim and Kamala got away or not. It's a total shit show."

He was right – it was a total shit show and they were the last act. She thought of the expression on her father's face as the marines marched him out to the SUV around the back of the West Wing and felt a rage she had never experienced before.

It felt like blood was boiling in her veins and that her head might explode at any minute. How could they treat him like that? That son of a bitch Davis Faulkner was going to pay for this, that was for damned sure – but how? She was talking about a man who had manipulated the entire US political system and the news networks to effect a coup of the world's most powerful country. How was *she* going to help her father and get back at Faulkner?

She was powerless, like a fly in the Vaseline traps her grandmother used to make when she was a child. There was only one way she had even the slightest chance of saving herself and rescuing her father and that was the

ECHO team, but she didn't even know where they were. The last she had heard they were lost in the Iraqi desert somewhere, up to their necks in sand and flies and being hunted by the Oracle's army of acolytes. It all felt hopeless.

"Take a left, Brandon."

"No, it's a right."

"I've lived here for quite a while now," she said. "We reach the car park if we go left."

"That's the car park everyone knows about, but there's another way out of here."

"I don't understand?"

"There are tunnels under the White House, accessible from several locations under the compound in case we have to evacuate the President in a hurry."

"In a situation like this, you mean?"

"Sure, just like this, only this time the tunnel in the Oval Office was out of the question because Faulkner knew about it and made sure the President got nowhere near it when he stormed the office."

"That bastard!" she said, holding back the tears. She could feel one of her anxiety attacks coming on and once again pursed her lips to push out long, slow breaths. "How far to our escape tunnel?"

"Not far."

"What if he knows about this one too?"

"I won't lie to you," Brandon said, glancing over his shoulder. "He's not going to take over the White House without knowing all about all the escape routes, but we're ahead of him, and the shootout in the West Wing looked like it rattled him. He waited to attack us when he knew we were all together there, so he wasn't expecting anyone to get away, least of all, all the way to the Residency. We're ahead of them, for now, but we don't have long."

"Please God, don't let them get us!"

She realized how pathetic she sounded, but Brandon didn't care. In the short time they'd known each other he'd become more than a secret service agent and they had struck up a good friendship. She knew that right now he wasn't just doing his job and saving the life of the First Daughter, but trying to protect a friend.

"We're here," he said, turning the wheelchair into a narrow corridor.

"This just goes to the kitchens."

"Wrong again, Reeve!"

Without warning and still at speed, he spun around in the corridor as they approached a storeroom cupboard door. He brought the chair to a stop and run his key card through a slot on the side of the door. The light went red and a buzzer sounded.

*

Kim Taylor kept her head down as she walked through the kitchens. As she walked past a pot of tomato sauce cooling on the side, she smeared a handful of it across the chef's whites they had stolen and pretended to be coming off shift. Joining a group of other cooks and waiters, she walked slowly through security.

Camacho and Agent Banks were right behind her, also disguised in the chef's whites and with their earpieces and palm mics discarded in case they were searched. Kamala planned to head out to the Ellipse where many of the White House staff parked their cars before coming into work in the morning, but whether they got there or not was another matter.

Extra security swarmed all over the grounds, including snipers positioned up on the roof of the main Residence building and at all the exits. "My car is parked at the west end of the Ellipse," she said. "Just keep your heads down and we'll be okay. They have a lot of shit going on around here, so we should be able to slip away."

They turned a corner and left the Residence, walking down a long parquet-tiled corridor leading out to the East Wing. Out of sight now, they stripped off the chef's whites and drew their guns again.

Camacho glanced over his shoulder. The coast was clear. "We're heading to the East Appointment Gate, right?"

Kamala nodded. "Right, and from there we go south on East Executive, past the Visitors' Entrance, and then we're almost at my car. From there it's a short drive to my apartment."

"And what then?" Kim asked.

"We have to presume they got Alex and Agent McGee," the senior Secret Service agent said. "So we have to get the hell out of DC or we're next."

"And how do we do that?" Camacho asked. "Our passports will already have been circulated to port authorities and airports."

"I have an idea," Kamala said. "Just leave it to me."

Making sure they were alone, they stepped out of a fire exit and left the East Wing, walking across the neatly manicured grass on their way to the exit. The atmosphere was electric and word spread across the city about what had just happened. Security was being amped up, and as they made their way to the exit, two guards swung the heavy iron gates closed and locked them up.

"Hold it right there," Kamala said, flashing her ID. "We need to get to the Treasury in a hurry."

The guard looked at her ID. "Sure thing, Agent Banks, but I'll need to radio through to the main building first. Just got an order that no one leaves the site without clearance from the Chief of Staff himself."

In a flash, Banks drew her weapon and pushed the

muzzle up against the guard's throat. "Open the gate, now."

"Woah! Take it easy!"

"Do it."

Camacho and Kim drew their weapons and covered the other man. "Do as she says!"

They unlocked the gates and swung them open again. Kim and Camacho slipped through onto the sidewalk as Kamala disarmed the men and took their radios. "Make a move toward us and you're dead. Got it?"

Their facial expressions said they got it, and the three fugitives sprinted down the sidewalk on their way to the Ellipse. Behind them, guards streamed out of the White House, into the Kennedy Garden, and across the South Lawn in pursuit of them.

"We need to get to that car in a hurry, Agent Banks!" Camacho yelled.

*

Alex Reeve swept her hair out of her face and tucked it behind her ears. Looking at Special Agent McGee with fear etched onto her anxious face, she could barely believe what was happening to her. "What's wrong?"

"They canceled my security clearance already."

"So what do we do now?"

Brandon's reply was to draw his weapon and aim it at the door lock. "Shield your eyes!"

She did as he told her and then she heard a tremendous explosion as the gun fired in the enclosed space. A cloud of wood and smoke burst out from the door, and then he kicked it open with his boot and rolled her into the storeroom.

She looked around the tiny space. Buckets, mops, cleaning fluid. "I think you made a wrong turn, Brandon."

"You don't have much faith in me, do you?"

He reached behind one of the shelves and pulled on a hidden lever and she felt her stomach go funny as the entire room started moving downward. "What the hell?"

"We're in an elevator." He stuffed his gun back in the holster.

They descended one floor and the doors pinged open to reveal a dark basement area with a polished concrete floor. Alex blinked twice and then saw the long line of black presidential limousines lined up in a neat row. There were twelve in all, but she could count only ten.

"We could take one of these," she said half-jokingly.

"Yeah right," Brandon said. "Something tells me we wouldn't get very far in the most conspicuous vehicle in the world."

"The tunnel's just over here."

He ran ahead of her and opened the door. Turning to her, he flashed a nervous smile but then it fell from his face and he drew his weapon.

"Brandon? What is it?"

She heard the savage crack of a gunshot and a bullet trace past her right ear. It slammed into Brandon's shoulder and spun him around in a half-circle. He slumped to the floor, grunting in pain as Alex turned to see several soldiers running toward them.

She spun the chair around and started pushing as hard as she could in the opposite direction. She knew it was pointless, but driven by instinct she pushed the wheels around as hard and fast as she could, blisters already forming on her hands.

But it was too late.

The men quickly surrounded Brandon in a hail of screams. "Down! Put your weapon down!"

He obeyed the directive and dropped his weapon. The men were on him instantly, flipping him over and cuffing his hands behind his back.

She knew it was over. She stopped pushing and closed her eyes, feeling the wheelchair slowly coming to a stop. One of the men walked over to her, gun raised into the aim.

"It's over, Miss Reeve. You're both under arrest and coming with us."

CHAPTER THIRTY-NINE

After receiving the coordinates from Alex, the team had flown north in a private helicopter arranged by Sir Richard Eden. Their crossing of the Iraqi deserts was uneventful and some even managed more sleep until they finally reached the Iranian border. Dawn was still hours away, and they landed on some flat scrub south of the foothills before setting up a makeshift camp and waiting for their rendezvous.

Zeke took the night vision monocular and tracked the passage of the two Land Rovers winding along the mountain roads to their west. "I'll bet you a dollar to a donut that's gotta be him. What do you think?"

He passed Hawke the compact optic and the Englishman took another look. "I'd say so, yeah."

"Good," Scarlet said. "Because there's fuck all else out here."

"How long do you think it took him to get here?" Lexi asked.

"Not long," Lea said. "He's only driving over from Mosul."

"It's him," muttered Hawke. "Look at the bloody awful driving. That's him all right, and he managed to get a second vehicle as well. Good lad."

They watched the two Discoveries wind their way through the winding roads of the foothills, behind them the mighty snow-capped Zagros mountains stretched up into the night sky like jagged razors. Hawke walked back to the area of flat ground where Eden's helicopter had dropped them moments earlier and gave the pilot the signal to leave. It rose into the night and turned south, its rotors no more than a faint beating sound cutting into the otherwise silent Iraqi night.

"They'll be here within the hour," Hawke said. "Everyone take some time out."

Hawke and Lea strolled along one of the goat tracks, their faces lit steel blue in the pale light of the desert moon. A breeze blew through the gulley below them, raising the fragrant scent of myrtle, scrub oak, and pistachio into the air.

Hawke turned to her. "How are you doing?"

She tipped her head. "I'm okay, all things considered. For me, this is about closure, and finding what my father wanted to find, but never did."

He nodded. "I know. Just don't be disappointed if we don't find it, or if we do but it's not what you expect. There are no guarantees in this world."

She looked back at the rest of their crew, gathered in the darkness waiting for the ride to what they all hoped and prayed would be their final destination. Scarlet, a woman running from ghosts as she chased illusions. Lexi, the quiet one with a locked heart full of dangerous secrets. Vincent "Reaper" Reno, the lost soul who drifted out of the French Foreign Legion and into ECHO, and who lived for his twin boys. Zeke and Nikolai were fitting in, even if the Russian was a little quiet. Only Ryan was missing, snatched from Mokrani's by the Athanatoi so they could use his mind. If any of them survived this mission, she knew they would be a very different team forever.

"Hey!" Zeke called out. "They're here."

She watched as the two Discoveries turned a hairpin bend to the north and pulled off the sealed road, crunching on the gravel as they parked up beside the team.

"Let's go and see how the old bastard's doing," Hawke said.

They walked back down the track. By the time they reached the group, Hawke's old friend was already out of the Land Rover and dragging on a Turkish cigarette. Ali al-Majid blew the smoke up to the full moon. "It's good to see you again, Joe. How long has it been?"

"Too long, old friend. All good?"

He shrugged. "Life has its ins and outs, you know."

"Ups and downs," Zeke said.

Ali looked from Zeke to Hawke. "Who the hell is this?"

"Meet Ezekiel Jones – one of our newest friends, and this is Professor Qasim al-Hashimi, our archaeological consultant."

Ali held out a hand. "I'm pleased to meet you. Ali is pleased to meet all of you. As Joe says, it's been a long time." The other man climbed out of the second Discovery. "And this is my brother Mohamed."

They shook hands. Hawke said, "How's Abiha?"

"She went to university in America. Now I only get a telephone once a month. She forgets about her old man."

Scarlet wandered over, cigarette hanging off her lower lip. "Fuck me, it really is you, Ali."

"Cairo Sloane! How long has it been?"

"Not long enough, you old fleabag."

They laughed and hugged. Ali took her by the shoulders and fixed his eyes on her. "I trust all is well in your life?"

"My life is the basket-case it has always been. What about yours?"

"Same old same old."

"Still hustling the markets of Mosul?"

A broad grin broke out on his face. "And what else would I be doing?"

He flicked his cigarette into the gravel and crushed it under his boot. "These vehicles are big enough for all of us and your weapons, and…"

Zeke said, "And it's such a shit heap it has the added benefit of drawing zero suspicion to itself?"

Even Nikolai smirked.

Ali shrugged. "I was going to say that they're yours for as long as you want them. The owner is in Iran on business and will not report their disappearance for at least a week if you know what I mean."

Zeke looked at the rusted panels and cracked windows. "Right, thanks."

Ali swung open one of the rear doors. "And there is this much storage in the other one as well – easily enough for the equipment I see here."

"Excellent work, Ali," Hawke said, heaving one of the ammo bags up into the back. The others slowly loaded the gear into the Land Rovers, working silently in the moonlight while Hawke and Ali wandered over to the cliff edge and looked down at the scrubby valley to the west.

"How long to the destination?" Hawke asked.

"As the crow flies, three hours, but the Zagros Mountains are a treacherous place. Winding roads, hairpin bends, avalanches… you call it."

"You name it."

"That's what I meant."

"Either way, old friend, the journey will go through the rest of night and that's supposing we don't come under attack from these people you talked about."

Hawke let the words drift into the valley. "Thanks for coming out tonight, Ali. Even when I told you how dangerous this could be, you never hesitated."

"For an old friend like you? Ali would do anything. You saved my life."

"And you mine. You don't owe me anything, but I would love to see these rings. They sound like something from another world."

"They are," Lea said. "In a manner of speaking."

Ali's brother walked over and the two men waited expectantly to see the ancient rings of the god-kings.

Lea handed them over to Ali and they studied them in the moonlight as the rest of the team packed the rest of their gear into the backs of the two Discoveries. When they were ready to go, he passed them back to her with a goofy grin on his face. "I have stolen many things in my time, but never have I seen such objects of beauty as these. To think they once adorned the hands of the gods is beyond my comprehension. Now I know why you must find this place! If it is filled with treasures like this, I cannot wait to get there!"

"Then lead on, mate," Hawke said. "You're the only one who knows how to get there, after all."

*

They drove through the night, drifting in and out of exhausted, troubled sleep as Ali wound them deeper and deeper into the Zagros Mountains. Desolation met them every time they looked out of the windows. Thickets of brush, wormwood, more scrub oak and kunar trees, and here and there an ibex in a ravine or a startled gazelle.

As they gained elevation and left the steppe behind, thornbushes and juniper trees thinned out to be replaced by acacia and dwarf palms scattered in the dunes. It was an alien landscape, bleak and uninviting and they all felt a sense of dread as Ali drove them further into its desiccated heart.

An hour after sunrise, they pulled off the unsealed track and Ali killed the engine. "This is the closest I can get to the location you gave me. The ground is too rocky for an airstrip, and we're too high for any helicopter to hover. It's on foot from now on, my friends."

The team checked their weapons and followed Ali into the shade of the oak and pistachio trees above the narrow winding goat track. "This is the best way if we wish to go up the mountain."

The march through the mountains was hot and hard and Hawke wondered how Ryan was bearing up over in the Oracle's party. He had trimmed up a lot since they had first met and he was tougher now, but he was without any formal military training, never mind the Special Forces fitness levels some of them could muster. He guessed he might be struggling, and Lexi was slowing down too. He kept it to himself, but even he was starting to get tired.

When he saw a sheltered gully, he knew what everyone wanted to hear. "We can take a break here."

"Thank God!"

Even Ali and Mohamed looked relieved, but Reaper was a different story. His energy was sometimes shocking to behold, and now he sprang up over the final rocks like a mountain goat and jumped down into the narrow gully. Taking it all in he gave a nod of approval and then lowered his pack to the ground. "This is a good place," he said. "We should be able to rest here. I think we can even disguise a fire in these walls, at least enough to hide most of the smoke."

"Great minds think alike," Lea said.

Zeke chuckled. "And fools never differ, sweetheart."

"That's why I chose it." Hawke started to gather the deadwood they had collected on the way and began building up a fire for later. "We stay here until we've recovered and then we move on again. We know the Oracle and his Athanatoi are in the area. We can't afford to go into this battle knackered, right?"

Lea cracked open one of the cans of food. "Too bloody right. We didn't come this far to get killed in the final bloody act, Josiah. We have a family to start."

Hawke gave her a startled look.

"Not *now* ya eejit. When we get home. When all this is over."

Hawke heard her loud and clear. The blood-soaked hopes and dreams they had lived with for so long were coming to an end, and perhaps sooner than he thought. When he turned the next corner on the track, he was shocked by what he saw.

A vast valley cut between two razorback mountains, littered with boulders and scree stretching away from them until fading out in a heat haze.

"Welcome to the Land of the Gods," Ali said, strolling over to the edge of the path and widening his arms to emphasize the enormous scale of the place.

Hawke reached out and grabbed his arm. "Get down!"

"Why?" Ali said.

"Yes, what is it?" Lea said, rushing over to him.

"Je vois!" Reaper whispered.

Hawke pointed across the final gully at a freshly blown hole in the mountain. A group of people was standing around it holding maps and compasses and weapons. The Oracle was clear to see in his broad-rimmed sun hat, and so were his Athanatoi lieutenants. Standing close to Wolff, one of them was holding a gun to Ryan's head.

"Looks like they beat us to it," Hawke said. "How the hell did they know this location?"

"I don't get it," Scarlet said. "They only have one ring – not even Ryan could decipher the Citadel's location from one of the rings. It took everything Alex had to work it out from the other seven."

Hawke frowned. "However they did it, they did it fast and they got here first."

Reaper scanned the gully with his binoculars. "Look over there, to the east."

"What is it?" Lexi asked.

"An Osprey."

Nikolai frowned. "A bird?"

"No, a Bell Boeing V-22 Osprey." Hawke took the binoculars from the Frenchman and studied the chopper. "It's a very powerful, multi-mission Vertical Take-off and Landing aircraft."

"I thought Ali said no chopper could hover up at this altitude?" Lexi said.

"He's right," Hawke said, "but this is no chopper. They were recently upgraded to be able to operate at much higher altitudes, including this one. At least we know how they got here so much faster than us, but the real question is where did they get it from?"

"What do you mean?" Nikolai asked.

"There are only around two hundred of them in service and as far as I know they're all with the US military."

"The Oracle has very high contacts," Nikolai said.

"But still…"

"I still want to know how he got the location," Lea said.

Nikolai pulled up the hood on his jacket. "Do not put anything past the Oracle," he growled. "He is capable of committing any evil to get what he wants."

"I can back that up," Zeke said. "Son of a bitch treated me like an animal in that damned dungeon. When I get my hands on him he's going to be one sorry bastard."

"We have to get to him first," Hawke said.

Lea linked her arm through his. "At least Ryan is still alive!"

Hawke nodded and watched as one of the monks dragged Ryan closer to the hole they had blown in the mountainside. "They're going in, everyone. Let's get moving – we haven't got a second to waste."

CHAPTER FORTY

The Oracle watched as his long life's mission reached its zenith, with the anticipation rising inside him like a lava flow. "You have done well, Bale," he said, turning to the hacker from London. "Without your hard work none of this would be happening, and we wouldn't be about to enter the Citadel."

Ryan said nothing. He looked like he was going to be sick as he watched the Athanatoi working like a well-oiled machine as they set about excavating the last rocks from the enormous entrance tunnel. Ahead of them, a slope receded into the darkness at the heart of the mountain. The Oracle didn't care about how the young man felt. He would be dead within the hour and the unimaginable riches of the Citadel would be his at last. After all this time.

"Perhaps if you swear allegiance to the Order, I will let you live."

"Who's the traitor?"

The Oracle turned to Ryan, cold dead eyes fixed on the young man's dirt-smeared, exhausted face. "What?"

"We're only here because you gave me photos of the other seven rings. There's only one place you could have got them, and that's from the ECHO team. Who is the traitor?"

"You presume too much, Bale. What if I told you I was able to get the images from the original owners of the rings?"

"I would say you are a liar. For one thing, there was no record of the Alexander ring until we found it in the

King's Tomb. The images had to come from ECHO, and that means we have a traitor among us."

"Or someone with a smart head for business. What would you do for ten million dollars?"

Ryan stifled his gasp. So it was true, someone in ECHO had sold out the rest of the team for ten million dollars. Shamefully, his mind instantly thought of Scarlet Sloane and her dream of a private island.

The Oracle was grinning. "I see I've put the cat among the pigeons."

Ryan kept his mouth shut. Could it be Lexi? They all knew she had many dark secrets, and just maybe one of them could only be kept locked away with millions of dollars. After all, what did anyone know about the mysterious Agent Dragonfly? Or Reaper? Surely not, and as for Lea or Hawke, the very idea was ridiculous. That left Alex in Washington, Zeke, and Nikolai. Had anyone else seen the rings?

A sharp nudge in between his shoulders nearly knocked him to the floor. "Move on!"

They walked closer to Ignatius and Absalom who were walking back up the slope, capering after their leader. They spoke with Salazar for a short while, and the senior acolyte turned and made his way over to the Oracle to make his report.

"The men are almost through," he said. "And it looks like the boy was right."

The Oracle felt his heart quicken. "How so?"

"Ignatius found some carvings on the stone floor within the first meter of excavation, and they're just as he described they would be. Eight icons with eight rings above their heads, like halos. This is the Gateway to the Citadel."

"Good, very good."

"But there could be a problem."

The Oracle turned sharply from watching the men down at the rockface and glared at Salazar. "What problem?"

"He also found this." He handed his leader the stone tablet.

"What is it?"

"We're not sure, Oracle. We found it set in the inner wall."

He snatched it from Salazar's hands and stared at it for a few seconds, his eyes crawling over the strange carvings as he desperately sought meaning from them. He relented after a few seconds and thrust the tablet at Ryan, who only just caught it before it crashed into his chest. "I can read the first symbols at the top, but I need your help for the rest. Feel free to decipher them instantly, or die."

He raised a Heckler & Koch P30 and pushed its cold muzzle into Ryan's forehead. "You could be a hero and refuse, but you'd only be a hero for a few seconds. If you help me, you may live another hour."

Ryan curled his lip. "Looks like I'm spoilt for choice."

"I thought you'd see things my way. Now, get translating – my men cannot proceed until we know the meaning of this tablet. It looks like some kind of warning."

Ryan set the heavy stone slab on the sandy ground and knelt in front of it. Like the Oracle, he also recognized the main line of symbols at the top. They were a simple set of pictograms he had gotten used to thanks to the golden icons they had found all over the world. They listed the gods' names and then a warning not to enter the Citadel. Reading the second line of symbols, he was able to extend his life by another few moments.

"It's a warning, but nothing specific. Loosely translated, it says we will incur the wrath of the gods if we continue on our present course."

The Oracle nodded and tightened his jaw. He ripped the tablet from Ryan's hands and smashed it against a boulder. "In that case, Mr. Bale, lead the way."

With a gun in his face, Ryan had little choice but to obey. Dusting himself off he got to his feet and started down the tunnel.

*

"It's time to move out," Hawke said. "Are we all good to go?"

Reaper hefted his submachine gun. "Oui. Mon ami. Let's get this done."

Nikolai leaped to his feet and dusted off his hands. "Just try and stop me. I've waited a long time to get my revenge, and now that time has come."

The exhausted team crossed the narrow river and made their way up the final slope, slipping and sliding on loose scree as they slowly approached the entrance.

"Hawke!" Zeke called out.

The Englishman turned to the Texan who was walking a few meters to his right. "What is it?"

The former tank commander hauled a dead mountain goat out onto the path. "Bullet to the head," he said in his thick Texan twang. "Fresh, too. I'd say they're less than a half-hour ahead of us."

"Then we need to get a wriggle on," Lea said. "We can't let those bastards get their hands on whatever the hell is inside this mountain."

When they reached the freshly blown hole in the side of the mountain, they cautiously followed Ali up the final stretch of the path and stepped inside the cool, dark interior.

They followed the tunnel in awed silence, noting the footsteps of the Oracle and his men in the dirt at their feet.

After another twenty minutes of marching in the damp darkness, Hawke saw something in the sweep of his flashlight beam and called back to the rest of the team. "Up ahead! I see an archway."

The archway was lighter than they expected due to the Athanatoi lamps and glow sticks scattered and dumped around the chamber. Cobwebs hung from gargoyles and a cold wind rushed through the narrow tunnel.

Hawke took it all in without slowing his pace for a second. Ryan was somewhere up ahead and like the rest of his crew, he had no illusions about what the Oracle would do when he had used him to reach the Citadel. His greatest fear was they had already found their way and no longer had any use for him. Every time he turned a corner in the tunnel or one of the vaults, he dreaded finding his friend's body lying in the dirt.

"Wait!" Lea said. "I see something."

She walked over to a chunk of flat stone and crouched lower as she swept her flashlight over its chipped, dusty surface. "I think we have something here, guys."

"It's some sort of stone tablet!" Nikolai said. "Without a shred of doubt – just take a look at it!"

He lifted the heavy tablet fragment and handed it to Hawke who took it and brushed some more of the dirt off its flat surface. "It looks like it's been smashed recently," he said. "I can just about make out what looks like some of their symbols carved into the rock but the damage is too bad to make any sense of it. There's only one person who could do it."

They all knew who he meant.

"But it looks like Ryan already worked his magic," Hawke said. "I'm guessing the Oracle had him translate this and then they smashed it."

"Why?" Zeke asked.

"Too heavy to carry," Scarlet said. "And they didn't

want us to read what it said."

"That's the bit that worries me," Hawke said, staring at the smashed fragments lying in the sandy dirt. "This could have contained any number of important messages – directions, some sort of guidance – a warning maybe."

"Merci, mon ami," Reaper said, his gruff voice rumbling in the vault. He looked from the fragments up at the ceiling of the vault and then down into the tunnel sloping away from them. "Now you have me worried, too."

"If we hurry, I think we can get ahead of them," Hawke said.

Lea looked doubtful. "Really?"

He nodded. "This place is vast. We must be able to find another way through to the actual Citadel, and avoiding their footsteps would be a good start."

*

The Athanatoi followed Ryan down the tunnel until they reached a gigantic cavern full of statues and ornaments arranged in front of a deep, black chasm. One statue towered above all else in the cavernous space, and the head of the ancient cult beheld the enormous object as his men's flashlights swept over its towering contours. In his long, meandering life he had seen nothing like it before. Half-man, half-monster, its dog nose, and snarling teeth took his breath away. "Like the Egyptian deities."

Ryan was confused. "You mean you don't know who it is?"

Salazar furrowed his brow. "None of us knows who or *what* it is. We are merely Athanatoi."

As the Oracle walked over to make a study of the statue, Ryan turned to Salazar. "*Merely* Athanatoi?"

"We are a simple priesthood, given the gift of long life

by the gods who built this civilization so we were able to serve them across the ages."

"Like servants?"

He nodded, the folds of his hooded robe obscuring his face from the flashlights dancing over the giant statue. "The ancients chose us to act like priests, a class of enlightened beings to spread their message to the mortals."

"Wait, you said you were given the gift of long life by the ancients."

"That's right."

"But that's not immortality."

Salazar smiled. "We are not immortal, but the years of our lives are counted in the thousands, so it appears that way to mortals like yourself. Even the ancients were not immortal. Their lifespans were counted in the tens of thousands of years. They gave us the gift of long life so we could serve them better."

"It's all starting to make sense now."

"To a person who lives ten thousand years, a life of even one hundred years is nothing. They could not develop a meaningful relationship with a person with that sort of lifespan. This way, our priest class could pass on their knowledge to their offspring and ensure the ancients were served properly. Four or five generations of Athanatoi across the lifespan of one ancient was the best they could do."

"And that's what the Oracle wants, a life of ten thousand years?"

"Not at all," Salazar said quietly.

"Not enough elixir?"

He gently shook his head. "The ancients did not restrict our lifespans, it was ourselves who restricted it, right here." He tapped his chest.

"I don't understand."

"Even with the elixir, our DNA can only withstand a lifespan of two or three thousand years. The Oracle is coming to the end of his long life. He is here to learn the truth about the ancients, not to seek more life for himself."

As the words sunk in, one question leaped to Ryan's lips. "So the ancients had different DNA?"

"Of course."

"Silence!" snapped the Oracle, turning with a ferocious look on his face. "Hold your tongue, Salazar, or I'll have it torn out and stuffed back down your throat until you choke to death on it."

Salazar crumbled instantly, bowing his head and begging his master's forgiveness, but his pleas were soon interrupted by Ignatius.

"The gods are smiling on us, Oracle."

"What is it?"

The monk raised his hand and pointed out across the chasm. "There, I see the entrance to the Citadel."

The Oracle almost fell to his knees. "Our destiny is before us, my loyal servants."

"Wait," Absalom growled. "There, to the south of the Citadel's entrance. I see movement."

Salazar looked on calmly. "It looks like they're going into the Citadel!"

"Have they seen us?" Absalom asked.

"No, but they have beaten us!" Ignatius said.

The Oracle stared into the gloom with his ancient eyes and when he saw the line of men and women moving toward the chasm. In the vastness of the cavern, they looked like tiny toy soldiers. He curled his lip and spat out one word. "ECHO."

CHAPTER FORTY-ONE

"My God," said Hawke as he swept his flashlight across the chamber and struggled to take in what they were seeing. "This is bloody unbelievable. I've never seen so much carved stone in my life."

"Is this the entrance to the Citadel?" Zeke asked.

"No." Qasim stepped forward. He had recognized the meaning of the carvings at once. "This is some kind of temple, and without a doubt, the entrance to the Citadel. The symbols are vaguely redolent of the much later cuneiform script of the Sumerian civilization, and like those, these are certainly phonograms and very complex ones." He shook his head, sweeping the flashlight beam along the length of the smooth rock. "These have been carved with some sort of stylus, possibly bone, and yet their symmetry is almost too perfect."

Lea leaned in and shone her flashlight on the beautifully carved symbols. "I see what you mean, Dr. al-Hashimi."

"It's incredible, isn't it?" he said. "But like the cut of the rocks themselves, they're just so accurate. It's as if they were carved yesterday using laser technology. This is incomprehensible, my friends."

"So is half of what you just said," Ali said.

Mohamed laughed, but the mirth was cut short when Qasim gasped, drawing the attention of everyone in the chamber.

Hawke broke the stunned silence. "Problem?"

The archaeologist shook his head in disbelief and took a step away from the wall. "I… this is *impossible!*"

"What is?" Scarlet asked.

"I'm not entirely familiar with the way this civilization is dating their epochs, but there are strong similarities with the way the Sumerians did it, not to mention later civilizations, including even us."

"You'll have to elaborate," Lea said.

Qasim looked like he was starting to panic; sweat beaded his forehead as he licked his lips and muttered to himself. Overwhelmed by the information in front of him, he was struggling to make sense of it all.

"I need you to focus, Qasim," Hawke said. "Our time is growing thin."

"I know… I know, but…" he reached a trembling hand out and traced his fingertips along the carved grooves, tears forming in his eyes. "The Babylonian calendar was based on the Sumerian one, and that one appears to have been based on this. If I am right in my interpretation, the Citadel beyond this temple is… no, it can't be!"

"What can't be?" Scarlet asked.

Qasim paled as he turned to face them. "At the time these carvings were made on this rock, the Citadel was already hundreds of thousands of years old. I don't think we're even capable of understanding just how old this civilization was, but we're talking *millions* of years. An entirely different civilization rising and falling right here in our world."

"Well, fuck a duck and call it Daisy," Zeke said. "And I thought Windsor Castle was old."

Scarlet rolled her eyes. "Coarse, but saved by your charisma… and the accent doesn't hurt."

He smiled at her. "You think I'm charismatic?"

"Don't push it, Tex."

"So what happened to them?" Lea asked.

Another shake of the head. "Something must have wiped them out."

"A plague, perhaps?" Reaper asked.

"Or a war," Lexi said.

Hawke felt his heart quicken. "Or some sort of out of control doomsday weapon."

"Wait," Qasim said. "It also speaks of three gates."

"Three gates?"

He nodded, staring wildly at the carvings. He ran his fingers over them as if his mere touch might help translate them. "*Only he who passes the three gates may enter the Citadel.*"

Hawke looked around the tiny chamber. "Must be through that door then, because there's no sign of any gates from where I'm standing."

"Joe's right," Lea said. "There's nothing here. It's all dead now," Lea said, looking at the ruins with a mix of awe and raw contempt. "Nothing left but dust and bones."

"I wouldn't be so sure of that…"

Hawke spun around just in time to see the Oracle's withered, gaunt face move out of the shadows of the entrance they had used to enter it. Behind him, Ryan's face also moved into the light of their glowsticks. What must have been a hefty whack to his face had produced a substantial black eye, and an inch-long cut snaked up from his top lip toward his nose.

"Mate!"

"Ry!" Lea said.

"Still alive and kicking," Ryan said, trying to smile.

The Oracle placed the muzzle of his handgun on the back of Ryan's skull. "Hand your guns over, or I'll put a bullet through his head within three seconds."

Giving his friends an apologetic look, Hawke's shoulders visibly slumped. "I'm sorry, but we have no choice."

"A heartfelt apology, I'm sure," cackled the Oracle.

Massively outgunned, he ordered the team to surrender

their weapons. Seeing Nikolai, he wandered over to him and cursed. "The filthy traitor from the monastery."

"Go to hell, Wolff."

"No, you're the one going to hell. I will kill you personally on the Citadel's altar. My first sacrifice to the gods in their very own temple."

"I bet you don't get bored at weekends," Scarlet said.

"Silence!" he yelled, and then to everyone's horror he turned to Ali and Mohamed. "My thanks to you both for providing the images of the rings."

Hawke looked at Ali with disgust. "What?"

An expression of realization spread on Ryan's face. "I *knew* it! So they're the traitors."

"I don't understand," Lea said.

"I do," Hawke said bluntly. "Back when we packed the gear into the trucks at the chopper landing site. They took the rings away to admire for a few minutes and that's when they must have taken the pictures."

"And that's not all," the Oracle said, beaming with pride at the deception. "Ali here also told me about the location of Mokrani's yacht as well. He has been a good servant."

"I'm so sorry, Joe," Ali said.

"But why?" Hawke demanded.

"The money. I have massive gambling debts."

"But we're paying you a million dollars!"

"And he's paying me ten million," Ali said.

"Wrong," the Oracle said. "I am paying you something *much* more valuable than a mere ten million dollars. I am paying for your journey into the afterlife."

He raised his submachine gun and aimed it at the two brothers.

"No!" Lea screamed.

It was too late. The rounds raked through Ali and Mohamed as if they were made of butter, and dropped both their corpses to the floor, dead on arrival.

"My God!" Zeke said.

The Oracle smiled. "They betrayed you. They were scum. Now, you take us through that door to the three gates," the Oracle said, his voice calm and in command. "And when we get there, you will pass through them first to ensure they are safe. Then, I will take what has been rightfully mine for several thousand years."

*

Passing through the temple's other door, they entered another world of twisting tunnels and caves. Stalagmites and stalactites turned harmless caverns into snapping jaws, and the drip-drip-dripping of underground water reminded them of a ticking clock, counting away the last few moments of their lives.

The tunnel took them into the center of the mountain, and the walk was long and arduous. Winding tunnels, narrow ledges giving way to bottomless chasms, and eerie underground lakes became their universe for the next hour. Exhausted and almost broken by the mission, Ryan tripped and slumped down against the side of a boulder, his legs collapsing beneath him. He searched through his bag for his water and took a long drink. "I'm about ready to drop."

"You just did drop," Scarlet said, glancing over her shoulder at their captors.

"Why is my pack getting heavier?" Lexi sighed and dropped her bag to the sandy ground before collapsing beside Ryan. She snatched his water and took a drink.

"Hey!"

"Mine ran out back there, *boy*."

"That's *my* nickname for him," Scarlet said, grabbing the same water bottle from Lexi's hands and finishing it off. "Anyone else using it is just taking the piss as far as I'm concerned, right *boy?*"

"I'm too tired to argue."

Absalom walked over and kicked Ryan's legs hard. "Get up."

Hawke pushed the Athanatoi monk away, but his show of resistance was met by the sound of multiple cocking handles and the sight of half a dozen submachine gun muzzles. "Back up!"

He followed the orders, hauling Ryan up as he went. Lexi staggered up after him. Hawke never said it, but he was concerned by what the trek had taken out of the team. As a former SBS man, he knew that the most common result to a long, forced-march through tough terrain was usually a bloody gun battle, or even a hand-to-hand, close-quarter knife fight, but Ryan looked like he was just about ready for bed. When it was time to take out the Athanatoi things were going to get nasty. Was his team up to it?

"Move on!" Ignatius yelled.

Another lengthy march down the sloping incline as they moved deeper inside the range, all the time covered by the small arsenal in the hands of the Athanatoi at their backs.

"Wait!" Ryan called out. "I see something up ahead."

"He's right," said Qasim. "It's another giant tablet."

They approached the ancient warning.

"What does it say?" Lea asked.

Ryan stepped forward, Qasim a step to his right.

"It's describing the three challenges, but the word they're using translates as *gates*, as Qasim here read earlier."

"Challenges?"

"Three trials that must be navigated successfully before we can access what they're calling the Way of the

Gods. The first of the three gates is called the Heart of the Gods, the second is called the Mind of the Gods and the third is called the Eye of the Gods."

"This is getting too real for me," Zeke said. "What the hell are we doing in this place? We have no idea what we are doing, or what we're going to find inside this mountain!"

The Oracle stepped forward, scowling. "What do we have to do, Bale?"

"Drop dead," the young man said.

Absalom delivered a solid back-slap and knocked him off his feet.

"Bastards!" Lea said.

Ryan crawled back up. Hawke clamped a hand down on Ryan's shoulder. "What does the first one say, mate?"

With a look of hatred at the Oracle, Ryan and Qasim began translating the second tablet in the ghostly light of the glowsticks and flashlights. Beside it, three narrow stone archways led to nothing but darkness.

"The first gate is the Heart of the Gods," Ryan said, at last, looking at Qasim for confirmation. The Iraqi archaeologist nodded hurriedly, and Ryan carried on as he walked closer to the archways. Pointing to the carved symbols above each one, he said, "The symbol above this archway means something similar to a *library*, the one above this one means *temple*, and the one above this one means *school*."

"What else?"

"There's a riddle here," Qasim said. "It says something like, *There is a room which you enter blind and leave with sight. What is it?"*

"We want the temple," Ignatius said curtly. "You go into a temple seeking enlightenment from the gods, and you get that through prayer." Pushing Ryan out of the way, he stepped through the archway and turned to call the others to follow him. “This way!”

“No!” Ryan yelled, but it was too late.

A trapdoor covered in dust and dirt, impossible to see before, now gave way and sent the Athanatoi cultist tumbling down into a pit of such blackness, none of them had ever seen anything like it before.

The Oracle and the rest of his acolytes started with a jolt and readied their weapons. “What the hell just happened?”

“Your man tried to go to the temple,” Lea said. “And it didn’t work out too well.”

His screams were still audible. “Mon Dieu,” Reaper said. “He has been falling for ten seconds and we can still hear his terror. That pit must be hundreds of feet deep.”

“And completely impossible to go around as well,” Hawke said.

“We don’t want to go around it,” Ryan said. “This riddle gives us the answer, and it’s not a temple.”

“What is it, mate?” Hawke said with a grin.

“School.”

The Oracle peered down into the pit. “And you’re certain?”

“Yes, because it’s an old Sumerian riddle, am I right, Qasim?”

The Iraqi grinned. “Yes, you are. I recognized it too. Not surprising considering that we now know the Sumerian civilization inherited everything they knew from this one.”

“If you’re so sure,” the Oracle said. “You go first. Seems to me that a library is also a room that can enlighten you.”

“I said it’s school,” Ryan said angrily.

The Oracle lifted his gun. “Then, time to go to class.”

Ryan took a deep breath and walked to the archway marked *school*.

CHAPTER FORTY-TWO

As soon as Brandon McGee regained consciousness, he knew one of his ribs was broken. His years as a wingback back in college football meant he was no stranger to the pain now radiating through his abdomen, only this time there would be no coach rushing to his aid with a stretcher to fix his broken bones. Instead, he received another hefty kick in his stomach, delivered by a steel toecap boot on the end of an unknown thug's leg.

He held the grunt in as much as possible. No sense letting these bastards know they could hurt you. Somewhere to his right, he heard Alex gasp in pain and scream *let go of me!* He heard the sound of struggling and kicking, and then another scream. Alex's voice again. Then the sound of an engine starting up. Sounded like they were in the back of some kind of SUV. Probably a Cadillac Escalade, he thought. They had knocked him out back at the White House so he had no idea of his exact location.

He called out in the darkness. "Are you okay, Alex?"

"Where are you taking me?" She sounded frightened, and who could blame her?

"Shut your mouths!"

Chaos reigned inside the back of the SUV. Like he guessed everyone else was experiencing, the nylon sack over McGee's head was blinding him to movements of the enemy. Now, he heard a muffled punch and then Alex's voice a third time as she cried out in pain.

"You sick son of a bitch!" he called out. "You hit a woman with a bag over her head?"

"Not just women," the low voice grizzled. McGee felt a solid punch pile drive into his stomach and he grunted in pain as he slumped to the floor.

"Jesus, we're in trouble…" he mumbled.

"Where's my father?!" Alex said.

"I told you to keep it down!" a voice said.

"This is treason!" McGee called out.

"No, President Brooke is the traitor."

McGee kept his mouth shut. No point giving men like this an excuse to beat you, because they would beat you hard and have no problem sleeping at night. He didn't recognize any of the voices now, so they weren't Secret Service personnel. He guessed soldiers from the rougher neck of the woods, maybe some sort of Special Ops guys Muston had dug up from a black project somewhere.

Either way, his job was still clear: protect the First Daughter at all costs, and if he got shot and killed there was no way he could do that. Keep it zipped, stay calm, remember your training and wait for the right moment, because sooner or later these guys would slip up and give him a chance.

Bide your time, Brandon.

Bide your time.

*

Alex heard the men piling into Brandon McGee and screamed for them to stop. They did, but so did her friend. He'd been silent for a long time and she was worried they'd knocked him out or even killed him. No way to tell under the nylon hood, she gently called out to him but there was no response.

The SUV turned corners, accelerated, and slowed. She was on the floor of the vehicle, and no sign of her chair anywhere. She felt vulnerable and scared. No way to know where they were going either, and no way to know if her father was still alive. Surely they wouldn't murder the President? Her mind pulsed with fear as she struggled to cope with the events of the day. How had any of this happened?

*

A few meters ahead of Alex and McGee, Jack Brooke was also in the back of an Escalade with a bag over his head and his hands cuffed behind his back. His mind raced. What had happened today was almost impossible to believe. Davis Faulkner, the man he had chosen to run as his Vice President and the man he had trusted as a safe pair of hands in the White House if something had ever happened to him had betrayed him in the worst possible way. He had effected a coup d'état against his administration and seized power. He had stormed into the Oval Office with a dozen heavily armed goons at his back and arrested him on trumped-up charges of treason.

It was ridiculous but worse than any of that was Alex.

That son of a bitch Faulkner had threatened the life of his daughter and scared the hell out of her as he hunted her around the Residence. For the coup, he would pay with his freedom, but for what he did to his daughter he would pay with his life.

CHAPTER FORTY-THREE

Ryan had never felt so nervous in his life, but when he passed under the ancient stone archway he knew at once in his heart he had made the right decision. The ground was solid with no trapdoors in sight and when the Oracle was also sure, he had the rest of the ECHO team march beneath the arch just to make sure.

Another lengthy trudge through a tunnel with their heads full of thoughts of escape, and they reached a spiral staircase built into the rock, twisting down into the darkness until the stone steps eventually vanished from view. They looked heavy and solid, but where they led was another question. The thought of stumbling and falling over the edge into the abyss made Hawke and the others debate the sanity of not finding another route.

"There's no other way," Ryan said. "This is it. This is the pathway to the second gate. The tablet was clear."

Hawke pulled a glow stick from his pack. He bent it in the middle, cracking the vial inside and mixing the hydrogen peroxide and diphenyl oxalate until a warm amber light began to glow. He dropped it down into the void and watched with the rest of his team as it fell through the air and disappeared. "Anyone hear it hit the bottom?"

"Not me," Lea said.

"Nor me," said Ryan.

"Then it's a drop of literally hundreds of meters!" Lexi said.

"We've been through worse," said Reaper.

"Yeah, think of all those hours trapped in a pressurized

aircraft cabin with Ryan," Scarlet said, this time offering the young hacker a wink.

He returned the favor by blowing her a kiss. "Thanks, *darling*."

"Hey, that's my line!"

"Enough talking!" Absalom said. "And more walking. Get going down the steps, now!" He slid the bolt on his compact machine pistol and raised it until it was pointing at Hawke's face. "You go first, hero."

Hawke lifted his hands in mock surrender. "Hey, take it easy, mate. I can take a hint just like anyone else."

With the rest of ECHO behind him, plus Qasim at the back, he started down the steps, acutely aware of the lack of any rail or rope, carefully selecting his footing before moving on to the next step. One slip and it was all over, and he hadn't come this far to die on the final furlong.

With only the artificial lights from their flashlights and glow sticks, they moved carefully in the darkness as they followed the curving steps down into the depths of the earth. After a few minutes of walking in circles down the spiral steps, Hawke called out from the front of the line. "I see the glow stick now – it's faint but definitely there."

Lea peered down over the steps and squinted. "Why is it so pale?"

"Probably underwater," he said. "Let's keep moving."

They reached the bottom another quarter of an hour later. Hawke had been right – there was a pool of water around the bottom of the steps and the glow stick was at the bottom now, covered in silt.

"Look!" Ryan pointed into the dark, sweeping his flashlight across another chamber, much bigger than the first. This time there were seven archways, each adorned with its own intricately carved symbol on the keystone.

"It's the second gate," Ryan said. "Another tablet and another riddle."

The Oracle shoved him closer to the wall with the stock of his weapon. "Read it."

Ryan closed his eyes and counted his rage away before turning his attention to the next tablet. "It's similar to the first but harder… much harder."

"What is it?"

"It's mathematical, I think. Do you agree Professor?"

Qasim leaned in and peered at the carvings. "I think so, yes. These are numerals, and that means this is out of my field."

Lea looked at Ryan, her eyes heavy with hope. "But not out of your field, right Ry?"

Ryan scratched his chin before he could reply. The Oracle walked forward again, flanked by his Athanatoi guards. "You had better hope not, Bale."

"I can do it, I think," he said with a heavy sigh. "But it's not going to be easy. "I think we're looking at something to do with ring theory."

Lexi laughed bitterly. "What is it with these guys and damned rings?"

Hawke rubbed his eyes and stared at Ryan in the gloom. "Ring theory, mate?"

He nodded. "In maths, we have something called algebraic structures."

"And here we go again," Scarlet said, turning to Salazar. "Got a cigarette?"

"Shut your mouth."

"Fair enough."

"Algebraic structures?' Hawke asked.

"It's hard to explain to…" he changed tack when he saw the look on Scarlet's face. "It's a tricky subject. Let's just say that there are various structures such as lattices, fields, groups, and rings. It gets more complex still with vector spaces but we don't have to go there now."

Scarlet sighed in mock disappointment. "Damn it."

Ryan shot her a glance. "Fine, so ring theory is the mathematical study and analysis of ring structures, and one of the unsolved mathematics problems we have is the Köthe conjecture."

The Oracle sighed. "I'm growing impatient and so are my men. If this is a delaying tactic, you should know I will start executing your friends one by one, starting with him." He nudged his chin at Zeke.

Absalom grabbed the Texan and hauled him out of the group, forcing him to his knees and putting a gun at his temple.

"You have three minutes."

Ryan was aghast. "Three minutes to solve the Köthe conjecture?"

"Two minutes, fifty-five seconds."

"But the greatest mathematical minds have been trying to solve this for nearly one hundred years!"

"Two minutes, fifty seconds!"

Ryan blinked in the darkness. "Will someone please hold the sodding light up at these symbols!"

Reaper whipped his flashlight up on the wall and Ryan started mumbling under his breath as his eyes scanned the ancient carvings.

The young hacker clamped his eyes shut as he struggled to work out the problem. "*The nil radical is the sum of all potential nil ideals...*"

"Is he speaking in Ryanish again?" Scarlet asked.

Lexi shrugged. "I have enough trouble understanding him when he speaks in English."

"*But if the ring hasn't any nonzero nil ideals then does that mean it hasn't got any nonzero nil one-sided ideals?*"

He was staring at Lea now, his eyes wide open again, but he wasn't seeing her. He was staring right through her into the middle distance. Suddenly he stopped muttering and spoke out loud. "That one." Ryan pointed to the fifth door from the left. “We go through that one.”

“How do you know?” the Oracle said.

“If I tried to explain it you would never understand.”

“An insult to my intelligence… not very wise.”

“It’s the truth.”

“Fine, but once again, you go first.”

Ryan looked defiant. “No problem. I’m telling you the truth.”

“I’m kind of nervous about what we’re going to find now,” Lea said.

“Tell me about it,” said Ryan. “The fact this civilization had thought of and solved the Köthe conjecture hundreds of thousands of years before we did does not fill me with confidence.”

Ryan walked down the fifth tunnel and when he was safely through the others followed him – like before, first the ECHO team and then the Iraqis and then finally the Oracle and his Athanatoi guard.

When Hawke finally reached Ryan, he found the young man staring wildly across another chasm, his eyes mesmerized by something on the far side. He followed his gaze and realized instantly what had transfixed his friend: the entrance to the Citadel was right in front of them, at the far end of a bridge crossing the chasm.

From behind in the tunnel, he heard Lea’s voice.

“Is that *light* up ahead?” Lea asked.

“Come and see,” said Hawke.

“There shouldn’t be any light down here.”

“Just come and see!”

She exited the tunnel and gasped. “Oh my *God…*” her voice was barely a whisper. “I’ve never seen anything like it before!”

“I know.”

“What are those holes around the outside?” she asked.

“Keyholes,” Ryan muttered. “For the idols.”

"What's the delay?" the Oracle barked, pushing his way past Qasim and Zeke. "Why have we stop… oh my *God!*"

As he stared at the vast circular portal, he knew immediately that they had found the Citadel. "Get the idols out," the Oracle snapped. "It's time to enter them into the locking mechanism."

Absalom padded over to Hawke and ripped the bag carrying the idols from his shoulder. Dumping it on the floor, the monk carefully unpacked the idols Eden had shipped from London and walked with them over to the circular gate.

The Oracle fixed his gaze on Ryan. "You! Insert these idols in the correct holes and unlock the third gate."

Ryan and Qasim studied the symbols above each of the holes and then started inserting the idols one by one. When the last one had been slotted into place, a heavy sigh emanated from the circular portal and the round portal clunked open in a cloud of dust.

"Looks like we made it," Hawke said.

Lea held his hand. "I always knew we would."

"Very touching," the Oracle said cruelly. "Now you can be the first to go inside."

Hawke and Lea exchanged a glance. "If we don't make it," he said.

She raised her finger to his lips and silence his words. "We'll make it."

As the Oracle cocked his submachine gun and yelled at them to get moving, Hawke and Lea stepped through the circular entrance and disappeared into the dust.

CHAPTER FORTY-FOUR

After an unknown time on the road, Alex heard the Escalade screech to a halt and the sound of the side door opening. She felt someone grab her by the arms and heave her up out of the footwell. His fingers bit into her arms as he pulled her from the car and told her to stop struggling. "Hey, take it easy! You're hurting me!"

"I'll do a lot more than hurt you if you don't shut up!" he barked.

When the man dragged her from the car and swung her over his shoulder again, she knew instantly where she was. She smelled jet fuel and heard the whine of jet engines. She knew from her time with the ECHO team that it was a small, private plane – maybe a Gulfstream or a Citation. She couldn't be sure, but maybe it mattered. With the bag over her head, she couldn't see the aircraft's registration number, but she had to do whatever she could to try and identify the plane.

The man carried her up the airstair and then she heard the door slam shut behind her as he threw her down onto a chair. "You asshole!"

"Alex!"

Her father's voice.

Thank God.

"Dad! Are you okay?"

"Not so much. I guess they have a bag over your head too, huh?"

"Yes. Where are we?"

"My best guess is Andrews, but maybe not."

She felt a surge of pity for her father. He was a good

man. A trustworthy, decent man, and he had been betrayed by those closest around him. Some of them, like that son of a bitch Faulkner would still be at the CIA if he hadn't hand-picked him as a running mate before the last election.

"What's going on, Dad?"

Now she heard McGee moaning in pain. At least she knew he was alive.

"It's a coup d'état, Alex."

She heard men laughing.

"It's the legal removal of a treasonous President from his office."

Was that Muston's voice?

"You can call it what you want, Josh, but we both know I have not committed treason. The very idea is ridiculous."

Alex felt like crying. "This can't be happening."

"What you call ridiculous, I call a great news cycle. Right now, images of the ECHO team murdering innocent Americans are plastered all over every news network, and the little ticker under those pictures is telling the public that you ordered them to do it – neat, huh?"

"You son of a bitch!" Alex's heart was beating too fast now. A panic attack was on the way if she couldn't fight it away and calm down.

"Easy, darling," Brooke said. "Just take it easy. No one's going to buy that bullshit. It's a total crock and everyone knows it."

Muston laughed and casually ordered the pilot to take off. "We're going, Captain Richards. The President just gave the order to take off."

"The President?" Brooke huffed out a cynical laugh. "That bastard couldn't preside over a damn thing, never mind this country."

"He seems to be doing fine so far," Muston said. "He's

already ordered a full investigation into your criminal activities and has the full support of the Cabinet and the Congress. They were very interested in the documents linking you to the international terrorist force, ECHO."

Alex recoiled at the words. "ECHO isn't a terrorist organization!"

Her father was much calmer. "You mean the documents you forged to frame me."

"You say potato, Jack…" he laughed.

Brooke's voice hardened like steel, but stayed level and clear. Alex knew he wouldn't give these men the satisfaction of knowing they had gotten to him. "When I get through this, and I will, you're going to spend the rest of your life in a federal prison sewing laundry bags. I hope you understand that."

A long pause. Alex had thought her father's words had struck a nerve, but when she heard Muston's voice as he returned from the cockpit, she knew the bastard had just walked off. "What was that, Jack?"

"I said I hope you're ready for a life behind bars."

"I'm not, and that's because I'm not going to spend the rest of my life behind bars. Sadly, the same cannot be said for you."

The plane finished taxiing and stopped momentarily on the runway as they awaited clearance for take-off.

"You live by the sword, you die by the sword, Josh. Know that."

"That's very wise, Jack, but it's you who's going to die by the sword. You might be the people's big hero, but the Presidency isn't there to serve the people. No government is there to serve the people. Governments are there to serve something darker, something older and nastier that cares only about itself."

"What the hell are you talking about?"

"You wouldn't understand, but know that we spend

our lives stopping wholesome family men like you from reaching the top. Sometimes we screw up, the zeitgeist blows the wrong way and then you just have to go. It's all very sad. If only people like you would accept there's no such thing as democracy. Those of us behind the curtain know it, and now you do."

"You sound like a madman."

"Hey, you're in good company."

"What the hell does that mean?"

Muston laughed, a loud cynical laugh. "What do you think it means, Jack? It means you're not the first president we had to remove from office. If any of you guys get into the Oval and we don't approve of you, or you won't do our bidding, then one way or another you're outta there."

"Oh my God..."

"Right, you get it. Good. You're a lucky son of a bitch, I know that. The history books were supposed to say you got killed in a terror strike on Air Force One over England, but Mr. Nine Lives went and survived it. Then you were supposed to have been killed in a freak tsunami in Miami Beach, but yeah, you guessed it – Mr. Nine Lives goes and gets out of that, too." He paused a beat as the aircraft ripped off of the runway and shot up into the air. "Let's just say that this time we took a different approach, a more nuanced approach, and this is where your nine lives run right the fuck out. You're done, Jack. Washed up. Out for the count."

"I can't believe I'm hearing this," Alex said.

"Take it easy, darling," Brooke said.

"Believe it," Muston walked over Brooke and leaned right over him. "And don't you think about trying to get up off the mat or your next stop is a coffin, for sure this time. And your kid here goes in one, too."

*

After hiding out in a side street out of the range of CCTV cameras for a short while, Kim, Camacho, and Kamala Banks were now making their way across to a parking lot south of the White House.

"It's right there," Kamala said, pointing at a white Chevrolet Impala at the end of the parking lot. "Let's hope Hank gave me the right keys."

"Hank?" Kim asked.

"A friend of mine – works as a steward in the Residence. I ask to borrow his car just before the shit hit the fan because I figured they'd be looking for mine."

"Smart move," Camacho said.

"We're almost there," Kamala said. "Keep going! I have a way we can get out of the city but we have to get to my apartment first because I need to get some pills. They're important and I can't go on the run to some foreign country without them."

"I didn't know you were on medication."

"No one does, but that's a story for another time. Keep running!"

Kim's lungs felt like they were going to explode. Never in her life had she run so fast, and now she was just about ready to collapse on the ground.

Kamala blipped the locks. "Thank you, Hank!"

They climbed in and she hit the gas, spinning the wheels and reversing the car at speed out of the lot. She spun the wheel hard to the right and the car surged forward. "We'll be at my apartment in a few minutes. It's not far."

She navigated the Impala through the streets of a panicked city, using her knowledge of the backstreets to make fast progress. When they pulled up on her road, they had calmed down and reloaded their weapons.

"So what's this idea about how we escape?" Camacho said.

"Yeah," Kim asked, heaving the words out as she struggled to get her breath back.

Kamala was fitter, but still fighting to slow her heart. "If we can get to the airport my brother can get us out of the country," Kamala said. "He works as a pilot for UPS flying cargo 747s. Goes all over the world. We just have to get to the airport and get through security to airside and we should be fine… for now."

"How far is your apartment, Kamala?"

"Not far, we'll be there in another five minutes."

Kim checked the news on her phone. "Dammit, it's already out there, guys. It says Brooke's been removed from office and arrested on charges of treason."

Camacho and Kamala both turned to her and spoke the same word at the same time: "What?"

Kim showed them her phone. "See for yourself."

"Holy shit!" Camacho said. "This is like a nightmare."

"Only one you can never wake up from," Kamala said, pulling her keys from her pocket. "We're nearly there. It's just up here on the right."

Kim glanced anxiously around the neat, narrow street. She did not see the black Dodge Ram pulling up at the end of the road.

Kamala pushed the key in her front door and turned the lock. "All right, I'll get the pills, and then we're out of here."

Kim felt the bullet tear right through her heart and burst out through her chest leaving a hole the size of a cantaloupe. She coughed, but no sound came out. She reached for the wound but there was just too much blood.

"Fuck!" Camacho drew his gun and crouched behind a parked car as he raised the weapon into the aim. "Kim? Are you okay?"

"Oh, *Jesus!*" Kamala rushed to her and caught her before she fell over. "Hang on, Kim!" She skidded to her knees and cradled her friend's head in her arms.

Camacho scanned for the shooter but saw nothing except the rear end of a black Dodge pickup slowly turning the corner at the end of the road.

Kim felt her body turn to ice, cold and stiff. She tried to move her head but nothing happened. Tunnel vision. Whistling in her ears. Looking up, she saw the kind, terrified face of Kamala Banks.

"I…"

Kamala swallowed hard and fought back the tears. "Hush, baby…"

"But…"

"You're going to be okay, Kim." But they both knew it was a lie. The sniper had completely blown her heart out.

Kim felt herself slipping away now. The ice had turned to water and she was numb all over. "Get… out… of… here…"

Her mind started to whir like a projector showing an old photo reel of her life.

Her father, her mother… but younger now – no lines around their eyes. The hopeful smiles of youth on their faces. She got it now. They were how she knew them when she was a little girl. She hadn't seen them like this for thirty years.

Still cradling her head, Kamala craned her neck to scan for any sign of the sniper. "Where are you, you goddam son of a bitch!"

"I think he's long gone," Camacho said, scrambling over to his old friend. When he saw the wound, he almost stopped breathing. "You're going to be fine, Kim… hold on."

The fresh green grass of her backyard. A blue sky with

not a single cloud. A kind, soft world bursting with possibilities. A yellow swing and a pink paddling pool. Her parents in each other's arms and play slaps and stolen kisses. She smelled home cooking and milkshakes. Laughter floated up into the air. Everyone was smiling.

Kamala had drawn her weapon and was still scanning the area for the sniper but could see no sign of him. "Stay with me, Hun."

When Kim's mother stepped out of the kitchen, she was carrying a birthday cake.

And when her father kissed her on the cheek and said, "Happy Birthday, darling," she smiled and closed her eyes forever.

CHAPTER FORTY-FIVE

When the dust settled, a world of unrivaled beauty dawned on Hawke and Lea. They had stepped into a vast chamber the size of the mightiest cathedral, with an intricate vaulted ceiling resembling the rib cage of some gigantic undiscovered beast.

The stone walls were perfectly smooth, hewn by masons over centuries, each giant block receding at the edges into a perfectly beveled camber and everything was bathed in a peaceful turquoise color by some kind of concealed lighting. In the center of it all was a large iron sphere set atop a golden pedestal.

Lea Donovan tried to gather an idea about its scale as she traced her eyes up to one of the many supporting columns until eventually reaching the intricately ornate vaulted ceiling hundreds of meters above them. Gently running her hand over one of the honey-colored blocks as she took in the impressive sight, she whispered something only she could hear. "I wish you could have seen this, Dad."

After a period of stunned silence, Hawke spoke. "Amazing."

"Reminds me of the time my parents took me to visit the Basilica in Rome."

"And yet it looks so *modern*," he said.

With the Athanatoi still behind them, Lea reached out for Hawke's hand. He took it in his and gave it a reassuring squeeze. "This is making me nervous, Joe."

"Tell me about it. We've seen a lot of tombs and temples but nothing like this."

"They're always dead places, dry and dusty. Brittle bones and chipped relics, but this… this is like something from another world."

Her eyes danced over the gleaming golden surfaces of the temple's interior, the impeccable and intricate ornaments, untouched by the passing of eons.

"It looks like something out of the movie *Alien*."

She turned to see Ryan behind her. They were all in here now, including the Oracle and his Athanatoi. Also stunned by the awesome spectacle, they meandered around the structure with open jaws trying to take it all in.

"Weird," Lexi said. "*Alien* was the first thing I thought of too."

"But it's not a ruin," Hawke muttered.

Reaper turned to him. "Hein?"

"It's not a ruin," he repeated. "These ancient tombs, temples, and chambers are always old ruins by the time we get to them. Hundreds of thousands of years old, they're crumbling old wrecks today. This place looks like it was built this year."

"It looks like it was built about a thousand years from now, more like," Ryan said. "I've never seen materials like some of this stuff. Look at the walls! Look at the way the ceiling arches are constructed. I don't know how any of this is possible."

"That's because you don't have the mind to know what you're seeing." The Oracle pushed past them and walked out into the center of the giant structure. He raised his hands in the air and when he spoke, he raised his voice to a shout and his words echoed eerily around the gigantic space. "This is the Citadel! The beings that built this place built it millions of years before humans even crawled out of the swamp! Their technology had reached levels we may not attain for thousands of years if we get there at all without killing ourselves. Now I am here to claim it all!"

"We're going into crackerjack territory again," Lea said.

"Silence!"

"The last thing I want to do is upset you, Wolff," Hawke said. "So before I do that I'm going to tell you what an arsehole you are."

The Oracle ignored the insult. "Your time on this planet is short, Englishman." He walked over to the towering iron sphere in the center of the building, carefully climbing the golden steps as if approaching a religious site. "I cannot believe I am finally in the Altar Room!"

"My destiny shall be fulfilled. Absalom! Start the search for the weapons."

"Yes, Oracle."

"Salazar, keep your gun aimed at the scum."

"Yes, Oracle."

The old man took the last few steps until he was parallel with the sphere. His eyes danced all over the dark iron ball in search of some unknown thing only he was aware of.

"What's he doing?" Zeke asked.

"You can never tell with him," mumbled Nikolai.

Laying his hands on the equator of the metal sphere, he began muttering some kind of prayer now, and the sphere began to glow blue at the poles.

Zeke took a step back. "This shit is way above my pay grade. This is voodoo."

"It's not magic," Nikolai said grimly. "It's technology."

"Could have fooled me, but then I'm just a tank commander, so what do I know?"

"No, he's right," Ryan said. "It's Clarke's third law."

"Clarke?"

"Arthur C. Clarke," he said. "The famous science

fiction author. His third law states that any sufficiently advanced technology is indistinguishable from magic."

"To dumbbells like us you mean?" Lexi said.

Scarlet raised an eyebrow. "Speak for yourself, darling."

The sphere was brighter now, a dull dark blue at the equator but a brighter neon color at the poles where it had first started glowing. When the Oracle screamed, his voice was a hoarse cry of insanity. "The world will be rent asunder by the powers this will give me!"

Reaper was in awe, moving closer to the sphere. "Mon Dieu! This color I have never seen before."

"Get back!" Salazar barked, lifting his weapon. "Or I'll shoot."

The former French Legionnaire looked at him like he was scum and took a step back into the line beside Lea and Ryan.

As the Oracle continued to chant his mantra, Absalom returned and nervously approached his leader. "The place is empty, sir."

The Oracle snapped, "Empty?"

"No weapons anywhere to be seen," he said. "No technology of any kind."

"Or knowledge. The libraries are empty."

"What? Search again!"

Hawke turned to Lea and lowered his voice to a whisper. "I'm looking for an egress point. Something tells me this is not going to end well, and when the shit starts flying, we're going to need to get out of here in a hurry."

"What about that over there?" Lea pointed to the west side of the sphere. "Looks like some sort of ledge with an archway in it."

Hawke shook his head. "That's no good. Look more closely and you can see it's on the other side of a chasm, at least twenty feet wide. I can't see the bottom but going by everything else I've seen around here I'm going to guess it's a long way down."

"No, further up there's a rope bridge."

He saw it now, barely visible in the darkness on the far side of the temple, toward the northern end of the vast space.

The sphere was humming now and glowing so brightly they had to look away. Somehow, the Oracle was able to stand right in front of it, his arms stretched out by his sides as he repeated his mantra over and over again, the alien words tumbling out of his dry lips.

Then the sphere exploded in light, almost blinding them all. When the bright blue flash receded, they all saw the sphere was now a circular gateway filled with spinning, swirling gases, and bolts of cyan electricity.

"Okay then," Lea said. "It's going to be one of those days."

Hawke turned to a mesmerized Ryan. "What's going on, mate?"

"Looks like some sort of plasma," he said nervously. "To be honest, it's beginning to frighten the shit out of me."

"Moi aussi," Reaper said.

"Over there!" Zeke yelled. "We got incoming!"

Hawke saw them next. At least a dozen men and women in white robes running through the arches at the rear of the temple.

The Oracle saw them too his face painted white with shock and terror.

"Who the hell are they?" Lexi said.

"I don't know," Hawke said, "but whoever they are it doesn't look like Wolff knows either."

"And what are those weapons?" Reaper said.

Lea took a step back. "They remind me of those weird crossbows Razak pulled out of the dirt back in the jungle."

The white-robed figures streamed out of the archways and began firing on the Athanatoi with a vengeance.

The Oracle's men took up positions of cover and returned fire, forcing the white-robed guardians into positions of cover on a ledge running above the sphere.

"We're out of here," Hawke said. "Zeke, check if we can get out of here the way we came in. Take Kolya."

"You got it, boss."

The team watched the two recruits as they jogged away into the gloom, not knowing if they would ever see them alive again or not.

A furious Lea turned to Hawke. "We can't just go! We don't know anything about this place! We have so much to discover!"

"You can't discover anything in the grave, Lea."

"What about my Dad?"

"We know where it is now," Hawke said. "We can return with a bigger force."

"But..."

"We know enough." Ryan reached out to her. "We know there was a civilization on this world millions of years ago. We know they had different DNA and could live for thousands of years. We know this was their capital, and we know they seeded the world as we know it, using their idols to create new societies."

In the center of the temple, the white-robed figures were gradually overcoming the Athanatoi. The firefight intensified, but the Oracle refused to take cover. Standing tall before the sphere, he was soon strafed by bullets and bolts of blue neon from the white-robed guardians' weapons, ripping into his upper legs and cutting him down where he stood.

His bloodcurdling screams made everyone turn and stare as he continued to crawl forward, blood pouring from the terrible wounds in his thigh. He stretched his arm desperately toward the glowing circle. “Please… show me the light!”

A thundercrack of electrical discharge and then he was wrapped in the blue plasma.

“Oh, Jesus!”

Hawke saw the Texan and Russian Athanatoi monk stagger back over from the main entrance and then a loud explosion behind them. “What is it, Zeke? Can we get out that way or not? Did I hear firearms down there?”

He stumbled over to them, a fresh bullet wound gouged into his shoulder. “We’re in deep shit, guys. That noise was the sound of around a hundred Special Ops making their way into the heart of this mountain right about now.”

Hawke darted his eyes over to the Texan. “Who?”

Zeke whipped off his battered and torn ten-gallon hat and wiped his brow. “Can’t be sure, but my best guess is the US.”

“Which makes sense given Faulkner is now the President,” said Lea.

“A hundred?” Scarlet said.

Zeke nodded. He looked nervous for the first time since they’d seen him. “At least, and those boys sure are tooled up. They have enough weapons to take Moscow. M134 miniguns at fifty rounds per second, pintle-mounted machine guns, swing-arm GPMGs, you name it.”

“We can take them!” Ryan said.

“No,” Hawke said coolly. “We can’t. We’re good, but we’re not that good. We’ve been on the road for a long time. We’re exhausted and we’re injured and we’re out of ammo. There’s no way we’re beating over a hundred Special Ops guys freshly fed and looking for a fight, especially as we also have those white-robes guys to think about.”

With the Athanatoi guards heavily pinned down under incoming fire, Hawke led the ECHO team behind the support columns and around the outside of the temple to the rope bridge Lea had noticed moments earlier.

"It's almost in sight!"

A white-robed man appeared on the other side of the chasm, a submachine gun in his hands. When he raised the weapon, Hawke screamed at the team to take cover, but before they had hit the dirt, the man in the robes was blasted off his feet by Athanatoi fire. With his white robes covered in deep red blood, he crashed down into the dirt on the far side of the chasm.

"Keep going!" Hawke yelled. "This is our only chance to escape this nightmare."

Barely alive, the man in the white robes crawled through the dust and gravel and filth, pulling a grenade from his belt. He pulled the pin and threw it at the chasm where it detonated and blew the rope bridge into a thousand pieces before slumping down to the ground.

Lea turned to Hawke, bullets tracing over their heads. "What now?"

"Wait, I've got a great idea!"

CHAPTER FORTY-SIX

Lea put her hands on her hips. "What's this great idea, Josiah?"

"Rope!"

Hawke tore off his pack and pulled out a length of thick climbing rope. He tied one end around the remains of the previous rope bridge and then grabbing the other end he sprinted toward the chasm.

"Is he crazy?" Zeke said.

"Yes." Nikolai shook his head, fully expecting the Englishman to fall into the void, but those in the team who knew him had more hope.

Drawing on his vast parkour experience and formidable strength, Hawke leaped over the chasm, flying across the bullet-streaked void and landing with a heavy crunch in the gravel on the far side. The mayhem that had unfolded since the arrival of the new soldiers was like nothing he had ever seen before. Foreign Special Ops teams, Athanatoi cultists, and this unknown new force now fought rucked and brawled wherever they found each other in the massive system.

With hot lead chewing into the rocky path all around him, Hawke launched himself into another parkour roll until he was behind the cover of a jumble of boulders at the base of the rock wall. Securing the rope to a hefty boulder, he created a way for the rest of the team to cross the startling void surrounding the Citadel.

One by one, the team monkey-crawled over the void while Hawke provided cover fire on the few Athanatoi who weren't engaged in a desperate fight for survival against the mysterious white-robes. Behind it all, the Special Ops team was fanning out and searching for something. Other Athanatoi tried to defend a position leading to an unknown corridor but the men in black combat fatigues dispatched them in seconds with their carbines.

With Lexi halfway across the rope, a vicious explosion detonated and blasted Qasim off his feet. With a terrible, bloodcurdling scream he tumbled down into the chasm, one of his legs blown clean off.

Lea turned away, unable to watch the horror as the mutilated archaeologist fell to his death at the bottom of the gaping chasm.

"Hurry!" Hawke yelled. "No time to think about that!"

Lexi landed behind him, sprinting over to his newfound cover as the enemy rounds bit at their heels. Ryan and Zeke were still pinned down on the other side of the chasm but managed to crawl through the dirt until they reached the bridge. One by one with Ryan in the lead they monkey-crawled over the void while Reaper and Nikolai were engaged in a terrible firefight further along the gaping crevasse.

Reaper stayed behind to pour cover fire on the enemy while Nikolai made it to the end of the frayed rope bridge and made his way across. When safely on the other side, the Russian returned the favor by firing on the soldiers while the former legionnaire ran at top speed across the wobbling, shaking bridge. Bullets tore into the suspender cables and blasted them apart. The bridge collapsed away, slowly falling into the chasm as the Frenchman sprinted for all his life to the other side.

With seconds to spare, Reaper leaped to the far side of the chasm and grabbed on with both hands as the rest of the bridge collapsed from under him, falling with a smack until it lay flat against the rock wall from where he was dangling.

Hawke saw it all with horror on his face. His old friend was a living target for the assorted soldiers and mercs on the south side of the chasm.

They turned their guns on him and fired.

"Your hand!" Nikolai screamed.

Reaper thrust his right hand into the air and the Russian monk grabbed it with all his strength, pulling the heavy ex-merc up out of the void as the bullets smashed into the cliff face all around him. Rocks exploded into dust as Nikolai finally managed to heave Reaper clear of the danger. Both men scrambled for the cover Hawke had established.

"That was too close!" Reaper said, turning to Nikolai. "Merci, mon ami. You have made a friend for life."

Nikolai saw the out-stretched hand and hesitated. Then, he took the Frenchman's hand and the two men shook hard. "You would have done it for me."

Reaper gave his customary one nod. "Yes, of course."

The moment was shattered by Scarlet's voice, harsh and cold in the chaos. "It's Lea! She's been wounded!"

Hawke looked across the chasm and saw her under heavy fire. Someone had almost killed her with a bullet but it looked like the round had created only a flesh wound. The problem was that the shot had knocked her off her balance and now she was tumbling back into a smaller gorge to the south of the chasm.

And it looked like it was full of water.

"Lea!" Grabbing his pack, he sprinted for the rope bridge with everything he had.

*

Lea felt herself falling deeper into the darkness. For a second, time stopped, and then she felt a hard smack as her body broke through the surface of the icy black water. Immediately she felt the cold, scratching at her like claws of steel as she plunged ever deeper into the water.

She wanted to cry out for help, but instinct sealed her mouth. It felt like a million needles were sticking into her body now, and her arms and legs were growing numb. She knew from her army training she had only a few seconds to get her bearings and swim to the surface before she lost consciousness.

Remembering what Hawke had told her about when he fell into the crevasse in Pavlopetri, she spun around in the water and blew out some air. The bubbles showed her the way home, and she started to swim up to the surface with all the strength her muscles could muster. The agony of pushing through the freezing water was almost more than she could bear, but now there was a faint light in the darkness.

Above her, on the surface, she saw a familiar face.

Hawke jumped in and grabbed hold of her, pulling her to the edge of the gorge and hauling her out of the icy water. On the dry ground now, he slung her over his shoulders in a fireman's lift. "Fancy meeting you here."

"You took your damned time, Josiah. I could have made a cup of tea in the time it took you to get your sorry arse over here."

"I'm so sorry about that."

"You're forgiven… what are you doing?"

With Lea still over his shoulders, he pulled his canteen from his pack and filled it with water from the gorge. "Just a hunch," he said quietly. "Now hold on tight!"

"Is there any other way to hold on to you?"

He rolled his eyes, and with bullets spitting at their feet and tracing past their heads, they made it back to the improvised rope crossing. "Listen, it's one at a time from here on, can you do it?"

She gave a quick nod. "I can get across their no problem, it's walking when we're on the other side that's going to give us grief."

He smiled at her. "We'll cross that bridge when we come to it."

"Eejit."

"Get across the bridge!"

She crawled across, with the team on the other side covering them while Hawke secured the other end of the rope.

"Hurry up!" Hawke fought with everything he had to keep the rope from slipping and hold the bridge in place. Pain tore through his body as the rope started to slide through his grip and scorch friction burns into his arms. Behind him, the Special Ops troops saw what was going on and started to make their way over. "I can't hold this thing for much longer!"

"I'm almost there!" Lea called back, ducking to avoid another strafing from the automatic weapons up on the ridge. "Just another few seconds."

When she was across, Hawke picked up the rope and sprinted to the chasm, once again leaping right the way across and smashing down into the dirt on the other side. A few back slaps of admiration from the team were cut short when a colossal explosion rang out in the center of the temple.

They turned to see the Oracle writhing like a dying snake in front of the sphere, now even brighter with the strange liquid-like plasma.

"Why doesn't he run away?" Zeke said.

"What's he doing?" Lexi asked. "He's crazy!"

"We already kind of knew that!" Ryan said.

The force of the blue plasma streams spun the Oracle around so fast his wretched, agonized figure became a blur to those watching his demise. Snaking together as they wrapped around him and covered his body, the neon plasma trails sparked and crackled and forced their way inside his eyes and his ears and his mouth.

His desperate screams for mercy went unheard under the heavy buzzing sound of the storm inside the iron sphere.

Lea Donovan felt like she was staring into the eye of God himself as the circle of flames increased in power and flooded the inner chamber with the neon blue light. It pulsed out an even mightier jet of plasma into the Oracle's ancient body and lifted him off his feet, holding him in the center of the chamber. Without any warning, the men and women in the white robes began retreating and fleeing the Citadel.

"They're leaving," Ryan said.

Scarlet nodded. "They know something we don't, that's for sure."

"And so is Salazar!" Lea said. "Look – he's going down one of the tunnels we came down when we arrived."

"He'll never make it," Ryan said.

For Lea now, time stopped. It crawled to a standstill like a dying friend as she drowned in the strange glowing light. Bewitched by the lights and only dimly aware now of the Oracle's terrified dying screams, she turned to see Joe Hawke beside her, his unshaved dirt-smeared face glowing the same ghostly blue that was seeping into the pores of everyone else in the chamber.

She felt like she was being hypnotized by the swirling blue and orange lightning bolts as they streaked around in circles and crackled and licked at the sides of the mysterious spherical monument. Unable to take her eyes away, she began to see the face of her father slowly forming in the electrical chaos in front of her. "I must be hallucinating…"

Another vast explosion, and when the light receded the Oracle was gone.

CHAPTER FORTY-SEVEN

The team shared a terrified glance in the silence.

"Where did he go?"

"Is he dead?"

"Or did he go inside the sphere?"

"It's... the... same... thing..."

Turning, they saw the man in the white robe at their feet, his body and face caked in drying blood.

"I thought he was dead?" Ryan said.

They gathered around the white-robed man. "Who are you?" Lea asked. "Part of the Athanatoi?"

The man's cracked lips turned into a half-smile. "Never."

"Then who?" Reaper repeated, scrunching his shirt up in a ball in his meaty fist and shaking him like a straw doll. "Who?"

He leaned forward, blood on his lips and his eyes rolling up into his head.

"We're losing him!" Lea said. "Dammit!"

"Have you heard the name Koru?"

Reaper shook his head and mumbled as he stared up at the others and then back down to the dying merc. "Non."

"You have now," he said weakly. "And you will be wise never to forget that name."

"What's so special about the name Koru?" Lea asked.

But the man was almost dead. He slumped limply down in Reaper's grip. The Frenchman laid him gently down to the deck. "Koru? What does this mean?"

"It means trouble... big trouble for you all."

"Bugger me," Scarlet said. "Not again."

"We are the chosen guardians of this place, or *were*… defending it for millennia, until this sacrilegious day."

Shots rang out behind them as the Special Forces gradually overwhelmed the dwindling numbers of Athanatoi. Turning, Hawke saw Absalom take a direct hit from a grenade and get blasted into the chasm. "Another one bites the dust."

Lea crouched down and cradled his head. "I'm sorry if we intruded into some sort of sacred place, but what *was* that thing?"

"That was the third gate," Ryan said, clambering up to his knees and dusting himself down. "Am I right?"

The Guardian gave a shallow nod. "That was the Eye of the Gods."

"A gate to where?" Hawke said hesitantly.

The guardian simply smiled.

Lea was stunned and struggled to find the words. "But what does this all mean?"

"You cannot win," the guardian said. "The treasures of the Citadel are gone forever, so are its weapons and its technologies and all vast libraries. All gone, hidden away by other Guardians in a place even safer than this."

"We mean no harm!" Lea said.

"It doesn't matter what you mean," the dying man continued. "You cannot be trusted with the technologies of this place. They are too advanced for the current level of your society. We swore to prevent this knowledge from ever falling into the wrong hands, and so we have done our duty. You will find nothing here. We have been watching you and the Athanatoi for a long time, and we have taken steps to ensure the secrets of this place never fall into the wrong hands."

They watched the life slip from his eyes, and he fell back limp in their grasp, this time stone cold dead.

"Oh *no*… now we'll never know!"

Scarlet was uncharacteristically somber. "What the hell happened here?"

Ryan scratched his head and shrugged his shoulders. "I don't want to say it, but just maybe it was exactly what he said it was. Maybe we just looked into the face of God himself."

"Heaven, you mean?"

Hawke lifted his chin and wiped the sweat from his forehead. "Let's not get carried away."

"Whoever, or *whatever* it was," Scarlet said, staring at the smoldering, blackened skeletons of the Athanatoi and the bloody corpses of the white-robed Guardians beside them, "it didn't seem very keen on that bastard getting through the gate."

Hawke agreed, but he was already wondering just how many levels they would have to fight through to reach the mysterious Koru, supposing he even existed. "Whoever these Guardians were, they weren't much of a match for the combined strength of the Athanatoi and those Special Ops forces."

"Speaking of which," Scarlet said. "They're on their way over here. I think it's time we made like bananas."

"Did you feel that?" Zeke asked.

"Eh?"

"The ground shook."

"Earthquake!" Ryan said.

With the vast structure crumbling all around them, the team sprinted into the northern tunnel network as if the devil himself was on their tail. The journey through the tunnels back up to the surface was an unforgiving punishment march after the fighting back in the temple, but with Faulkner's Special Ops on their tail, taking a moment to rest would have been a fatal error.

When they reached the entrance, night had fallen. A vast dazzling grove of stars lit the mountain range like

Christmas lights. A cold breeze whipped across the plains and into the gullies, biting at their noses and ears and making them shiver as they staggered down the slopes on their way back to reality.

For a long time, no one spoke. The slaughter they had witnessed was unlike anything any of them had seen before, but the elephant in the room was the Oracle's epic destruction inside the sphere of plasma. No one, not even Ryan, could begin to explain what they had seen tonight, and in their hearts, they now carried a heavy memory and a thousand new questions.

Scarlet lifted a cigarette to her lips and lit it with trembling hands. "What the buggering *fuck* do we do now?"

"We go back to Dubai," Hawke said without hesitation. "We touch base with Rich and take it from there."

CHAPTER FORTY-EIGHT

Brooke tried to strike out but his arms were handcuffed behind his back and his legs were cuffed together. "You goddam son of bitch, threatening my daughter! When I get out of here I'll skin you alive, you bastard!"

Muston laughed as the plane leveled off.

Alex fought back the tears and tried to stop the panic attack from taking over. She was starting to sweat and felt dizzy. She hated hearing her father get so angry. She hated seeing these traitors mocking and humiliating him like this, and now they were threatening his only child. "Just leave him alone, you asshole!"

"Better keep it zipped, Alex, or I'll have one of my men stick some duct tape over that big yap of yours. You want a nice peaceful flight to your new home, right?"

"And where might that be?" Brooke asked, calming again now.

Muston sucked his teeth and sighed. "Strictly need to know."

"A CIA black site then."

"You're not as dumb as you look."

"Faulkner was a long-time CIA man," Brooke said, his mind whirring. "It's the obvious choice. The question is where."

"You have no idea."

"We're flying southwest," Brooke said quietly, almost to himself. "Several sites across various states spring to mind."

Muston chuckled. He was enjoying himself. The deed was done, the king was killed and he had somehow survived to become Faulkner's Chief of Staff. He could relax a little. "You're presuming we're keeping you in the US."

Alex's panic grew stronger. Not in the US? Where the hell were they taking them – Mexico? Nicaragua? She felt her blood run cold. Colombia? She knew all about Colombia. "My father has the right to be tried in the US!"

"Any trial is a long way off, Alex. President Faulkner has a full domestic and foreign policy agenda to roll out, not least of which is increasing the war on terror, including against foreign forces like ECHO."

They heard another chuckle.

"You can't do this!"

"We already did it," came the dry reply. "And believe me when I say there's no way you're escaping from where you're going, no way at all. You will stay there for interrogation until the President is satisfied you're not harboring any secrets threatening the vital interests of the United States and then you will be brought to trial to answer for your crimes. Some of the more hawkish are pushing for the death penalty, but between you and me I think it's just a few centuries in prison for both of you."

Brooke laughed. "You think you're going to pull this off, huh?"

"As I said, we already did. There's no one out there coming to save you, Jack. No one at all. That little thing you used to command – the US Armed Forces – guess what? They all work for President Faulkner now. None of your little Special Forces buddies are ever going to know where you are, never mind bust you out. And as for ECHO, you can forget about them too. They're already on the FBI Most Wanted and similar lists in every country around the world that wants to do business with the US." He laughed. "And that means everyone now, even North Korea."

Alex fought the panic attack off and calmed herself. This was no time to fall apart. A few hours ago she was researching possible locations of the elixir for the ECHO team in a bid to try and get her legs working again, and now her father had been deposed and the two of them were being flown to an unidentified extraordinary rendition site somewhere in Latin America or maybe even further away from home.

And the bastard Josh Muston had been right. With Faulkner as the new sworn-in Commander-in-Chief, the entire US military was now under his command. No one was going to look for them. No one was coming to save them.

Their only hope was Hawke and the rest of the ECHO team, and not only would they now have to work without any support or resources from the US Government, but they were also actively being hunted down as an international terrorist group.

She sank back in her chair and closed her eyes. At least that way she could forget about the bag overhead.

"Don't worry, Alex," her father said gently. "We'll get through this."

She sighed. "You really think so?"

"Sure, why not?"

"Listen to your father," McGee said quietly.

"You have a plan, Agent McGee?"

"No plan, sir, but I have a phone. I smuggled it in. You don't want to know how."

Brooke actually laughed. "Good work. Don't let them know we have it."

"No sir, Mr. President."

"See, darling?" Brooke's voice was calm and measured. "We're going to make it."

"Jesus, Dad! Look at us!"

"You can't think like that, Alex or these bastards have

already won. They already beat you when you start thinking like that." His voice got serious. He wasn't talking to her as her father anymore, but as a soldier, an army officer, a president. "Whatever they do to us, however much they cheat, however much they harm, however they much hurt, however much they use corruption and nepotism to crush us and get us out of the way… you know what you do with that?"

"What?"

"You curl it all up into a ball and put it inside your fist. You know what you do next?"

"I think so."

"Right, you smash that goddam fist into their faces and you keep smashing until they're dead."

*

Jack Camacho nodded a curt *thank you* at Captain Michael Banks as they trotted up the airstair and stepped inside the 747's top deck. The flight was simple: Washington DC to Luxembourg City and there a change onto another cargo flight piloted by one of Banks's closest friends. No passports. No questions. This would take them to Dubai where they could meet with the rest of their team. It was the only hope they had now.

He climbed into his seat and buckled up, still in shock. He'd never been on a cargo 747 before and was surprised by how cramped and basic the jump seat area was. A dozen not particularly comfortable seats and no-frills anywhere. The rest of the enormous aircraft was packed full of goods being exported to Europe.

But he had no complaints, just a deep and irrepressible horror about what he had witnessed in Georgetown outside Kamala Banks's apartment. The power of the high velocity round and the terrible violence of his old friend's death.

The rage swelled in his heart. He had known Kim for more years than he could remember. They had shared so many good and bad times it would be almost impossible to believe she was dead if he had not seen it with his own eyes. How Joe Hawke and the rest of the ECHO team would react he could only guess, but he knew one thing – whoever had taken her life was a dead man walking.

The plane's mighty engines roared and seconds later they were in the air and leaving Washington airspace. It banked sharply to the right, and he saw Kamala was looking over at him. "I'm so sorry, Jack."

"Me too," he said through gritted teeth. "But not as sorry as the son of a bitch who killed her."

*

Jessica Clarke's drive back to the airport was uneventful. She couldn't believe what she was hearing on the radio about the President. It all sounded too crazy to be true, and she vaguely wondered if it had anything to do with her latest mission. Maybe, maybe not. Garcetti and the rest of those pen-pushing slobs never told her anything.

Talking of the devil, when Garcetti had sent her a text changing her mission from Iraq to Washington, she had breathed a massive sigh of relief. To her, it made no difference who was the next target – they were all equal as far as she was concerned. The big difference was time away from Matty. A flight to DC meant she could be there and back to LA in less than a day, but Iraq meant leaving her son on his own and badgering Mrs. Kowalczyk to keep an eye on him.

She drove away from the mayhem. Already she could hear the sirens and the police and ambulances scrambled to the site of her hit. A tragedy for the evening news – *and tonight, the brutal slaying of a woman in Georgetown…* she doubted it. Judging from what was going on inside 1600 Pennsylvania Avenue today it was unlikely the murder of Kim Taylor would make any news at all. They'd probably cover it up as a mugging gone wrong.

Not her problem.

The truth was, she was getting closer to her paycheck, and that meant getting closer to her dream. That was three down now – Devlin, Lund, and Taylor – and this was the sort of professional progress her employers expected, and why they had hired her to execute this contract. No one else could do it like this.

She cruised through the streets and drew closer to the military airfield where her plane waited to take her back to LA. Three down was good, but there was still a long way to go and plenty of ECHO teammates to take out before she got her money and her new life. At some red lights, she checked her box of bullets for the next target and raised her eyebrows in expectation when she read the name.

Logical really, when you thought about it.

Green lights, and on her way again. Soon it would be four down.

Another funeral.

Another wake.

Another day closer to her Mexican dream.

CHAPTER FORTY-NINE

"Burn them," he snarled. "Smoke them out and burn every one of the bastards."

"You're asking US soldiers to turn on their own, Mr. President."

"Camacho?" Faulkner said with a cynical laugh. "That son of a bitch is a traitor to this country. He turned his back on his nation when he went to ECHO. He gets no special protection from any American Special Ops. If anything he's even worse, just like Kim Taylor. What happened to her?"

"Cougar took her out a few hours ago."

"Good," Faulkner said without emotion, running his fingers along the edge of his desk. "If there are any survivors from the fight in Iraq, I still want her to continue with the mission and hunt them all down one by one until they're all gone, got it?"

"That's the plan, sir. I'll contact Pegasus immediately."

The new president gave a nod of satisfaction before spinning around in his leather swivel chair and facing the rest of the top brass assembled in the Situation Room. These were the world's most powerful men and women and they had all sworn to obey his orders.

And that put him in nearly as good a mood as when the Special Ops team had reported their success in securing the Citadel. Details were sketchy. The fighting was brutal, apparently, and the building was partially destroyed by some kind of self-destruction mechanism. The team reported that there was enough left to study, to pull apart, to analyze, but the real news was the death of the Oracle.

Gone to hell, probably.

Now he and he alone commanded the most devastating military force on the planet, at least until the missing treasures of the Citadel were discovered, and then he would control them as well as all the nukes. For a moment he almost felt giddy with the thought of such unbridled power resting in his hands. If the legends were true, and he found what the Oracle had told him awaited them in the Citadel, he would be the first person in history to control the entire planet.

Now the Oracle was dead, of course.

Muston put the phone down and walked over to the new Commander-in-Chief. "That was General Patterson, sir. President Brooke and the others arrived at Tartarus a few moments ago. They're being transferred from the aircraft to the underground detention center as we speak."

"Jack Brooke."

Muston was confused. "I'm sorry, sir?"

"You said President Brooke."

"It's customary to refer to…"

"Not with him it's not," Faulkner snapped. "The man's the worst traitor in American history. He's to be stripped of the title President, got it?"

Muston looked around at the blank, inscrutable faces of the men and women commanders around the long table. None of them offered him any hope of a way out. "Yes sir, Mr. President. I'll look into it with the Attorney General right away."

Faulkner looked away and started flicking through more images, this time of memos.

"What are they?" Muston asked.

"These are Presidential memoranda ordering the transfer of more weapons and technology to the ECHO team. All signed by Brooke."

They shared a grim smile.

"Yes, sir. The signature is almost perfect."

"Naturally. See to it that they get into the press."

"Yes sir."

Out of nowhere, Faulkner laughed a loud, booming laugh and reached around to slap Muston heavily on the back. "I know I can trust you, Josh." He stared at the generals and admirals at the table. "He's one helluva guy, right?"

A murmur of agreement rippled around the low-lit room.

"What sort of force they got down at Tartarus?"

An admiral spoke up. "Three thousand troops, sir, plus a small civilian staff of two hundred and around fifty medical. The island is airbrushed right the hell off all maps, including all satellite imagery so no one's finding it – not on paper maps or Google Earth. It doesn't exist."

"An island that doesn't exist, that isn't on any maps and is guarded by three thousand US troops," Faulkner said, steepling his fingers. "Sounds like Brooke's not going anywhere until we're ready for the trial."

"Yes, sir, Mr. President. Makes Gitmo Bay look like a Sunday School picnic."

"You tell General Patterson that Brooke and his daughter, plus McGee are traitors awaiting trial for high treason and that he is to guard them with his life. If anyone busts them off of that island, Patterson and his entire top team are spending the rest of their lives there, and not as guards but as prisoners. You tell him that."

"Yes sir."

Faulkner started to relax for the first time since ordering the coup. Now, with Brooke well and truly out of the way, the head of the snake was decapitated and the threat of a counter-attack was all but dead. And Muston's suggestion of Tartarus was inspired. An artificial island built in total secrecy and never registered on any maps, not even classified military ones, there was no way the goddam ECHO team was getting their asses there to save their hero either.

He breathed a sigh of relief and pushed back into his chair. He felt his shoulders slope a little as the tension bled out of his body. He had done it. Brooke was arrested and out of the country on a prison island that was so remote, it could only dream of being in the middle of nowhere. The ECHO team had failed to secure the treasures of the Citadel and most important of all the Oracle was dead and his army of crazy monks scattered to the four corners of the earth like the ashes from a thousand burned temples.

Facing the military commanders, he lit up one of his fat cigars and took a deep puff, chewing the smoke in his mouth before blowing it up into the low lights over the desk.

"Ladies and gentleman, we have a world to take over."

Muston looked smug. With the mysterious Oracle out of the way, there was no one to stop them now. His mind drifted to the Special Ops reports… how the dying guardians had screamed the name *Koru* in their last breaths. Probably nothing, he thought, all things considered. Maybe worth looking into when they had control of things here in DC. Turning to his boss, he saw the grinning face of the cat that got the cream. "What's the first order of the day, sir?"

"That's easy. I want the President of Iraq on the phone right now. When the devastation clears around the Citadel, we're going to need to secure the entire location and go in once again. Something tells me we haven't even begun to scratch the surface as far as that place is concerned and it's vital to our national security interests that it's a secure US-Iraqi facility. No Russians, no

Chinese, no Brits, no French, or anyone else. If there is any missing technology from that civilization, or weapons, or knowledge, I want it and I don't want anyone else to have it. Got it?"

"Yes sir."

Faulkner smacked his hands together and dragged heavily on the cigar.

"Good. Then let's get to business."

CHAPTER FIFTY

A day later, the ECHO team had flown south over the Persian Gulf and checked themselves into a penthouse suite in one of Dubai's most luxurious hotels.

Hawke leaned on the balcony rail outside and watched a tug from the United Emirates Navy tow the yacht they had fought on back into port. There was no more smoke billowing from it now, but the fire damage was harsh and he guessed it was a clear write-off. But what did that matter now?

After the battle of their lives, the Oracle was dead. Burned to death in a savage plasma blaze. When he closed his eyes, he visualized his blackened bones crushed inside the iron sphere or under one of the shrines he so longed to find. The man who had become kingmaker to so many governments around the world was now no more than a pile of ashes, as were his leading acolytes and cult members. ECHO had ended the threat they posed and shut down the endless series of terror attacks and relic plundering that had characterized Otmar Wolff's depraved reign.

But Hawke was tired. During this war, he had aged like anyone else. His bones ached and his muscles burned. His stubble was growing more silver by the week. It took longer than it ever did to get out of bed in the morning. The recovery time for his injuries was also stretching out. What used to take one night to heal now took a week. He looked at the younger Ryan Bale or Nikolai with envy.

"That was epic," Zeke said, cracking a beer.

Scarlet was two bottles ahead of him. "You can say that again."

"So what's next?" Lea said. "If you ask me… wait – my phone's ringing."

Lexi rolled her eyes. "Oh *God,* what now?"

Reaper watched Lea's face as she read the caller ID.

"It's Alex," Lea said, her eyes flooding with panic. Lea wiped a tear away, exhausted and broken and with no end in sight. "Alex, go ahead – you're on Facetime."

Hawke turned to Ryan. "Trace it, now!"

"On it."

"Alex, are you okay?"

"I've been better," she said.

"Why can't we see you?"

"I've got a hood over my head. We all have. Me, Brandon McGee, and my Dad."

"Jesus."

Hawke heard Alex's voice contort with fear. "He's invoked the Twenty-Fifth, Joe! They arrested my father for treason!"

"How are you speaking with us?" Ryan asked.

"Agent McGee managed to smuggle me a phone. He's loyal to Dad."

"This can't be happening," Scarlet said.

Lexi shook her head. "This is really, really bad, Joe."

"So what's happening right now?"

She started to break down.

"Hold it together, Alex," Lea said. "You can do this!"

"Where are you now, Alex?" Hawke asked.

"On a plane. They're taking us to a place called Tartarus. It's some kind of prison island used for extraordinary renditions and terror suspects. I don't know anything anymore. As I said, I'm on a plane with no windows. There's no light. It's so dark. Dad's on here too.

Agent McGee says Tartarus is some kind of black site and that we seriously do not want to go there. He doesn't know the location or he'd tell me. I trust him." She took a long breath and tried to calm herself. "I trust him! Who else can I trust?"

"You're not alone, Alex," Camacho said. "Hold tight."

"They're coming after all of you," Alex said. "You're on the list too, Agent Banks."

"Oh my God," Kamala said.

Hawke said, "Alex, I want you to contact us when you land. Unless they're flying around in circles to throw you off the scent we might be able to use the time in the air to work out the location of this Tartarus."

"Sure thing, Joe. Wait, someone's coming! I have to go."

"Alex, wait!"

The image jumped all over the place and then smacked into the floor with the camera facing up. They all saw the roof of an aircraft – vents, lights, overhead bins. Then they all saw something else – a boot heel come out of nowhere and smash into the camera's lens. The signal cut immediately and the screen went black.

Hawke felt a sickening feeling in his stomach, crawling up his throat.

Alex was gone and the call was cut. They stared at the dead, black screen with horror on their faces. "Looks like she lost the phone," Lea said.

"Damn it!" said Hawke.

Kamala was stricken with fear and confusion. "She said I was on the list."

"I'm so sorry," Lea said. "It's because you tried to save Kim. You're one of us now, whether you like it or not."

"I don't know what to think. I have to get back to America. My family!"

"You're looking at your family," Reaper said gruffly.

"Bienvenue, ma nouvelle amie." A cloud of smoke drifted up to the wires where the smoke detector used to be. "Bienvenue."

Kamala shook her head and collapsed down onto the bed. "This can't be happening."

"It's happening all right," Lexi said. "Now you run with the shadows just like the rest of us."

"I'm not a fugitive!" she protested. "I've dedicated my life to law enforcement. I'm in the Secret Service."

"Not anymore, you're not," Ryan said.

"Shit," Zeke said. "Guess that means you're stuck with me too."

Scarlet pursed her lips, drew her eyes away from his biceps. "We can probably fit you in."

"Well, I don't know about us but you…" Ryan said, preparing one of his best lines, but then he stopped talking and took a sip of his beer instead. "Sorry, now's not the time for cheap gags."

"Said the senator to the escort girl," Scarlet said, deadpan.

A ripple of subdued laughter went around the hotel room.

"Cheerfulness in the face of adversity," Hawke said. "That's what we say in the Royal Marines."

"Come on, you heard Alex, Joe!" Lea said. "Faulkner has put us on the Most Wanted! We're outlaws for God's sake."

"Us versus the world," Ryan said. "Who wants a beer?"

Nikolai rejected the offer of a drink. "I drink only water."

Scarlet's jaw fell open. "But this is ECHO."

"Hell, gimme his!" Zeke said, snatching the bottle from Ryan's hand. "I could sink about thirty-five of these babies right about now."

"Thirty-five?" Scarlet asked, lifting an eyebrow. "That's fighting talk, Tex."

He grinned and blushed. "Maybe just six, sweetheart."

Hawke measured the temperature of his team and saw things were getting too hot. They'd had a lot to process. Danny, Magnus, and Kim were all gone – murdered by the sniper, most likely Alfredo "The Spider" Lazaro. Alex Reeve and her father President Brooke were gone too, but thankfully still alive. Whisked away by Faulkner with Brandon McGee to an unknown Black site.

But they'd had their victories too. The Oracle was dead. None of them understood what they had seen back in the Altar Room deep inside the Citadel, but they all knew it was the end of Otmar Wolff. They also believed Nikolai when he told them that without their leader the cult would start to crumble and crawl back into the holes they came from.

Who the mysterious, unaccounted force was at the Citadel – none of them knew, not even Nikolai. They had vanished as quickly as they had arrived and seemed more focused on guarding the Citadel than attacking ECHO.

And new friends had joined them, proving their loyalty and showing their mettle in the heat of war – Ezekiel Jones, the former tank commander, Athanatoi acolyte Nikolai and Kamala Banks who had risked her life to stay with Kim when an active shooter was in the vicinity.

Lea's phone rang again. "Eden."

Hawke sighed. "Something tells me he's not going to like our report."

Lea told him about Alex's report and then flicked the phone to the speaker. They all heard Eden's upper-class English voice as he said, "And something tells me you're not going to like what I have for you, either."

Hawke braced himself. "We can take it, Rich."

"I can confirm everything Alex has told you, and

there's more bad news. Things are moving fast. Faulkner's freezing our assets wherever they can find them," Eden said grimly.

"Our money?" Scarlet asked.

He nodded. "We need money for everything we do, from paying for jet fuel to bribing officials to buying weapons and ammo. Without money we're powerless."

"A good job you have Nikolai on your team, my friends," the Russian said. "I never needed money to get whatever I wanted in life. You tell me what you want and I get it."

Reaper gave him a hefty pat on the back. "Merci, mon ami."

But it's not going to be enough, Hawke thought. Nikolai might be able to use his skills to acquire food or hotel rooms for them or to hire cars or gasoline, but he was going to struggle when it came to providing private jets or submachine guns, or fake passports. Still, it was better than nothing.

"Thanks, Kolya," Hawke said. "We appreciate it."

"Stealing food to survive?" Zeke said. "Shit, I thought this was going to be like James Bond and now you say we're eating out of trash cans."

Nikolai tutted. "Never! Not with me around."

"And not with me around, either," Hawke said, steeling himself for the oncoming battle. "We've been through too much together to be starved like rats and snuffed out by a scumbag like Faulkner."

When the room's heavy Bakelite telephone rang, everyone jumped. Lea was closest. She picked up the phone between the beds and spoke in hushed tones for a few moments before hanging up and turning to the others. "That was the front desk. They say our cards have been rejected. They say we have an hour to pay for the rooms or they're going to throw us out."

A grim silence filled the room.

Scarlet was first to speak. "So it's already started."

"What cash have we got?" Hawke asked.

They turned out their pockets and threw it on the bed.

Ryan scanned the pile in a few seconds. "Less than a thousand bucks US."

Kamala stared at the messy jumble of bills and coins scattered in a heap all over the bed and gasped. "How does he *do* that?"

"Don't go there," Lea said.

Lexi blew out a breath of frustration. "That's not going to take us very far."

Nikolai took off his gold ring. "This is worth two thousand."

"And this watch is a thousand euros," Reaper said as he unbuckled the strap.

Lexi took off a ring. "Maybe a thousand… I can't stop thinking about Alex."

"I still can't believe she said we're on the FBI's Most Wanted Fugitives list," Lea said. "That's not just public enemy number one in the USA, but the entire world."

"What – us versus the entire world's military?" Ryan said. "That seems a little unfair."

"He's right," Scarlet said. "They don't stand a chance."

"So what do we do now?" Zeke asked.

"Yeah," Ryan said. "What do we do about Alex and Jack Brooke?"

Reaper gave a long Gallic shrug and started to search through the pockets of his denim jacket for his tobacco tin. "The answer is obvious, mes amis."

"More than obvious," Hawke said, his jaw tightening. "We go and get them, is what."

THE END

AUTHOR'S NOTE

Land of the Gods represents the closing chapter in the ECHO team's latest struggle and the beginning of a new adventure that has been a long time in the making. Ever since Faulkner's first appearance in *The Aztec Prophecy* back in September 2016, I've been developing the storyline of his seizing power and isolating the ECHO team, starting with his destruction of their HQ on Elysium in *The Secret of Atlantis* two months later.

Planning long arcs like this is challenging but a lot of fun and it's great finally to be able to roll it out. I hope this is working in a way that you enjoy, and keen-eyed readers might have noticed a few loose ends that might have to be tied up in the future. With this in mind, Hawke's brand new adventure begins with *The Orpheus Legacy*, a lean, superfast thriller that releases in early 2019, and I'm looking forward to you being able to get into a brand new adventure!

Also on the way are the adrenaline-fueled Raiders series, continuing like a rocket in *The Apocalypse Code*, and Cairo Sloane's second installment *The Gods of Death*, which is also screeching towards us like a runaway train. In other projects, I'll also be working hard to release the third Avalon Adventure before the year gets too old. I'm starting to miss Decker and the rest of his crew.

As ever, if you enjoyed this book, please leave a review & until next time, Dear Mystery Reader

Rob

Printed in Great Britain
by Amazon